I0549104

VISIONS

LEAVING EARTH

VISIONS

LEAVING EARTH

CARROL FIX

LILLICAT PUBLISHERS
USA

VISIONS
LEAVING EARTH

VISIONS: Leaving Earth *Copyright © 2014 by Carrol Fix*

"Heaven's Mountain" Copyright © 2014 by J.J. Alleson; "Retribution" Copyright © 2013 by Harry Alexiou; "Star Climber" Copyright © 2013 by Mike Boggia; "Drifting to the Moon" Copyright © 2014 by Clement Chow; "Five Days and Nights" Copyright © 2014 by Douglas G. Clarke; "Cavia Porcellus" Copyright © 2014 by D.A. Couturier and Timothy Paul; "The Jewel" Copyright © 2013 by Carrol Fix; "Tumbleweed" Copyright © 2013 by Carrol Fix; "Life Lift" Copyright © 2014 by W.A. Fix; "My Name is Millec" Copyright © 2014 by W.A. Fix; "Murphy's Ride" Copyright © 2014 by Gary Hanson; "Babel Ascension" Copyright © 2013 by Ami Hart; "Elevation" Copyright © 2014 by Alan D Hickerson; "Enough" Copyright © 2014 by Thaddeus Howze; "I Ride the Night" Copyright © 2014 by Thaddeus Howze; "I Never Scream" Copyright © 2014 by J. Richard Jacobs; "Time is Up" Copyright © 2014 by S.M. Kraftchak; "After-Life" Copyright © 2013 by Randall Lemon; "Ascent" Copyright © 2013 by Andy McKell; "R&R" Copyright © 2014 by DC Mills; "No Man Left Behind" Copyright © 2013 by Karl Morgan; "Odd One Out" Copyright © 2013 by R M Pala; "Godzilla and Icarus" Copyright © 2013 by Amos Parker; "The Climb" Copyright © 2013 by Jon Ricson; "Spacelift" Copyright © 2013 by Jot Russell

Cover art Copyright © 2014 by Victor Habbick Visions, artist and photographer with a broad palette of styles. Vhabbick@mac.com www.victorhabbick.com

All rights reserved. No part of this book may be used or reproduced by any means, graphic, electronic, or mechanical, including photocopying, recording, taping or by any information storage retrieval system without the written permission of the publisher except in the case of brief quotations embodied in critical articles and reviews.

Lillicat Publishers books may be ordered through booksellers or by contacting:
Lillicat Publishers
www.lillicatpublishers.com

Because of the dynamic nature of the Internet, any web addresses or links contained in this book may have changed since publication *and may no longer be valid. The views expressed in these works are solely those of the individual authors and do not necessarily reflect the views of the publisher, and the publisher hereby disclaims any responsibility for them.*

ISBN: 978-0-9916426-3-2
Ebook ISBN: 978-0-9916426-6-3
Printed in the United States of America

This book presents exciting stories by a broad range of artistic talents from around the world. Both professional and undiscovered science fiction authors write using American English rules, British English rules, and/or write with English as a second language. The unique flavor of each creates an international tapestry for the enjoyment of science fiction fans everywhere.

Contents

EVER FOREWORD

Leaving Earth. As a species, we've barely begun this milestone achievement of finally expanding our limits beyond the planet of our birth, an event as significant as when our ancestors took their first steps out of Africa. We've been to the moon. We've spent months on space stations in orbit around Earth. We've sent robots to Mars and beyond. We've even sent a probe outside our own solar system. But we have yet to point to any human beings who can truthfully say, "I'm from the Moon," or "I was born on Mars."

Leaving Earth has been a mainstay topic of science fiction for decades. This anthology of short stories that you are holding in your hands (or tentacles) demonstrates why. The concept, much more than any typical trope, offers an enormous range of story lines that appeal to every writer and reader.

As a long-time magazine editor, especially as editor of *Perihelion Science Fiction Magazine* during the late 1960s when it was a print publication and since 2012 when it was reborn as an online magazine, I've had the opportunity to read maybe hundreds of stories dealing with the concept of leaving Earth. I've broken them down into six primary categories: outside forces, unusual escapes, technical progress, encounters, prevention, and necessary evils.

Outside forces involve situations where humans leave Earth involuntarily. For example, in the morning the protagonists are lounging by the pool, soaking up some rays, planning on a restful day topped by dinner out at a fancy restaurant. Instead, by evening, they are light years away from Earth facing the muzzles of some fierce ray guns. This is not at all what they expected. A classic story in this category, if not quite as melodramatic as my example, is Jules Verne's *Off on a Comet*. In the Verne tale, the characters experience what they believe to be a simple earthquake. In truth, a comet has gently kissed the Earth and taken with it a huge chunk of real estate including several cities. The characters eventually realize they have left Earth because of a number of physical anomalies: the sun sets in the wrong direction; days and nights are shorter; lesser gravity; different star configurations. One of the main characters is a scientist, obviously.

The category of unusual escapes are intended escapes, otherwise the stories would belong in the first category, except they involve methods not normally expected to produce escape velocity. I wrote a bit of flash fiction some time back where a special formula of beer was loaded into the engine of an old VW Beetle, providing enough thrust to launch two passengers equipped with hardhats, ham sandwiches and, fortunately, parachutes, into the stratosphere. The brew was more potent than the inventor anticipated because, expecting a leisurely cruise several thousands of feet among the clouds, the car instead streaked headlong into outer space; the passengers had to use their parachutes for an emergency exit back to Earth.

Technical progress is the least fanciful and most realistic category of scenarios for leaving Earth. Sometime in the near future, generational ships are developed which enable humans to embark on a journey to colonize other planets. This is one storyline. You will note that it is scientifically correct and will without a doubt occur one day, presuming we don't wipe ourselves out beforehand. Or we could perfect the science of terraforming and emigrate to Mars. This is also a certainty. Authentic technical progress as the background for exciting space adventures was a familiar and successful formula for many of science fiction's legends: Arthur C. Clarke, Isaac Asimov, Larry Niven, to name a few. With them, learning the scientific details behind the stories was as interesting as reading the stories themselves. This is what makes tales of technical progress, the hardest of science fiction, most enjoyable.

This brings us to the category I like to call encounters. It is the most hopeful and encouraging category. Full of all kinds of warm and fuzzies. Humans are on the verge of leaving Earth by themselves. Given a few decades, up to a century, and we predictably can accomplish this historical feat. But there are no guarantees. We could succeed. Or not. The consequences of success are enormous. The results of failure are devastating. We aren't the only ones who realize this. I can envision a Council of Extraterrestrial Species (of course that is not what they call themselves) meeting on a distant planet to discuss the Human Race—

"That's still not enough reason to commit resources and lifepower to a contact mission," gurgled the Liaison from Neffrig, its green body-bristles stiffening. "Leave them be!"

"But they are intelligent," protested the Liaison from Ooieai. "Aren't you the least bit curious how intelligence could develop way out in the fringes?"

"You Ooieai are curious about everything," the Liaison from Neffrig scoffed. "You'd investigate a large gumrock if it looked interesting."

"Floor! Floor!" The Liaison from Drmlgtrz flashed and blew smoke rapidly.

The Liaison from Neffrig passed the cup-o-palaver to the Liaison from Drmlgtrz who took it in a bony claw, then set the cup down on a nearby surface.

"I too am not convinced that a contact mission with, what do they call themselves, Urth, is in the best interests of this magnificent Assembly. Our close encounter probes have shown the planet to be mostly water. Our hydrophobic colleagues will have our skins if we show this planet any undue considerations. The life is carbon-based, so it has a tendency to smell. The atmosphere is rank. The planet is way overpopulated. What are we going to do with it? The planet has nothing to offer. Aside from water, it is mostly aluminum and silicon, for gripe sakes. Aluminum and silicon! With an iron core, to boot. We need another iron core planet like we need a hole in the skies."

"Why does everything have to be useful?" questioned the Liaison from Ooieai. "Pure science is a lofty goal all by itself. Didn't only a few orbits past we deploy a contact mission to the No species?"

The Liaison from Neffrig's body-bristles stood on end again. "The No are right down the block. They'd already colonized their own nearest planet. We had to act, despite the fact that they are, no offense, of no value."

Several Assembly colleagues reacted mirthfully to the pun.

"Supposing we did mount a contact mission to this new world? Help them along. They will be leaving Urth and emigrating throughout the galaxy soon enough on their own. With our assistance, they can avoid any tragic errors. Like becoming hostile—"

In this encounters category of leaving Earth stories, friendly and advanced aliens take us humans under their aegis and help us to spread throughout the universe in a non-confrontational manner, more quickly than we could have without mentors, avoiding tragedies for all involved. This was the plot of the movie *Star Trek: First Contact.* The *Star Trek Encyclopedia* explains: Zefram Cochrane (portrayed by James Cromwell) is the first human to create a warp drive system, and in 2063, his successful light-speed flight draws the attention of the Vulcans, leading to humanity's first official contact with an alien race. From that point on, the Vulcans become Earth's guidance counselors, so to speak. This relationship is explored throughout the *StarTrek: Enterprise* TV series.

On the flip side of this is the prevention category. Briefly stated, the other intelligent life forms in the galaxy are hesitant about humans leaving Earth. They deem our species, with just reasons, to be too violent, too greedy, and too prone to a host of other sins to be let loose among the stars. We may be permitted to pollute our own solar system, but that's it. Anything beyond Uranus (although we have no idea of other life forms' verdict regarding poor Pluto) is strictly out of bounds. Borders are patrolled and violators are persecuted with the harshest methods imaginable. Various stories have us benevolently corralled humans reacting to the gatekeepers in a number of different ways. Curiously, this sometimes leads to interplanetary war with sometimes us violent humans winning! I guess the aliens were right.

The last category is necessary evils. We *have* to leave Earth. The planet is either overcrowded and running out of resources, or dying from global warming, or infested with zombies. In the movie *When Worlds Collide*, (1951), based upon the novel written by Phillip Wylie and Edwin Balmer, produced by George Pal and directed by Rudolph Mate, the star Bellus is on a collision course with Earth and certain to wipe out all of humanity. A select group of men and women, young, fertile, supposedly intelligent, healthy, and with good teeth and haircuts, are selected to leave Earth in a space ark, which will travel to Zyrus, a supposedly earthlike planet orbiting Bellus, where people can pick up where they left off, so to speak. Cheesy, but fun.

Many of the stories in this collection were written by authors who have also contributed to *Perihelion*. I can attest to the quality of the writing, the imagination behind the narratives, and the enjoyment you'll have reading each and every tale. So leave Earth and don't look back.

Sam Bellotto Jr.
Editor
Perihelion Science Fiction Magazine
October 31, 2014

MOVING TO SPACE

1. TUMBLEWEED

Carrol Fix

I don't know why I agreed to do this. I'm usually a smart guy, but now I'm standing here, in the middle of a shopping mall at the top of the Space Elevator, with this 12-year-old kid looking at me as if he's about to cry. Seemed like he was tough, boarding the SE—never even blinked when it started, and that was some serious bucking.

His mom should be here, not me. Just because we're cousins doesn't mean I have to do this for her kid. I could have refused to come with him, but who in their right mind would give up the chance of a lifetime? Okay, her—but she never dreamed about space like me.

I never thought it would come to this. All I planned to do was go along for the ride—and what a ride it's been! At least, until I had to tell him, "No way, dude!"

"I promised Grandpa," he says to me and shows me the damned box with the tumbleweed. How the hell do kids manage to do that, make you feel mad and guilty all at the same time?

Yeah, I loved Uncle Jim. He was about the only one who made me feel like a real person when I was this kid's age.

3

He could roughhouse and tease as well as my cousins and me, without trying to show us how much bigger and stronger he was. Uncle Jim was in the game for the fun.

He got rich, too. My mom said he got lucky, but I think hard work and caring about what he was doing was the real secret. After the money came, he and my mom sort of drifted apart. Mom was jealous, but she couldn't see that she was. Sibling rivalry, I guess. He knew and didn't push— just sent gifts for birthdays and Christmas, but nothing big.

This is his only grandson, and I know how much he must have loved that kid.

When he died, there was some money for my mom and me and my sister. Not a huge amount, but enough so we knew he cared about being remembered. And, Mom was bitter. What can I say; she is who she is.

Anyway, Sarah called me and asked if I would go with her son on this trip. Seems Uncle Jim left two tickets and one was for his grandson. Alvin wasn't old enough to go by himself. Alvin, can you believe it? Who saddles a kid with a name like that? Anyway, the powers-that-be decreed 18 as the magic number of years that would get you a single seat on the Space Elevator. Any less than that and you got a combined, double seat with another person over 18, as long as that person was legally responsible for you.

I'm definitely over 18, 36 last April, so I must be responsible. Not enough for a wife, maybe, but still responsible for the kid—and, I guess, for the tumbleweed— but I don't have any idea how we'll manage to toss it into space, even if he does say he knows how to do it.

Years ago, if you wanted to get to outer space, you had to sit in a hot little can attached to the top of an exploding rocket and just pray that the whole thing didn't blow itself apart. Getting there was only half the fun. To get back home, you had to take that same can and drop it through the atmosphere like a marshmallow over hot coals.

Then came the Space Elevator. Talk about a difference! Here we are, 22,000 miles above Mother Earth, without one ounce of sweat. After the initial lift, when it was a little rough, what with all that weight gaining momentum—that inertia thing they talk about—and the swaying from the pressure on the string thing we're attached to, it finally smoothed out and we zipped up that line like flying on a plane. I had just gotten used to the constant feeling of going up, when we came to the top and I had to readjust. The kid didn't even seem to notice.

I first met the kid when his mom handed him over at the airport in Los Angeles. I flew in from upstate New York and they arrived from Denver. Sarah looks like her mother, dark hair and chunky body, while Al is lean and angular like his granddad, Uncle Jim. I inherited the same genes as Uncle Jim, so Al and I look a lot alike. We both have wavy, auburn hair and, what one of my old girlfriends described as, a nose like a boat's prow, adorned with a prominent bump at the bridge.

The flight took eight hours from L.A. to the Space Elevator Base, 800 miles southwest of Hawaii. Seems like they could put the thing closer to shore. Must be expensive as hell to ship the stuff they lift every day, all the way out to the middle of the Pacific Ocean. It's supposed to be for safety reasons, I know, but you would think they could figure something else out. Of course, if that string breaks, hundreds of miles of it could fall down to earth and cause a lot of damage.

Near the Base, there's a city with an airport on a manmade island. They have stores and tourist attractions— everybody wants to see the SE, even if they can't go up in it. Cruise ships dock there and luxury hotels are full most of the time.

We had to get there a day early and there was a two-bedroom suite reserved for us in a first class hotel, with all the bells and whistles you could ask for. Even the kid seemed excited. We were on the fortieth floor and had a huge picture window with an awesome view of the Space Elevator.

We watched the SE going up, and the one on the other side coming down. One Elevator car goes up every day and one comes down. The trip takes about a week one-way, so there are always seven Elevator cars on the up side and seven on the down side. For the return at the top, they switch the up cars over to the string on the down side, and then they move them around again at the bottom. I don't know how they do it, but it must be something like switching trains on railroad tracks or something. The string isn't really a string, of course. They call it a nanotube, I think, or maybe it's made up of nanotubes, but I'm not sure. Ask the kid, he'll know. The two sides make it thick enough that you can see it from the island, but it sure looks flimsy compared to the size of the cars.

While we waited, we had to take the anti-radiation pills they gave us. Those things are wicked. We took turns in the bathroom for about 16 hours. They're supposed to make you absorb and flush the radiation out through your bowels, but your body has to adjust to the chemicals. You have to take them every day, and since they don't want you doing that adjusting on the Elevator, they make you take the pills every 12 hours, starting 24 hours before you leave. I guess I see their point.

We rode a helicopter from the hotel roof to the SE Base, where we boarded the Elevator car. It kind of reminded me of a hospital emergency room, grays and blues, but with much nicer furniture. There were about 40 individual rooms around three sides of the car—20 upstairs and 20 downstairs. There are two more levels for freight down below. We had our own compartment, with two small beds for sleeping and we could sit in the lounge or the upstairs restaurant the rest of the time. Meals are free, but not anything to brag about. The kid sent pictures to his friends on his cell, so I sent some, too. He watched me, kind of sideways, as if he wasn't sure if I really knew how to do it right. He didn't talk much on the way up—didn't give me any clue about what he planned.

When he finally sprang it on me, we were getting ready to exit the elevator for a stroll through the shops on the GeoDeck. That's what they call the station at the geostationary level of the Space Elevator. You know how communication satellites always stay in the same spot in the sky all the time? That's geostationary. Anyway, he said he needed to find the shop where his grandpa had told him to pick up a box. Okay, I says, no problem. Yeah, like I knew what I was saying.

The shop was the same as all the others along the corridor, a couple of small display windows and a narrow door leading into a deep, brightly lit room filled with trinkets and postcards, flashing signs, colorful artwork, sparkling jewelry, scarves, hats, t-shirts with Space Elevator pictures, cheap carpets, and probably a hundred things I didn't notice.

The guy at the counter scowled at the note the kid handed him before signaling another guy, who came over, examined the paper, and then motioned us to follow him. He led us into a back room and pointed to a table next to the wall, where a large cardboard box sat surrounded by leftover merchandise and dusty stacks of paperwork. Large, red, hand-written letters on the sides of the box declared "Do Not Touch." The shopkeeper handed the unimpressive three-foot cube to the kid, who took it easily, thanked him, and headed for the door. Frowning a little, the man followed us out, watching as the kid headed further up the corridor. I think he looked sad, but I could be wrong.

That's when I started to get mad. I caught up with the kid and asked him what the hell was in the box. He stopped right there in the corridor and showed me. I stared down at it with my mouth hanging open and listened to Al explain how his grandpa took him on a trip through Wyoming when he was just a little kid. They saw tumbleweeds rolling across the highway in the wind and my Uncle Jim stopped the car and caught one for his grandson. It became a symbol, between him and Al, of his life and their relationship. When he died, he had the thing shipped up here and wanted it released into space as his memorial to all the generations of his offspring, rolling forward into the future. The thing was, the International Space Administration had rules and laws preventing the average Joe from dumping things into space. Of course, he knew it was illegal, so he arranged for several people to help his grandson make it happen. Must have cost him a fortune.

People walking by were staring down at the box, so I quickly closed it, hoping no one had gotten a good look inside. At first, I told him no, and then he told me about his promise. That's when his eyes got big and wet looking and now I'm standing here thinking of Uncle Jim and all he had meant to me.

"Does your mom know?"

He nodded.

Damn. She set me up. I had to admire that woman—she always was sharp. She knew I was better at this kind of thing than she was. After all, what did she know about sneaking around, skirting the edges of the law? My whole family knew my history—from smoking pot in high school, to a recent cross-country Harley ride with a group of Hell's Angels. Not a bad bunch, those Angels. We had a great time and any one of them would have given me the shirt off his back, or his favorite babe, if I asked. Of course, I didn't ask—had my own babe, at the time, and a nice wad of cash from a temporary side gig marketing my favorite herb.

"Yeah, okay. Let's do it."

He smiled for the first time since I met him and it was a nice smile.

I have no idea how many years Uncle Jim worked on this, but he left the kid with detailed instructions. The owner of a very expensive GeoDeck restaurant had agreed to expel the tumbleweed into space with the restaurant's debris. I thought that meant it was a cinch and everything would just fall into place from there on. No such luck.

We found the business with no problem, but the owner was "down below," as they call it when someone goes back down to the planet. The second in charge was his son, who needed to contact his dad on a secure line before he would even talk about it. I wondered aloud why Uncle Jim hadn't made sure the guy was available when we needed him, but that seemed to upset Al, so I shut up.

The son put us at a table to wait while he made the call. I ordered a burger and was half way through it, when the guy finally came back. The kid wasn't hungry and sat sucking on a glass of Coke, watching me eat. I could tell Sonny wasn't happy. He sat down and stared at his hands clasped together on the white tablecloth. He said his dad apologized to us, but things had changed and he couldn't take the chance of losing his restaurant because of a promise he had made years ago. He said he was sorry, but the kid's grandfather was dead and couldn't do anything about it now. Sonny looked up then and met the kid's eyes. Al just sat there, pale and silent. I was about to speak up, say something about maybe forcing them to honor the agreement, when the kid reached into his pocket and handed Sonny a letter, never breaking eye contact.

Sonny nodded when he finished reading it and handed it back, mumbling something about his dad thinking we might have it. He acted like he was relieved, giving the kid a hint of a smile as he looked down at the box on the floor by the kid's chair. Al said he had one more thing to do and that we would be back in an hour.

Carrying the box, the kid headed out to the corridor, moving fast and not saying anything, with me tagging along. We came to a cross-corridor and he turned right, walked awhile, and turned left. I was getting pissed. We made two more turns before I grabbed him by the shoulder. His eyes were sad, but hopeful, when he answered my question. The envelope held a letter from Uncle Jim and the deed to the restaurant, made out to the kid and his mom. Sarah had already signed the transfer of ownership and all it needed was the kid's signature with me as witness. Once they met their part of the bargain, the restaurant ownership would officially transfer to Sonny's dad.

So, what were we doing here? The kid pointed to the end of the deserted corridor we had just entered. Closed doors on both sides didn't tell me anything. He grinned and picked up the box again, striding to the blank wall at the end. I didn't even notice the emergency fire extinguisher, until he started fooling with it. He unlocked the holder with a key he had, then took the extinguisher down and turned it upside down. There on the bottom was a sticky label with Uncle Jim's name on it. He looked at it for a minute and there were tears on his cheeks. He hugged that fire extinguisher as if it really was his granddad. Finally, he pulled the top of the box open, pointed the nozzle inside, and started spraying the tumbleweed.

"Hey," I yelled, "What the hell are you doing?" I reached for the nozzle and he batted my hand away.

"Leave it alone!" he growled.

I backed off and he glanced another warning in my direction, before reaching down inside the box to turn the tumbleweed over and spray the other side. The foam was sticky and gray, making the thing look like a grimy, flocked Christmas tree. When he had emptied the sprayer, shaking it several times to make sure he got all of it out, he knelt down beside the box, weeping silently.

"Okay, Grampa," he whispered, "it's time to go."

He folded the top closed and stood up, holding the box and looking at me hard. I looked back at him and touched the box in his arms.

"Yeah, I understand." I stroked the box gently. "I know he thanks you."

He twitched a smile and then headed back toward the restaurant. I shoved the empty canister into the corner with my foot, and then followed the kid. If, and when, anyone had any questions about it, we would be a long way from here.

Sonny was waiting, and took us through the kitchen to the disposal area. He had shut off the burner on the incineration unit and removed the screen over the exit hatch. It was a tight fit, even without the box, but the kid pushed the tumbleweed against the hatch and stepped back. Sonny closed the unit, checked again to make sure there was no heat, and triggered the vacuum ejector. We all looked at each other for a few seconds, and then Sonny turned it off. When he opened the unit, there was nothing there.

I don't know for sure what happened to that tumbleweed when the vacuum of space sucked it out of the hatch. Maybe it broke apart—maybe the pressure stripped off Uncle Jim's ashes—maybe it kept its shape.

I like to think of Uncle Jim and that tumbleweed sailing out the hatch together—rolling through space eternally— circling our old Earth and watching down over his family from among the stars.

Carrol Fix is a passionate reader of science fiction and fantasy, an innovative website designer, computer analyst, and a publisher. A former computer consultant, who has lived in six different States, Carrol currently resides near San Diego, California, USA.
Carrol is a short-story writer and novelist whose science fiction work includes the award-winning novel, Mishka: Book One of the Quadrate Mind. *She is currently writing the second book in the* Quadrate Mind *series, while working on a young-adult fantasy novel,* Worlds Apart. *Her first place flash*

fiction entry in the April 2012 Science Fiction Microstories Contest, "Time of the Phoenix", appeared in the May 2013 issue of **Perihelion Science Fiction.** *CarrolFix@LillicatPublishers.com http://www.mishkabook.com*

2. THE JEWEL

Carrol Fix

I was sitting in my apartment, browsing the Web and drinking my fourth cup of overheated coffee, when my phone rang. I didn't know why the guy contacted me—making that reference to my "background," like he was accusing me of something—but I hadn't had any money coming in since my last jaunt down to Mexico, so I listened to his offer. He said he heard about the stunt the kid and I pulled on that Space Elevator trip. I told him it was the kid's idea, not mine.

"Yeah," he drawled, "smart kid. I need some help like that and I'll pay a lot for it. I think a round number with five zeros attached would buy you."

The guy sounded like a character in a low-budget detective show. I should have been insulted, but it's hard to be offended by someone offering that kind of money.

He wouldn't give me his name, just said he wanted me to get some information from a woman. How hard could that be? Turns out, the woman was in space. The money kept me listening. She had the ephemeris positions to a small asteroid that he claimed was his. I wasn't sure how he could own it and not know where it was, but his money was still talking to me.

12

"Just so you know," I said, "I don't beat up women. Not for any amount of money. If that's part of the deal, count me out."

"No, no," he said, "You have to get it without her knowing. You get the numbers and I can get to the asteroid, so she can't steal it from me."

I started making noises as if I might not take the offer, but he just laughed at me. What could it hurt to hear the rest of his offer?

"Pick up the car reserved for you at the rental place up the street. Under the front passenger seat, you'll find a package. Open it and then call me." He hung up without waiting for me to ask how he knew where I lived.

What he offered made it worth checking out—if it was ligit—so I did as he asked. The car was a slick sports model and I got behind the wheel, looking forward to having some fun. I pulled into a store lot and dragged out the package, which held a cell phone, a key, a pencil, and a pad of paper with a phone number and "write notes here" hand-written on the first page. Just what I would expect from this guy. I shook my head and dialed the number.

A recorded message gave an airport name and a locker number, repeated three times. The second time through, I remembered to write it down and after the third time it disconnected. When I called back, there was no answer and a message said the number was no longer in service.

The airport was about an hour away. Enjoying the power and luxury of the sports car, I arrived in less than 45 minutes. The locker contained half the money he had promised, two plane tickets, two space elevator tickets, a credit card, a key to an apartment at Top Elevator City and instructions. I would get the second half of the money when I turned over the coordinates.

I wasn't happy to see that one set of tickets was for the kid.

It had been three years since my cousin's twelve-year-old kid and I first rode the Space Elevator. He probably would want to go up again, but I wasn't sure that was such a good idea. Don't ask me how, but word got out and we were kind of celebrities, although the authorities hadn't hunted us down. According to my new employer, the woman knew about our little escapade and was a fan. She would be at the GeoDeck level when we arrived and would be much more approachable if the two of us were there together. I stomped on my conscience and called the kid's mom, Sarah, and lied about wanting to take the kid on another Space Elevator trip. I could hear him in the background doing the *"Please, Mom, please!"* bit. He was fifteen now and, with a little persuasion, she seemed pretty much okay with it.

It wasn't easy, but I managed to get the two of us all the way to the top within two weeks. In three years, the shopping mall had grown into Top Elevator City. Our first stop was a visit to Sonny. Happy to see us, he ushered us to the only empty table in his restaurant. Packed with a hungry lunch crowd, it was the only available restaurant and there were twice as many tables as I remembered. The kid was quiet, thinking about his grandpa, I guess, so I told him I needed to talk to Sonny and left him sitting at the table.

Sonny said he couldn't tell me anything about how the details of our previous visit had gotten out. I asked about the woman, Moira Haskell, but he claimed he didn't know her. He suggested I look her up in the directory, which I had already done when we first got to the apartment, without any results.

Back at the table, I found the kid staring down at a rock he was holding in his hand. He passed it to me, frowning. "A lady and a man were at that table over there and she dumped some stones out of a little bag. They started arguing and he reached for one of them. When she batted his hand away, her sleeve dragged one off the table and I saw it bounce under that other table. She put the stones back in the bag and looked around on the floor, but they were still arguing and she rushed off before she saw this one. I was going to stop her, but by the time I got it from under the table, she had disappeared."

I had been looking at the stone while he talked. It wasn't just a stone, it was a rough diamond—probably four or five carats. "Hey, kid, this is a diamond!" I said, rolling it around on my palm. "You just struck it rich!"

14

He gave me one of those patient looks I was used to by now, and I readied my sigh.

"You know we have to try to find her, right?" he said, in that tone parents use with their kids. He took the diamond, stuffing it into his pocket. "This belongs to her."

I released the breath I had been holding, trying to make it sound gruff and not like I was agreeing with him. Damn kid is so honest. "Yeah, okay."

It took some time, but the kid had a good description of her and we finally tracked her to a hotel near the ship docks. As we came close to the entrance, she came out, carrying a bag and dressed in a ship jumpsuit. The kid walked right up to her and held out the stone.

"You dropped this at the restaurant," he told her.

She had taken a step backwards when he approached, but now she took the rock and looked at him for the first time. Her lips were parted and she looked from him to me and back again, as if she wasn't sure if she heard right.

"Thank you," she said and two lines formed on her forehead. "Don't I know you from somewhere?"

"I'm Al Jenkins and this is my cousin, Paul Riley," the kid said, before I could stop him. I don't usually introduce myself to strangers, but the kid didn't know that.

She smiled. "Aren't you the two who brought the tumbleweed up here?" When we glanced around, looking guilty, she laughed. "Don't worry, I won't tell anyone. I'm Moira Haskell."

Of course, the kid didn't know anything about her, but I almost choked. Things were beginning to make sense. Diamonds, an asteroid, and a beautiful woman. I cleared my throat.

"Were you going somewhere?" I smiled back at her, placing a fatherly hand on the kid's shoulder. He was grinning all over like a puppy waiting for someone to throw a ball.

She paused, seeming to think, while I concentrated on looking harmless and accessible.

"I was just going to check on my ship. What do you think, Al, would you like to take a look at her?" she finally said.

15

"You, too, of course," she added for me. I think the kid's eager acceptance was more obvious than mine.

She was a babe, all right. Her jumpsuit showed all of her curves and long legs. Dark shoulder-length curls, caught up in a sort of twist on the back of her head, just begged to be loosened and let fall. Her easy acceptance of us made me wonder if I was doing the right thing. Of course, I would owe a lot of money, if I didn't follow through.

Towering above the metal flooring of the huge cargo hold, the jungle of catwalks leading from docking ports to elevators was alive with robotic and human workers. We took the elevator up and then walked across the catwalk near the top row to Moira's access hatch. Through a viewport, I could see a smallish pear-shaped ship, with obvious marks of age, nestled against the station. I had seen ships like this on the news, built for two or three-man crews of asteroid prospectors.

"She's beautiful, isn't she?" Moira and the kid had come up beside me. "I call her *The Jewel.*" She had the soft-eyed look mothers have when they show you their new baby. Beauty really is in the eye of the beholder. The kid agreed so quickly, she didn't notice my lack of enthusiasm.

Inside, the bulkiest part of the ship held three levels, with the small end sealed off for the drive unit. We entered through the main hatch onto the nearly empty cargo deck, which contained several large pieces of securely fastened robotic equipment. We climbed a narrow spiraling stairwell to the upper deck. Prompted by the kid's non-stop questions, she led us to the seating and eating areas, the control room where display screens covered one wall, and then to the lower deck, where two sleeping cabins and operational systems rooms filled every space.

The kid checked each of the electronic systems—life support, communications, propulsion, emergency backups, main computer, every one of them triggering a barrage of questions. I never knew he could talk that much, or that he was so familiar with space ship systems. His mother had told me he was in the gifted student program at his high school and was taking college classes, but I still was surprised at how much he knew. Moira seemed impressed.

16

Having gotten a pilot's license when I was younger, which I managed to mention, some of the computerized systems in the control room looked familiar to me.

I knew she was thinking about taking us with her, but before she had a chance to say anything, and using my best "didn't mean to bother you" tone, I said we should be leaving. I started moving the kid toward the exit and, sure enough, she made up her mind and asked if we would help her out. She said she had just fired someone who was trying to steal from her and she needed a replacement. I winced, but managed to sound reluctant before telling her we couldn't leave a nice lady like her to fend for herself. The kid was in heaven.

I wasn't qualified to help her much, but, at the time, all I really wanted was to find those coordinates. With access to the control room, I could locate them in the navigation system. I was ready to pitch in with the preparations, when she said everything was set to go and we would leave as soon as Al and I could get our things together. I tried to stall, but the kid was eager and Moira said we had to go right away. What could I do? I would have to transmit the info from the ship.

Back at the apartment, while the kid was getting his stuff, I called the guy and told him what was happening. He wasn't happy. I couldn't even tell him which way we would go. He swore for almost a minute, before finally saying, "Okay, forget about the coordinates. Someone will hand you a package on your way back to the ship. Put it in your carry-on."

"I'm not taking a bomb on board," I told him.

"It's just a harmless tracker. You can open it and look at it."

I was getting worried. If he were tracking us, what would happen when we got to the asteroid? There was no way he would let Moira keep it. Whatever he was planning, we were all in big trouble.

Glancing quickly toward the kid's room, I lowered my voice. "Look, just leave this to me. Forget the tracker. I can get the information from the navigation system. I'll send the coordinates and you'll get the asteroid." I was beginning to sweat when the kid came into the room carrying his bag.

Finally, the guy growled, "I better hear from you within eight hours," and hung up.

The kid looked at me and I laughed, smoothing the back of my hair with one hand, telling him his mom wasn't very happy with our little side jaunt. He didn't smile and I think he knew I wasn't telling him the truth. I went to shove my stuff in my bag.

Moira was ready when we buzzed the entry com. As she disengaged and navigated away from the station, I sat near her and watched, explaining that I wanted to be able to relieve her at the controls. It didn't take long to identify the navigation system and learn the codes to work it. The kid was watching, too, and I got the feeling he wasn't there just to learn. I found out, when he cornered me in the mess.

"What are you doing?"

I stopped pouring, my coffee cup half-full. I didn't have to ask what he meant. I looked into wide questioning eyes and knew I couldn't let him down. I put the cup down and replaced the coffeepot, turned to lean back against the counter and crossed my arms across my chest.

"Jesus, kid, I think I really screwed up this time." I couldn't look at him, as I told him the whole story.

"You know he lied to you, don't you?" He didn't sound as mad as I expected. I nodded and reached for my coffee. "We have to tell Moira," he added.

I choked on a mouthful of coffee. He was out the door before I could set the cup down and try to talk him out of it.

Moira's response was not quite so lenient. The look she gave me was a mix of fury and disappointment. The words she used raised the kid's eyebrows, but he smiled at me with a satisfied nod. She stomped around for a while, waving her arms and shouting, then settled down enough to ask what I intended to do.

Since I hadn't figured that out, I just shook my head. Again, the disappointed, almost sad, look on her face. She turned to the kid. "We need to get back to the station. Can you use the scanners to see if we're being followed?"

He nodded and we headed for the control room, just as a piercing whistle split the air, signaling that we were too late.

"Damn," she cried, "proximity sensors. They're boarding us. Follow me!"

She raced down the stairs, with us close behind. Near the cargo hold, she slapped a palm sensor, opening a weapons locker. With quick motions and few words, she showed us how to use them. The kid seemed more comfortable with his blaster than I did with mine.

"They'll enter through a hatch. Al, you stay here and shoot at anything that moves through the cargo hatch." She grabbed my arm, dragging me toward the stairwell. I looked back, meeting the kid's scared but firm gaze. I tried to smile, but I felt like I probably needed more reassurance than he did.

"Hurry!" she yelled, disappearing down the stairs. She showed me where to hide, with a good view of the aft maintenance hatch.

"Can you use that," she asked, pointing at the weapon in my hand. Her eyes were concerned and her voice almost gentle. I looked at her for a moment, and then grinned. "Don't worry. I've got it handled."

She smiled as she dashed for the stairwell. I heard her curse as a clanging contact rocked the ship.

One remaining hatch opened in the hull near the control room. The pirate vessel was attacking there. I'm no hero, but I knew that we might die if I didn't do something. Taking aim, I fired at the hatch cycle control, sealing that entrance. I have experience with weapons; I just hate using them.

I ran up the stairs as fast as I could. Weapons fired above and I leapt upwards, two steps at a time. At the top, I turned left, carefully easing around a corner to where I could see the breached hatch. The crackle of blasters sounded in the other direction. Moira was doing a good job of holding them off from the control room, but she needed help.

Moving quickly, I slid along the wall toward the battle. Peering around the curve of the wall, I spotted three men crouched behind furniture. As I watched, one of them circled to the wall next to the control room door. He motioned with his hand and the other two fired high through the opening. I took him out just as he stepped into the doorway and aimed. Before the others could react, I fired again, removing the final threats.

"Moira," I called, "are you all right?" My heart did a funny flutter when she hesitantly poked her curly head around the doorjamb and then rushed to hug me.

"I thought you were dead!" I was amazed to see tears in her eyes. "I heard a blast and I thought they came in there and killed you."

"Not yet," a voice said from the corridor—a familiar mocking voice. We turned and saw a hard chunk of a man, barely taller than the kid he clutched next to him. "I want those asteroid positions. If I don't get them, now, one of you will die." He bared his teeth, shaking Al roughly. He must have searched for me and found the kid watching the cargo hatch.

I knew he wouldn't let us out of this alive. The kid knew, too, and he looked down at my weapon, and then held my gaze, as he moaned and buckled his knees, crashing to the floor at the guy's feet. The kid's shirt jerked out of his hand and his blaster wavered. My shot caught him between the eyes. The kid and I must watch the same bad movies.

Turns out, Moira's dad discovered the asteroid, and then died mysteriously. She suspected our dead pirate murdered him, but could never prove it. All of that, and the illegal boarding of The Jewel, cleared us of any charges over the bodies we hauled back to Space Elevator City.

Moira was generous. After she staked and filed her claim on the asteroid, she gave us each half of a percent of that chunk of rock loaded with precious gems. If things go well, we could be rich.

I took the kid home and his mom threatened to get a restraining order against me. I don't think she'll go through with it.

Carrol Fix is a passionate reader of science fiction and fantasy, an innovative website designer, computer analyst, and a publisher. A former computer consultant, who has lived in six different States, Carrol currently resides near San Diego, California, USA.

Carrol is a short-story writer and novelist whose science fiction work includes the award-winning novel, Mishka: Book One of the Quadrate Mind. *She is currently writing the second book in the* Quadrate Mind *series, while working on a young-adult fantasy novel,* Worlds Apart. *Her first place flash fiction entry in the April 2012 Science Fiction Microstories Contest, "Time of the Phoenix", appeared in the May 2013 issue of* Perihelion Science Fiction. *CarrolFix@LillicatPublishers.com* http://www.mishkabook.com

3. TIME IS UP

S.M. Kraftchak

Cara slid her hand protectively over her swollen belly as the doctor walked into his office. She met his strained smile with a creased forehead.

"How are you doing since the accident? I'm sorry I couldn't attend Sean's funeral. I was called away on an emergency."

"I'm doing okay. Still sore, but that's to be expected. It was a small service. We hadn't been on planet very long." Cara tried to smile as her chin quivered.

"Is the baby active?" the doctor asked.

Biting her lip, she yanked a tissue from the box on the desk, dabbed her eyes and nodded. "Quite," she said wiping her nose before looking into the man's blue-gray eyes. "Dr. Rock, I don't mean to be rude, but why am I here? You and the research doctors gave me thumbs up earlier this week."

It was Rock's turn to bite his lip as he opened the manila file folder on his desk. "Well, your latest tests indicate that the Teranor virus is no longer responding to protocols. In fact, it has escalated by a factor of ten."

Cara wrapped both hands around her belly. "But the baby . . . it's still . . . ?"

Rock raised his bushy eyebrows. "Yes, the baby appears to be fine. No virus is crossing the placenta from you to the baby, but it won't matter."

"I'm sure I can convince the research doctors to increase my treatment. I only have a few more months and the baby—" Cara stopped suddenly as Rock closed his eyes and shook his head.

"It's not that simple. Your time is almost up. At the rate your numbers are increasing, I estimate that you have only two weeks to live . . . unless you're on the next space elevator to the United Medical Space Treatment facility in orbit."

"That's fine. I'm not scared. I'll go." Cara slid to the edge of her chair.

"The UMST will not permit you unless . . . "

"Unless what?"

Rock dropped his head and hid behind his salt and pepper hair, took a deep breath and then looked up.

Cara's face paled as she met the doctor's pained eyes. "No!" Her voice was a harsh whisper.

Nodding slowly, Rock said, "You'll have to give up the baby."

"Absolutely not. If they increase my treatment, I can—"

Rock shook his head. "I've already done some discreet inquiries, hence this unconventional file," he said and handed Cara the manila folder. "I discovered that they are planning to terminate your pregnancy without your knowledge or consent because they believe it's interfering with your treatment."

With trembling hands, Cara took the folder and read the single paragraph on the sheet of paper.

RECOMMENDATION for treatment of escalating Teranor Viral involvement in patient #27, Cara Benner: Terminate pregnancy to eliminate high levels of hormones that appear to be preventing effectiveness of treatment protocols. With a drastic increase in viral levels, successful treatment is dependent on slowing the viral replication by sending her to a low gravity environment at the UMST, which will not permit gravid patients. Recommend mixing Pitocin with the patient's protocol to eliminate the

23

emotional stress of the patient having to make the decision to terminate her pregnancy and allow her to believe that the protocol was responsible for the miscarriage.

Dr. Bosque

Tears streamed down Cara's face as she looked up. "They wouldn't dare . . . "

"It's already scheduled for your next treatment, and as your consulting physician, I've signed off on it," Rock said and then rolled his lips over his teeth.

Cara jumped to her feet, threw the file on the desk, and turned toward the door before pausing to turn back to Rock. "How dare you?" Her voice was deep and threatening. "How dare you conspire to murder my . . . ? You know how much this baby means to me!" she said then lurched toward the door.

"Wait, Cara," Rock said rushing around his desk to grab her arm.

"Leave me alone!" Cara tried unsuccessfully to yank her arm away.

"Cara, I won't let them take your baby."

"But you just said . . . "

"But you didn't let me finish," Rock said softly, as he raised his bushy eyebrows.

***

Leaning close to Cara's ear, Dr. Rock whispered, "You need to smile. They are going to save your life."

"But they also want to kill my baby," she said, swallowing hard to keep from crying.

"But you aren't supposed to know that."

"Ah, Cara, how are you feeling today?" Dr. Bosque approached with his hand extended. "Is that a little fatigue I see?"

Cara smiled and inhaled deeply. "Yes, I'm tired but doing pretty well."

"No side-effects from the accident?"

Cara pursed her lips and shook her head.

"Good. And this must be Dr. Rock." Bosque grabbed Rock's hand between both his and shook it firmly. "You're a lucky lady to have such a renowned doctor in your corner at a time like this. Good to finally meet you, Dr. Rock."

"I see my reputation precedes me. I hope it's not all bad," Rock said.

"On the contrary, but we'll have time to talk later." Dr. Bosque turned to Cara. "I'll be personally administering your protocol today. I'm sure it will be a turning point in your treatment."

"Wonderful. Does this mean that you think I can go full term?" Cara said, raising her eyebrows.

The man opened his mouth, looking between his patient and the other doctor before finally smiling broadly. "I'm sure this will sustain you until your time is up. Dr. Rock, would you mind taking her into treatment room six, while I go pull her protocol?"

"Not at all, we'll see you in there."

Seated in the contoured treatment chair, Cara looked up at Dr. Rock with tear-filled eyes. "Remember, you promised."

Dr. Bosque burst into the room with a small tray holding a hypo spray and covered with clear plastic. He stopped when he saw his patient. "Are you well?"

Cara sniffed and wiped her nose with a tissue, then nodded. "I just wish Sean . . . he was so excited to be . . . "

"I am sorry," Bosque said, glancing at Rock as Cara began sobbing.

The two men tried to look anywhere but at Cara for several minutes and then Rock pulled Bosque back to the door.

"Would you allow me to administer her protocol and then take her to my private facility for the . . . after effects? We can care for her quite adequately there. She's like a daughter to me."

"That's not usual procedure; however, if you think it will make things easier on her . . . I can even send one of our nurses with you. The sooner we get this done the better. I'm seriously concerned with the sudden escalation of the virus. I've added a double dose of the . . . you know, to make sure it happens quickly and completely. The next space elevator leaves tomorrow at sunset. If all this is to be worth . . . the cost, she needs to be on it," Bosque whispered with a heavy sigh and a glance over Rock's shoulder at Cara who was starting to quiet.

25

"It's not necessary to send your nurse. I have mine on stand-by. I'll log the protocol results via the guest id you gave me. I understand the urgency and will make sure she gets there."

Bosque clasped Rock's hand. "Thank you and good luck."

 ***

Dr. Rock helped Cara from the public transport vehicle. "Easy does it. I know you're a little loopy but it will make the trip easier."

"What did you give me last night? I can barely remember my name," Cara's words slurred slightly as she allowed Dr. Rock's strong hand on her upper arm to guide her. "Where are we going?"

"You're going into space. You need to continue your Teranor treatment there or you will die."

"But I can't go . . . they won't allow the baby . . . " Cara ran her hand over her smooth belly and stopped, jerked her arm free, and caught her balance at the last second. She looked up at Dr. Rock with her mouth agape. Her eyes suddenly filled with tears. Her voice a strangled rasp, she screamed, "You did it, you son-of-a-bitch!" before taking a wild swing at him, which only landed her on the ground.

As Rock tried to lift her off the ground, he scanned the plaza in front of the space elevator station and spotted a single security droid targeting them. "Stop it!" he said in a loud whisper. "You know what I had to do. Now get up and walk."

"No, I don't care anymore. I don't want to live without . . . " Cara blubbered and rolled into a fetal position on the ground.

"Fine, but I do care and you're going to finish your treatment. At least, then, you may be able to thank me before your time is up," Rock said as he wrangled Cara into his arms.

"May I be of assistance?" the security droid's synthesized voice was monotone as they approached the entrance to the space elevator station.

"Yes, I am Dr. Rock. I am delivering a patient for Dr. Bosque. Cara Benner is scheduled on the next lift."

26

The droid paused and then, "Thank you. I have verified passage for Cara Benner, and I have verified all the appropriate paperwork documenting the termination of her pregnancy. She may enter."

"Given her current state, I'll need to deliver her to the elevator," Rock said raising his voice above Cara's sobs.

"That is highly unusual. Permit me to get my supervisor." Another longer pause and then the droid spoke with a more human voice. "Dr. Rock, please take the patient to the elevator and secure her in her seat. We depart in twenty minutes."

Five minutes later, Cara sat silently and benignly compliant with her face tipped away from Rock as he secured her harness. His hand slipped around the back of her waist as he bent forward and whispered in her ear. "I hope this gives you the time you need and that one day, you can thank me for this."

As Cara felt the band around her abdomen tighten slightly, she turned her blood shot eyes on Rock and said, "Go to hell."

He paused with a half-smile and searched her face before saying, "I might yet. I've activated the extra gravity band which should make the trip safer and more comfortable given your tender condition," he said and raised his eyebrows.

"It doesn't matter. Nothing matters anymore," Cara said.

"Dr. Rock, I'm going to have to ask you to exit the elevator. We'll take good care of her. There is a UMST facility employee waiting to receive her on the space platform. Ms. Benner, we are about to depart, so I need to put your breather on," a uniformed male attendant said.

Ten minutes later, Cara closed her eyes to delay more tears as the launch of the elevator forced the air from her lungs. While gravity forced her body deeper into the reclined seat, her thoughts wandered. *This space elevator is anticlimactic. It's nothing like the videos of astronauts taking off in a shuttle where they're shaking violently as they lay on their backs.* She felt the band around her torso, adjust and squeeze her high under her breasts and tighten around her hips. A voice spoke from the speakers in the seat on either side of her head. "Ma'am you need to breathe or you will pass out."

I don't care, she thought, ignoring her body's need for air, just like when she fell out of a tree and knocked the wind out of herself when she was a kid. Tears spilled from her eyes as adrenaline surged through her body, urging her to breathe. She had no desire to obey the voice or her body as the urgent voice became more distant. "Breathe, ma'am."

Cara was vaguely aware when she felt hands quickly unbuckling her harness and squeezing her jaw open to release the breather from her mouth. "Is she breathing?" she heard a woman's voice.

"Yes, she is now. Some of them can't remember how to breathe under pressure and black out even though we've escaped atmo and the pressure stops." Cara thought she recognized the voice of the man who had given her directions after Dr. Rock had left.

"Thank you. I'll take her from here," the woman said to the man, and then closer to Cara's face, "Give it a minute, and you'll feel like yourself again, only lighter."

Cara opened her eyes and looked at the woman, who had blonde hair cut close to the sides of her head, with about an inch and a half of hair spiked on top. Even though her mouth pulled into a tight pucker, the woman's crystal-blue eyes seemed to smile behind the transparent full mask clinging to her face. Cara read the woman's embroidered name on her jumpsuit. Dr. Evelyn Wynn.

"Here, let me help you," the woman said and pulled Cara to her feet, gently lifting her by the upper arms. "Once we get you settled in your room, we'll get this band off and you'll be more comfortable," she said, as her hand moved to Cara's back and pressed.

"Oh," Cara said as the pressure on her abdomen suddenly shifted. "It almost felt like—"

"Sometimes it does, but that's normal. Everything is readjusting to where it belongs. Escaping atmo is the tough part."

"But I thought I felt—"

"Hush, you need to focus on walking right now. It's a little tricky at first in low gravity. We'll talk when we get to your room and start checking your vitals," Dr. Wynn said, with a shake of her head.

Cara had expected to find the UMST as busy and bustling as the treatment center on planet, but they passed no one. She understood why, when Dr. Wynn said, "Here we are, your room," and Cara read, ISOLATION, on the glass door as it slid into the wall.

"Why—"

"Ssshhh, save your breath. I'll explain in a few minutes."

Even though it had not been hard to walk in the low gravity, Cara sighed as she lay down in the reclining, contoured chair that could extend into a flat bed. She watched as the doctor hooked up the monitoring system, examined all the readouts, and nodded. Cara opened her mouth to talk, but Dr. Wynn shook her head and held up one finger to stop her. "One more thing," she said then returned to the doorway and pressed the button marked, "WINDOW". Suddenly, the see-thru front wall of the room became frosted glass.

Dr. Wynn returned to Cara's side and smiled. "Now. How are you feeling? Any pressure?"

The corner of Cara's mouth pulled down and she turned her head away. She turned back suddenly when she heard the woman laugh.

"You really don't know, do you?"

Cara swallowed hard as tears burned her eyes.

Dr. Wynn leaned close to her ear. "You're still pregnant."

Tears suddenly spilled from Cara's eyes as she gasped, wide eyes examining the woman's face. "But Dr. Rock . . ."

". . . is a very good liar and an even better administrative manipulator. You will remain in isolation and only have contact with me until your time is up or the cat is out of the bag, so to speak, but by then it'll be too late for the UMST to take any action against you. We'll continue your protocol as planned, to give your baby as much time as possible."

"But the doctors on planet said that they could arrest the Teranor's progression up here. Why are you talking like I'm going to . . ."

Dr. Wynn's smile suddenly faded to a tight frown. "As long as you are pregnant, the protocol will not arrest the viral progression, even up here. The research team will think their hypothesis that your pregnancy was interfering with the protocol was wrong, until the truth comes out in the end. Dr. Rock and I have bought your baby time because we believe that something unprecedented is going on with your child—your baby may hold the key to curing the Teranor virus . . . that will kill *you*."

Cara stared, blank faced, at the woman as she processed the words. "I don't understand."

"As your body fights the virus, assisted by the protocol, it seems to be causing your baby's body to make the antigen that is preventing her from contracting the virus."

"Her?" Cara's face flushed with emotion. "Sean always wanted a little girl." She looked into her lap for a minute and then looked up. "Is there any way you can safely take antigens from her to help me?"

Dr. Wynn shook her head and eased onto the edge of the chair, took Cara's hand and smiled sadly. "It is the progression of the virus in you that is making her immunity stronger. If we try that, she may contract the virus and then . . ."

Nodding slightly, Cara smiled and took a deep breath. "I understand. How much longer do I . . . does my baby have until you'll have to take her?"

"We think we can get you to thirty-two weeks, but not much farther. Her lungs should be mature enough by then, especially up here, giving her pretty good odds."

Cara's chin suddenly began to quiver and tears fell from her eyes. "Will I get to meet her?"

Dr. Wynn swiped at her own tears, gave a tight smile, and tipped her head to the side. "I think you will."

Cara smiled. "Thank you," she whispered and then rolled away from her doctor.
***

"Dr. Rock, I'm glad you could make it," Dr. Wynn said extending her hand to the man stepping off the space elevator platform.

"So am I. How is she doing?"

Wynn tipped her head to the side and shook it. "She's quite a fighter. I expected her to be too weak by thirty weeks, but to make thirty-four weeks . . ."

"She's always been a tough kid. How's the baby?"

Wynn stopped and looked up and down the corridor before answering. "Very active. Tests show her immunity is incredibly strong. Lab trials are showing that her antigens immediately attack any introduced virus, but I found something strange I need you to look at. I haven't even shown the research team yet."

"Now or after?"

"Probably better now. It won't take long. They are prepping Cara for the C-section."

As Dr. Wynn lead the way into her office, an intercom on her desk sounded. "Dr. Wynn?"

"Yes?"

"Cara Benner is asking for you, before she will allow the techs to give her any sedation."

Wynn looked at Rock then said, "Tell the techs to hold off, and assure her I'll be there in just a few minutes."

"Thank you, Dr. Wynn."

"Not a problem," she said as she escorted Rock to the vid-board on the wall. She tapped it and a picture of active cells appeared.

Rock's brow creased as he examined the display. "Is this a combination sample?"

"No, it's just the baby's."

"But there's both antigen and virus side-by-side. Where did the virus come from? Is it mutated or has the antigen stopped working?"

"She's a typhoid Mary. She holds both a cure and the virus," Dr. Wynn said softly.

"How is that possible?"

Shaking her head, Wynn said, "My best guess is that since Cara was infected before she became pregnant, that the virus somehow entered the early fetus and, since Cara started receiving protocol soon after, it allowed the baby to

31

develop the antigen. Furthermore, I've been looking back and I believe that when Cara's numbers jumped, her body began filtering the virus from the baby."

"I thought we calculated that the virus was not crossing the placenta?"

"I think it has been crossing from child to mother but not from mother to child." Wynn tapped the screen and it went dark.

"And the antigen?" Rock asked as they entered the corridor. "Is it too late to . . . ?"

"Yes. Her time is up. I've promised not to put her to sleep for the surgery, to only give her a spinal block so that she can meet her daughter, but I don't expect Cara to make it out of surgery." Dr. Wynn's voice wavered as they arrived at the surgical suite.

"Dr. Wynn?" Cara called out, as she tried to turn to see who had entered the room.

"Yes, Cara. I've also brought a friend," Dr. Wynn said as she appeared on Cara's left and Dr. Rock appeared on her right.

"Hope you're not still mad at me," Rock said with a smile.

Dr. Wynn waited silently as she watched Cara smile for the first time in weeks, weakly lift her arms with dangling IV lines and monitor cords, to ask for a hug from Dr. Rock. The man laid his cheek on Cara's and allowed her to hold him close as she whispered in his ear. After nearly a minute, he nodded and pulled away. Cara turned and smiled at Dr. Wynn.

"Thank you," she said squeezing the woman's hand. "Now, my time is up. There's a baby that needs to be born."

Fifteen minutes later, Cara gasped in tearful wonder, as they laid her blonde-haired baby girl on her chest. She gently covered the infant's back with both her hands, amazed at the tiny, bright-blue infant eyes that met hers. After a suspended minute, Cara closed her eyes and allowed her face to relax.

"Promise, Dr. Rock?" Her voice was a loud whisper.

"Promise," he said laying his hand on hers.

A moment later, shrill alarms sounded and the baby began to cry. Dr. Wynn reached over and turned the alarms off. Dr. Rock lifted the newborn into his arms. With eyes full of tears, he put a finger in her tiny grasping hand.

"What was the promise?" Wynn asked.

"To name her baby, Hope."

S. M. Kraftchak notes: As a writer who spends most of my time in other worlds with dragons, elves, and the occasional alien, I still enjoy sunrise on the beach, sunset in the mountains, and portraying Elizabeth Tudor. I have two dogs, who think they are footrests, a cat who thinks she's a blanket, and three awesome daughters. My husband is my best friend, my harshest critic, and my most fervent supporter.

Writing is my passion. You can read two of my flash fiction stories in the newly released anthology: **The Future Is Short: Science Fiction in a Flash,** *published by Lillicat Publishers. In "Time is Up", Lyla has an agonizing decision to make. Could you endanger your child's life to save your own?*

4. STAR CLIMBER

Mike Boggia

Fault deliberately jostled the child, abruptly ending Tommy's exuberant kangaroo-like dance, causing him to careen into the stainless steel gate, face first.

"How dare you!" Starr Portman's eyes flashed fire. She dabbed Tommy's swollen, bloody lip and kissed the top of his head.

Fault snorted. "Keep that misbegotten half-breed away from me, slut."

A round trip on the space elevator was the dream of every child in the Uranus Support Colony. The elevator was reserved for explorers, colonists, and researchers. To ride it was a yearly privilege for essay contest winners. Tommy's essay brought him and his mother to Tether Station 2, where Darwin S. Fault, space explorer extraordinary, ended his elation with one swipe of his elbow.

"Tommy, we're boarding now. I'll get a heal strip and you'll be good as new."

The boy wiped tears away with webbed fingers and cowered against his mother. "Why'd he do that?"

Because he's an arrogant, son of a Centauri muck sucker, Starr thought. "He doesn't have manners, dearest." She guided Tommy through the gate and into the hold of the elevator.

"Will daddy meet us?"

She shook her head. "You know he's on a mission."

"I hoped he'd come to the docking station."

Starr and her forbidden lover had broken the all mighty Pure Earth Federation Code. The father Tommy idolized was condemned to a life sentence shuttling cargo through the void of space, never to see them again. A seven-year-old was too young to understand, or to suffer the trauma and impact of that forbidden love.

"Yo-Yo Boy, you still driving? Figured you'd be flying beyond the Milky Way by now." Fault slapped Denton's shoulder, dislodging his aviator's glasses that were a tribute to a distant grandfather, a B-52 pilot.

Denton remained focused on the array of screens before him. *Ignore it and it will go away.* His fingers tightened on the armrests of his chair.

Fault's deep and disturbing laughter rattled the small control room's green matte walls and the intricate instruments.

"Sorry, I forgot, crips like you don't get to fly real missions, do they?" he mocked.

"The Pure Earth Federation needs us as much as they need you."

"It must be fun, riding up and down, day in, day out, shuttling cargo and people, dreaming and never getting anywhere, Yo Yo Boy."

I hope a Tactillion sticks a tentacle up your butt and plucks your glorious innards. Call me Yo-Yo Boy one more time and so help me, I'll fillet you. Denton's black thoughts shifted to flaming crimson.

"We're about to ascend. Please exit the control room." Denton kept complete control of his voice.

Fault departed, leaving Denton with an overpowering urge to disinfect the bridge. He glanced at the mechanical climbers ascending the cables, taking him and his precious cargo into the gravity-free zone, where he then would launch ships on voyages beyond imagination. It occurred to him that he held the power of life and death over the passengers, and even the crews of the ships docking with the station.

The space elevator gleamed; two saucer shaped cargo pods on either side of what resembled a tubular paraglider wing. The tube contained bedrooms, an entertainment center, cafeteria, lavatories, and a small shop carrying exotic treats, clothing, and toiletry items. The climber car hung suspended from the cable by tethers running from the fore and aft crawlers.

Tommy and Starr followed Professor Townsend along the corridor, listening as he described features of the climber. They visited Container Pod-A and the cafeteria.

"I wish he'd move faster." Tommy tugged at his mother's hand.

"Hush. He's elderly, and we'll be aboard two days. You'll see everything on the elevator."

Townsend paused at a hatch with NO ADMITTANCE stenciled in red. He pressed a button and a lock clicked. The door slid open and the professor beckoned Tommy to enter.

"Go upstairs, Thomas. Portman, there's only room for your son, so we must wait here," Townsend said as the portal shut.

At the top of the steps, the boy found heaven. Tommy's eyes darted left to right, up and down as he caught his breath. The small room was the heartbeat of the elevator and the man seated at the console was its keeper. Through the windows, he saw the cable stretching out of sight, the mid-climber, and a panoramic view of the space elevator's layout. The blackness of space and countless stars overwhelmed him. Eagerness danced in the child's sapphire eyes, his fuchsia skin glowed with excitement.

Denton swiveled around and raised his eyebrows. This was not what he expected. The boy was a hybrid. A human had sinned, mated with an alien, and this was the result. He rose from his chair, clung to the armrest with his left hand, and extended his right.

"Welcome aboard, Thomas."

Tommy stretched out his hand, expecting the man to drop his at the sight of his webbed fingers. Denton grasped the small hand in his and smiled.

"So, you won the essay contest this year?"

Tommy nodded. Myriads of questions bounced in his brain, short-circuiting his tongue.

"Bet you want to know all about these gizmos, screens, buttons and toggle switches, don't you?"

The boy nodded. He stepped closer and noticed the man's right leg was twisted and half the size of the left one.

"Crashed an ore carrier head-on into an asteroid, ten earth years ago. Saved a stranded transport ship and eight hundred people. The ore carrier and I were totaled. They told the public that I was a hero, but, now, I can't fly anything except the elevator—if you can call this flying." Denton's mouth snapped shut and he turned away.

The passengers on the antiquated transport ship were colonists and deemed expendable. I didn't see it that way. Because I destroyed a valuable ship and its cargo, rather than see people die, the Commission denied reconstruction of my leg. Instead, a half-blind Cygna witch doctor treated my mangled limb.

"Sorry, you want to know about the elevator. If you look out there, you can see the mid-elevator climber. You know there are two others, one at the top and one below. We're now traveling at Mach 1, even though we appear to be standing still. Took seventy years to get it right, and now, we're able to travel across galaxies."

Tommy edged up to the console and studied the screens. One of the dark ones lit with the face of a ship captain requesting the elevator's ETA with the docking station. Denton checked a small screen at the bottom right of the console and told him the arrival time.

"Any questions? Don't be afraid, I've heard them all."

"Can you talk to all of the ships out there?" Tommy pointed toward a swirling nebula to his right.

"A few of them, if they have an open channel."

"Can I talk to my daddy?"

Denton's eyes widened. "First thing, Tommy, I'd need to know the name and number of his ship's call sign. Second, he'd have to be within range. The elevator's transmission system isn't geared for long distance communications."

"Oh." Tommy unzipped a pocket on his jumpsuit, dug in his pocket, and removed a piece of wrinkled paper. "Please try."

"Where did you get this? Paper is obsolete."

"Mom had it."

He took the scrap, felt the soft, worn texture and read the clumsy lettering. "We can't tie up the channels, so you'll have to be brief, okay?"

Tommy nodded and waited while Denton's signal traveled across the solar system.

"I never saw him," he muttered to himself.

Denton bit his lip. The child's father was an outcast, condemned and banned from any contact with his earthling lover and offspring. Denton had broken the Code by sending a message to ship StCii556cygnaX. Chances were the ship was beyond their range and he'd done his good deed for the trip.

"Why doesn't he answer?" Golden tears filled Tommy's eyes. "I want a daddy, like the others have."

"It takes time for the signal to reach him and equal time to return to us."

A buzzer sounded and a red light blinked below a screen showing the door Tommy had entered. It slid open to reveal Fault, pushing his way past the professor and Starr. Denton swore and turned toward the stairs.

Fault's eyes narrowed at Tommy's presence.

"What's that piece of excrement doing here?"

"Part of his prize from the contest."

"Just like you, Yo-Yo Boy, to flock with your kind." He leered at Tommy. "What do you plan to do when you grow up? You know, there's no place in our society for you. I hope they castrate you. Someone should have aborted you, little crap-dog."

"Shut up, Fault." Denton glared at the explorer. "State your business and get off my bridge."

"Okay, my ship has to be the first one launched, immediately upon our arrival. Is that clear, Yo-Yo?"

"Yes, sir, clear."

"It's polluting the place." Fault jabbed a finger at the child. "I'm out of here."

When he had gone, Tommy buried his face in his hands and sobbed.

Denton placed his hand on the boy's shaking shoulder and struggled for words to soothe the youngster.

38

A screen at the top left of the console glowed, brightened, and projected a face resembling Tommy's, though more mature and darker in color.

"Space Elevator, U-2-Alpha, StCii556cygnaX responding. What is your message?"

By a fluke of solar wind or magnetic storm, the broadcast reached the ship. Denton swiveled the screen to Tommy and tapped it.

"Tommy Portman wishes to speak with his father."

The alien started back from the screen, brushed webbed fingers across his face, sapphire eyes wide. He uttered a series of garbled words and turned away from them.

"Are you my daddy?"

"Captain Wargonsee, here." He turned to face the screen, golden tears staining his cheeks. "My son? I have a son!" He babbled for several moments, cleared his throat, and smiled. "Tommy, your mother, how is she?"

"She misses you. We look at your pictures every night and she tells me about you." Tommy placed his hand on the screen.

Wargonsee kissed the screen. "I thought she was dead. I didn't know I had a son. I've found a haven where I can take my wife and son. You know what lies ahead for him, don't you, Denton?"

Denton groaned. *I'm going to be in deep Martian muck for doing this.* "Need to disconnect. U-2-Alpha, over and out. Sorry, Tommy." Denton tapped the screen.

"Daddy." The boy threw himself at the console in a desperate attempt to capture the fade-out image.

Tommy's cry tore Denton's heart. "You need to go back and finish the tour. Don't tell anyone about what I did for you, please."

Denton got the message less than five minutes after Tommy left the bridge—Command Center Alpha ordering him to report to headquarters upon landing.

It's coming, the end of my career. He snorted. *What career, Yo-Yo Boy? You'll be grounded, work in a box, stare at endless rows of lights, and never see the stars again. I'd rather die!*

I could use the laser guns, the ones for destroying stray space debris threatening the elevator, cut the cable and let us free fall or float free. Death before confinement!

Denton swiveled the lasers and took aim at the cable, a fiendish grin on his face. He jumped at the sound of footsteps behind him.

"Tommy, what are you doing back here?" Reality returned and he released his grip on the laser pad.

"I'm sorry."

"It's okay, little guy." He looked at the boy and knew he had to help him—his own sanity, and even his life, depended on it. He made a decision.

"I'm busy right now, but if you can come back in, say fifteen, I'll put the climbers on manual control and let you operate them. I'm going to let you drive us all the way to the docking station."

The rainbow light in the boy's eyes is payment enough for the pain and humiliation I've endured since the crash.

Alone, Denton sent a message into the void of space, fingers crossed.

Tommy sat on Denton's lap and operated the climbers. The intensity in his expression, mirrored in the console, brought a smile to Denton's tired face.

"Let's bring your mom on the bridge. We're almost at the platform."

Tommy turned. "You said only two persons on the bridge."

"Don't you think we can squeeze her in here?"

"She'd like to watch me run the climbers."

"Touch that screen, it opens the door. Call her."

The docking station loomed before them. The name was a misnomer. It was more than that. It served as a repair depot, hospital, resort, storage area, and conference center for those who rarely set foot on planets.

Tommy caught his breath and leaned against the console in an attempt to get closer to the windows.

"You'll fall through," Denton laughed. "Once we dock, I'll take you and your mother on a tour of the station."

"Your leg?" Tommy frowned at Denton.

40

"We'll be in an almost zero gravity situation. It's not a problem for me."

The elevator connected without a sound. Denton swept his fingers over the control panel, picked up a credit card size instrument, and led them from the bridge.

He brought them to the observation deck, within touching distance of the ships. A lone figure charged through one of the transparent air locks to a nearby vessel. Denton's communicator clicked.

"Yo-Yo Boy, I'm aboard. As soon as my crew and staff board, launch us. Get me away from that. . ."

The ship catapulted into space. A terrified wail faded from Denton's communicator as Fault's craft streaked beyond range of the handheld.

"How'd that happen?" An innocent, wide-eyed, startled look crossed Denton's face.

"This way, double time." He grabbed Tommy and Starr's hands and charged through a narrow passage, opening into one of the transparent air locks.

Starr tried to pull free. "What. . ."

"No questions. Run." Denton launched them through the open hatch of the rainbow-hued ship and tumbled after them.

In the semi-darkness of the hold, beings grabbed them and belted their bodies into seats. Seconds later the ship streaked into deep space.

The lights brightened and a figure appeared in the doorway.

"Welcome aboard."

Starr and Tommy unbuckled and threw themselves into Wargonsee's arms. Denton shut his eyes and relaxed. They were going to a new world. He didn't know or care where. It was a place where the four of them would find freedom.

Mike Boggia
I've loved science fiction since my childhood when a family friend gave me a paperback book filled with wonderful stories. I read and reread Theodore Sturgeon, Ray Bradbury, H. G. Wells, and more. From that day, I continued to read science fiction, as well as any other book, fiction or nonfiction. I still seek old books in Bookman's and at yard sales.

My parents owned a dairy farm and I was the youngest of the family. I was left to my own devices for entertainment when my chores and school work was done. When the weather was too rainy or snowy and cold, I spent time reading, or if I didn't have a book, I wrote my own stories. Now retired, I can devote more time to writing and reading.

As with any short story, characters and plot revolve in my brain and suddenly inspiration strikes, be it from a picture, a piece of music or a memory. Out tumbles the story, sometimes like a raging river, or at other times in drips and drops. The story written in this book reflects memories and a picture.

My desire is to entertain, maybe make the reader think, or shiver.

5. LIFE LIFT

W.A. Fix

Dean Martin stood in the safety of the North American Elevator Airport Terminal, watching the sand storm blast everything not shielded by the building and its heavy glass windows. The storm had raged for two hours. If the winds didn't die down soon, today's lift would be canceled; only the third time in seventy-five years that North America would miss a lift. The whole point of building the facility in the southwest corner of Arizona was the weather—340 days of sunshine a year and when it rained the lift shuttles could still fly. The only thing that stopped them was sand. Sand, driven by forty to sixty mile an hour winds, would destroy the six massive ramjet engines propelling the shuttle. Old technology combined with the latest advances in fuel designs allowed the shuttle to lift, and return, 500,000 pounds of payload to forty thousand feet, with less than a hundred pounds of pollutants released into the atmosphere.

Scanning the scene outside, Dean saw no sign that the storm was weakening. He strained to see directly across the field at the four football-stadium-sized hangers that each housed a shuttle in the lift rotation.

The rotation was simple. While passengers and cargo unloaded, the shuttle inspection process began. Every rivet, every nut and bolt, every weld, piece of equipment and

43

electronic device was checked for operability, stress and fatigue. Identified problems were repaired within three days. The teams could replace and test an engine in thirty-eight hours, so there was nothing that would stop the rotation. Twelve hours for loading, eight hours of preflight checks, and the shuttle was ready to fly—twenty-four hours before its scheduled launch time. If the shuttle ahead couldn't fly, this ship was ready. One hour before take-off, the two hundred passengers went aboard and the ship was sealed.

However, it didn't look like that was going to happen anytime soon.

"Ladies and gentlemen, may I have your attention, please?" echoed the public address system. "This is Sidney Cotch, Director of North American Elevator Flight Operation. Due to weather conditions, today's shuttle flight is rescheduled for tomorrow's Lift. We know this is an inconvenience, but it is unavoidable. All flights have been slipped twenty-four hours. Shipping manifests and boarding passes, dated for today and the next five days, will be accepted for that lift date plus twenty-four hours. Thank you for your patience."

"Ahh, crap," said Martin as he activated his phone implant, selecting his boss from the call list on his right contact lens. Jay Yond answered within three seconds.

"Dean, what's up?"

"Sand storm canceled the shuttle. There's no way to avoid it—we're going to be twelve hours too late. Our five friends will be useless in thirty-six hours. What do you want to do?"

"Sand storm! Are you fucking serious? What the hell is a *sand* storm?"

Martin rolled his eyes. "I don't know, Boss, the wind blows hard, it picks up sand, a lot of sand. I'm looking at it right now and I can't see more than a hundred yards. The wind must be blowing 40 miles an hour." As Martin watched, the sand seemed to clear then picked up again, rolling several tumbleweeds past the window and into the massive cloud of red sand.

"Of course, it had to happen on a day we're doing a transport," said Yond. "Jesus Christ, what a mess, I don't know what to do. Get hold of whoever is in charge and explain the problem. I'll contact the lab and see if we can do anything here. I'll let the hospital on the Neil Armstrong know there's a problem and we're doing what we can. Dean, was this avoidable?"

"I don't think so, Boss. Sometimes the wind blows and there's no problem. Other times, like this one, the sand goes a couple thousand feet up in the air, along a twenty-mile front. No one could predict that."

"Okay," said Yond, "I'll get back to you in an hour. Let's see where we stand then."

"Passenger Dean Martin, please report to the check-in counter," said the female public address announcer for the second time.

"It sounds like someone looked at the cargo manifest," said Yond. "Good luck."

As Martin approached the check-in counter, the attractive clerk's smile got broader. He stopped in front of her and she said, "Mr. Martin." She stopped and almost laughed. "I'm sorry Mr. Martin. It's just that you actually look like him. I mean, Dean Martin, the old-time singer."

"He was my great-great-grandfather and my mother had an odd sense of humor and before you ask . . . I can't carry a tune in a bucket."

The smile vanished, "I'm sorry if I offended you."

"Hey, don't worry. I get that all the time. Actually, it's kind of fun." And it had been, since the resurrection of mid-twentieth century music; he had even been interviewed and asked to pose with a group of "Rat Pack" look-alikes.

"Our Director, Mr. Cotch, would like to speak with you. Would you come with me?" He followed her through a door and down a hallway, enjoying the view with every step. She led him into an office, where a moderately tall and slender man stood in front of a wall monitor, sorting through what was clearly the cargo manifest.

"Director Cotch, this is Mr. Martin," she said.

"Thank you, Julie," said Cotch.

Dean quickly turned to her, smiled, and offered his hand. "Thank you, Julie. I hope to see you again." Their eyes met and, hesitating slightly, she accepted the handshake with a hint of a blush. Dean thought, *Thank you, Great-Great-Grandpa.* She turned and walked out of the office.

Cotch moved to Dean, shaking his hand. "Hi. Sid Cotch. As you can imagine, things are just a little hectic. Dean, can I get right to the point?"

"Please," said Dean.

"As I understand it, you're transporting five eight-hundred-pound crates to the Neil Armstrong Space Platform." He walked to the wall and touched a 3D box to display a holographic image of the five crates. The crates flashed red with a message "Bio Degradable" and a clock counting backwards from 35h: 19m: 44s. "I also understand that Hartford Medical Laboratories has insured each crate for one hundred million New Global Dollars. We're unloading the crates, as we speak, so you can get them back to your facility and protect the contents. We'll provide any transportation, security, or assistance you require."

Dean sat in a guest chair, and said, "Well, Sid, actually *you are* transporting them. There is no one who can accept those crates on this planet. If you don't make delivery in," he glanced at the clock, "thirty-five hours seventeen minutes and fifty-four seconds, North American Elevator will pay us the insured amount."

"Our attorneys will have to sort that out. We certainly respect your privacy and we know you are not required to allow access to security recordings of packing, but if we knew what was in the crates we might be able to find a solution to our problem."

"Mr. Cotch," Martin paused. "Our attorneys have already sorted it out. It's not *our* problem. Hartford Medical Laboratories will do everything we can to help you make that delivery and solve *your* problem."

"Let's assume you're correct, and it *is* solely our responsibility. What makes those crates worth five hundred million NGD?"

"The contents are worth twenty percent of that. The other four hundred million will cover our financial liability, if the delivery isn't made." Martin stood and moved to the wall.

"May I use your display?" Cotch nodded and Martin placed his palm against the wall, activating his secure link. He touched the 3D box labeled "Hartford Medical Laboratories." Several other boxes opened and he selected "Transplant Cloning Shipment." Instantly, a transparent holographic image of a naked human male stood next to him.

"This is the contents of crate 1 of 5. It's called a Transplant Clone. It's genetically neutral—organs or body parts will take on the genetics of a host, only after it's implanted. It has no cerebrum and only a very limited cerebellum to maintain life support and assist in muscle tone development." Dean touched a red ball that floated next to the image. Internal organs, arms, legs, portions of the scull, several of the vertebra, eyes, internal, and external ears, and large patches of skin lit up in pastel colors.

"Eighty percent of this clone is scheduled for implant. The colors indicate the different recipients and the associated organ or body part that will be harvested. The five clones, male and female, represent one hundred eighty-three different patients from earth, and as far away as the asteroid belt. All of them have been in zero gravity for at least a week, waiting for their transplants. Zero gravity keeps them alive by reducing stress on failing organs. Many will die within a few days, if the transplants aren't performed."

Cotch interrupted weakly, "How many?"

Dean touched a spot marked *critical* and displayed a list of patient names. "As you can see, fifty-six people will die if this delivery is not made."

"Well, order up some more of those clone things. We'll replace this order with the new one and we'll have them there tomorrow. One day can't hurt," said Cotch in a tone betraying that he knew it wouldn't work.

"Sorry, Sid, 'those clone things' are cultured over four weeks and the next set won't be ready for two weeks. Anyway, the configuration would be wrong. You know— men, women, ears, no ears. We try not to produce products we're not going to use."

Dean left the display where it was and looked around the office. "You got anything to drink?"

Cotch looked at him blankly, then said, "Oh, yeah, there's bourbon and some glasses in the cabinet next to you." He looked back at the fifty-six names.

Dean smiled. "Ahh, bourbon, something else I inherited from my great-great-grandpa." He found the bottle and two glasses, poured himself five ounces and half that for Cotch. He didn't want to get the guy drunk, just relax him. Handing one glass to Cotch, he took a swallow of the amber liquid.

"So, what are you thinking, Sid? Got any more ideas? I've pretty much given you everything I can." Dean took another pull on his bourbon.

Cotch sipped his drink, shaking his head slowly, deep in thought. He activated his phone implant.

"Mike, how many pilots are on site? Good, bring all three to my office immediately. Set up a conference link with Lift Command. We need to solve a serious problem."

There was a short pause. "Julie, Mr. Martin needs to be on site tonight, so get him one of the VIP suites, and have his luggage sent over. I'll be here all night. No, I won't need one. Thanks, Julie."

He took another sip. "I want you to know that we'll do everything we can to find a solution." He paused, looking at the list. "And, Dean, it's really not about the money."

Dean touched the "close and clear" spot on his link and it vanished, replaced by Sid's original link.

"I know, Sid, the money just gets your attention and helps focus on the important stuff." He set his empty glass down. "Thanks for the drink. Thanks for the room. You know where I am, if you need me. I'll just check with Julie," and he walked out.

Two hours later, Yond called back.

"So what's the news, Boss?"

"Absolutely nothing," said Yond. "All the lab and the hospital on Neil A. can do is wait. Please, give me some good news."

"I wish I could. I've got them motivated, but there may not be anything they can do. They'll contact me, if they come up with anything. I'll let you know."

At 3:00 a.m., Sid called. "How many can you save if we get everything there seven hours before the deadline?"

"Probably everyone. Robots do almost everything. The longest surgery takes about an hour. I think we could do them all, if we used every surgical robot on the station. Can you give me seven hours?"

"Maybe even a little more. The shuttle takes off at 9:00 a.m., four hours ahead of schedule. We'll notify the other passengers. I'll talk with you later." The line went dead.

"Was that Sid?" Julie asked sleepily.

"Yeah. It sounds like he has a plan." Dean leaned over, kissing her on the cheek. "Go back to sleep. I need to make a few calls."

At 7:50 a.m., Dean stood with the other 199 passengers outside the main terminal, waiting to board the shuttle. It was a beautiful morning; the sky was clear with not a hint of wind. Two hundred yards away, the massive aircraft sat on the tarmac, looking like a combination of the old SR-71 and a huge cargo plane. The tail section was open and four people waited at the ramp.

"Excuse me, Mr. Martin?" Dean turned and met the gaze of a pleasant looking man in his early thirties. He nodded and the man continued, "I'm Mike Fisher, Mr. Cotch's Deputy Director. We're ready for you now."

"I'm sorry? . . . You're *ready for me now*?" said Dean skeptically.

"We need to get you suited up before take-off, sir. We don't have much time, please follow me." Mike put a hand on Dean's shoulder and indicated the direction with the other.

As they walked, Dean frowned, looking over at Mike, "I really don't like the sound of this. What do you mean 'suited up?' I think I'd rather ride with the passengers." He looked over his shoulder at the crowd filing onto the passenger ramp.

"Sir, Mr. Cotch is waiting for us. He'll explain everything." They were crossing the tarmac to the aircraft cargo ramp and an enthusiastic Sid Cotch.

"Dean, good morning!" Cotch shook Dean's hand vigorously.

"Sid, what's going on? Shouldn't I be riding with the other passengers?" Dean looked around nervously.

"No. You're going to love this. I talked to our Board of Directors last night and they approved our plan, as long as you travel with the cargo. We did a little checking of our own and you're the only person who *can* accept delivery of the cargo. You need to be at the hospital as soon as the cargo arrives." Sid almost laughed with excitement. "You are so lucky. God, I wish I could go with you."

"As you know, the Space Elevator Lift Wing lowers into the atmosphere on cables from space. The stations that operate the three elevators are orbiting above the equator, moving in the same direction as earth's rotation. Their orbit speed is slower than the earth rotates, so the Lift Wing, when in the atmosphere, seems to be flying 40,000 feet above the surface at around 330 miles per hour, bringing an elevator over the same latitude every twenty-four hours. A single lift is two operations: drop the previous day's shuttle and lift today's shuttle, which takes about four hours. There will be no shuttle to drop today, because yesterday's shuttle dropped on schedule and landed after the storm died out.

"South America's shuttle hook up is scheduled for four hours before ours. If we use their drop cable, bypassing the normal maintenance between hook ups, we can hook up to the Lift Wing four hours ahead of our normal schedule. The Lift can take both shuttles into space on South America's rotation. At about one hundred-twenty miles, the cargo bays open. You and your crates transfer to a space tug and are ferried directly to the hospital-landing platform, where you take delivery. In the meantime, the remaining cargo and passengers are spending another twelve hours, completing the lift, clearing customs and transporting to the Neil A." Sid could barely contain his excitement. "So what do you think?"

Dean smiled and said, "It all sounds pretty good. You've cleared all this with customs?"

"They reviewed the crate packing recordings and, given the circumstances, authorized a one-time free pass for you and the cargo."

"It all sounds great. Now, what about this mid-lift transfer . . . exactly how is that going to work?"

"Oh, don't worry about that . . . Paul! Hey, Paul! Come over here!" Sid yelled to one of the crew.

"Paul, this is Dean Martin. Paul is our loadmaster. He's normally in charge of the entire cargo, from loading to unloading. Today, he's in charge of you and your five crates. He's all yours, Paul"

"Come on, Dean, we've got to get suited up," said Paul.

As he walked up the ramp into the massive belly of the shuttle, Dean asked, "So, why do we need to get suited up?"

Paul smiled. "Well, when we transfer, we have to open the tail doors. You need to be in a space suite when that happens."

"Oh," said Dean. "Won't that damage the cargo?"

They were walking between the fuselage and the cargo stacked and secured in the center of the cargo bay.

"They're all either vacuum packed or pressure controlled containers. Everything inside the cargo hold works with, or without, atmosphere." They came to an oversized crate with a door in it. When they entered, lights were on inside where Dean saw seats and two space suits on a rack against the wall.

Twenty minutes later, the engines started and Dean couldn't hear anything Paul was saying. Paul finally gave up trying to instruct him and helped him finish putting on the suit. As soon as the helmet sealed, the noise vanished. Paul strapped him into one of the seats as the shuttle began to move. It took Paul less than five minutes to get into his suit. When he put his helmet on, Dean could hear every word.

"Okay, nothing to do until we hook up. You want to listen to the Com?"

Dean nodded and suddenly he could hear what was going on in the cockpit.

"NAE S zero 3, you are clear for take-off. Have a good flight."

Dean felt the deep rumbling in his bones. He was pushed heavily into his seat as the shuttle rolled faster, until it seemed to float up and the vibration of ground contact vanished.

51

"Speed 170 knots, heading West-southwest at 20 degrees. Climbing to 10,000 feet . . . request clearance to 20,000 . . ."

The chatter continued until Dean drifted off to sleep.

"Hey, Dean, wake up! We're getting ready to hook up."

"NAE S zero 3, you are in the slot. Hold current speed and position. We are bringing the docking clamps to you . . . Engaging clamps . . . Docking complete. Throttle back."

There was a brief shudder as the Lift Wing took over the aircraft.

"NAE S zero 3, we have you. Shut down all engines and systems."

The lights flickered and returned, signaling that the elevator's Lift Wing powered all systems and life support.

"Lift in . . . Five . . . Four . . . Three . . . Two . . . One" There was a slight jerk. "Lift initiated . . . Freefall in six zero minutes."

Paul's voice cut in, "Come on, we've got a lot to do."

They unbuckled and headed back the way they had come. When they reached the tail doors, Paul said, "NAE S zero 3 cargo bay to Lift Control. We are ready to begin decompression."

"Roger, cargo bay. Decompression initiated."

Dean's five crates were on the first pallet, ten feet from the bay door. Paul began disconnecting the pallet from the bay floor and inspecting the attached stabilizing rockets. He noticed Dean having difficulty moving around in the suit.

"The suit's pressurized and it'll be even harder when we reach freefall. You'll have trouble getting enough leverage to bend the joints. I'll help, if you need me. We have ten minutes till freefall." He pulled Dean to the crates and, using carabineers and loops on the suit, hooked him to the heavy straps.

"We don't want you to float away."

"What the hell do you mean, 'float away'?" Dean demanded.

"All personnel, this is Lift Control. Prepare for Lift stop and ten minutes of freefall. Secure all items and cover all liquids." The message repeated every two minutes, until Dean felt his feet leave the floor.

Paul was a crazy man, flying around Dean with ease, releasing the final restraints for the pallet.

"Lift Control, this is NAE S zero 3 cargo bay. Open bay doors," said Paul.

"Roger, cargo bay. Doors initiated" Dean watched the doors slowly swing out as the ramp dropped down. The earth was well over a hundred miles below. Dean had seen this from the passenger cabin, but never like this. All he could do was stare in open-mouthed awe. Paul pushed off the floor and grabbed the crate strap just above Dean's head, securing himself atop the crates.

"Okay, Dean, old buddy, time for you and me to go for a little ride."

"Little ride? What the hell are you talking about? Where's the tug to take us to the hospital?" Dean yelled.

"We're going to wait here, while the Elevator clears the area. Our ride can't pick us up until they're gone. Hey, don't worry, I've got you. It'll be fun."

"Fun, my ass. What do you mean You've got me? Who's got *you*? Nobody, that's who."

Paul produced the holographic controls to the stabilizing rockets and, the next thing Dean knew they were floating toward open space.

"Lift Control, we're clear," said Paul.

The raft of crates spun around for a better view. As the doors closed, the shuttle and Lift Wing moved away, appearing to simply . . . shrink.

To their left was the massive cylinder of the Neil Armstrong Space Platform, with its two hundred thousand residents—over a thousand miles away, but Dean felt like he could reach out and touch it.

"Dean, what do you think of that view?"

"I think, if I live through this, I'm going to kill Sid Cotch," said Dean.

Dean had no idea how long they waited—a few minutes, a few hours—time seems to crawl when you have your eyes closed. The small craft arrived and Paul threw a line into its cargo bay. The crates reeled in, the doors closed, and they headed to the Neil A., at 2500 miles an hour. In thirty minutes, they docked at the hospital receiving area. Under Earth level atmosphere and gravity, Dean signed the manifest and accepted delivery of "his" cargo, which disappeared into the hospital. That was the last Dean saw of it.

"If you ever do this again, Dean, let me know. It was fun," said Paul.

"Thanks, Paul. When you talk to Cotch, tell him I owe him a drink. I'm bringing the bottle."

Dean walked through unfamiliar doors into the hospital and stopped a nurse to ask directions. She paused before answering, smiled, and blushed, ever so slightly.

"Do you know you look just like Dean Martin, the old-time singer?"

W.A. Fix is a retired information technology professional, who lives with his wife and three cats in the suburbs of San Diego, California. He has "toyed" with writing all his life and recently became more serious about the craft. Several of his works are available on online magazines throughout the Web. He has two stories in an anthology of flash fiction, The Future Is Short: Science Fiction in a Flash, *also published by Lillicat Publishers. Read flash fiction by W.A. Fix at* The Story Shack Magazine, www.thestoryshack.com, *where his works, "Born to Play," "Nin's Glory," "Mitzi," and "Testament" are featured.*

DISASTERS

DISASTERS

6. I NEVER SCREAM

J. Richard Jacobs

About two months back, I'd had a particularly nasty day. You know, one of those days where everything was screwed royal. When I pulled into the drive, I guess I wasn't paying attention and ran through my garage door. That's right. Just drove right through the damned thing. The day and my garage door and my car all piled in on me as I headed for the house. On my way up the steps, I dropped the papers I was supposed to review before going back to work. You could say I was right on the edge of total torque by the time I reached the porch. The feeling that I needed to kill something was percolating to the surface.

My wife greeted me at the door—she never does that—and she was smiling one of those smiles that makes a guy want to get back in the car. What made it particularly bad was that it was rare for her—the smile—and I suppose I should have been appreciative, but I wasn't. I was tired and borderline berserk after a long day in the idiot bin, I'd wrecked my car and my garage and, dammit, she was wearing one of those smeared on smiles, you know the kind, and holding a large, gray envelope in her hand. I was not in the give-me-revelation mood. The first thing that went through my mind was, who was cutting us off for what and why the hell was she looking happy about it, or what was it I had done and what was I in for?

"We won," she said through a giggle that gurgled.

"Won what, Meg?" I said warily as I draped my coat over the arm of the couch.

"The lottery, silly. I sent our entry in last month. You don't remember?"

"No, dear, I don't. For how much and when do we get it?"

"No, not the money one. They announce those things through the system. We won two tickets for a ride up on the El and a week at Earth Station One, all expenses paid."

"Oh, great. Are they round trip, or one-way?"

Like I said, I was in no mood. Okay, I know what you're thinking, but you're dead wrong. Why the hell did I choose that phrase? Never mind. Anyway, I'm not a natural born smart-ass. I'm actually kind of conservative. I don't go out with the guys, carousing at all hours. Hell, I've never even cheated on Meg. Thought about it a couple of times, but I didn't do it. Anyway, I thought it was a reasonable and logical question at the time. No way did I want to become a permanent resident of the ES-1 that orbited just a few miles beyond the thing they call the dumbbell, whatever that is. I'm a homebody mostly. Well, I was up until a few weeks ago.

"They're round-trip, Phil. Why would they give anybody a one-way ticket?"

She had me there. Why would they do something like that? I guess it was a stupid question, but I wasn't thinking all that clearly. Cutting through the chaff, the prize included arrangements with my sadistic employer at the asylum for the terminally stupid for a couple of weeks off and the lottery would pay my wages. Such a deal. Not even I could refuse an offer like that. I was tempted, you know, but I didn't. I was rapidly on my way to straightjacket land at work and I could use the break. Any break. Even something as stupid as going for a trip into space. Who does that, right? It's not natural.

We had two weeks to prepare for the trip. They had included a list of the things we needed to do so that we would be allowed to board the El. We had to go for a medical exam that would be transmitted directly to the El powers that be. We were to limit what we brought with us to forty kilos or less. Why forty kilos? That one was a problem for me. What the hell could I take and what of those things that I hedonistically treasured would have to be left behind? I mean, there's stuff, and then there's stuff. Like the important stuff. How could I survive without all those little things that make a guy comfy? And for two weeks?

Anyway, we accomplished all the little tasks they required. There were forty irritating and rotten little things they wanted. I wondered if someone at the El office who handled these things had a hang up for the number forty. You know, like forty days and forty nights. I don't remember boot camp being that restrictive. When the time arrived for us to be picked up by the El, Inc. limo, I had finally made all my decisions about the stuff I'd take and was weighing it all when the chauffeur rattled our door com.

"Phil, honey, hurry up. He's here."

I packed all my junk in their official, made-to-spec carry-on case with the abandon of the damned. In the limo, I couldn't get rid of the idea that I'd forgotten something critical. Some bit of stuff I couldn't live without.
***

The flight to El Center Complex was uneventful and smooth, considering. I've been supersonic, of course. Everyone has. Never hypersonic, but I knew a lot about it and even though there were no windows, I could clearly see in my mind the leading edges of the wings glowing white-orange. My nerve endings had taken up a perch on the tips of every body hair I had. My stomach, full of acid, set up housekeeping right behind my tongue. Then the seatbelt light winked on and scant seconds later we were on the ground and nestled all cozy like against the debarkation tube. My stomach sank back to its normal place after a while and my nerves scrambled back where they belonged. Well, most of them.

The people pads transported us smoothly and briskly to the main waiting area where a group of reps from El, Inc.

stood in front of a large vidscreen. One of them stepped out from the cluster and raised a hand.

"Ladies and gentlemen," she said, "will you all please take a seat and we will begin your orientation."

Orientation? What orientation? It's just an elevator, right? Was I in for a surprise, and I could tell by Meg's expression that she felt the same tension. The first thing that came up on the screen was a sentence in very bold, intimidating letters in blood red.

A soft voice issued from the screen to explain the statement flashing on the screen.

"There is a radiation hazard warning light in the front of the lift pod above the doors. It is green in color to differentiate it from the other notice and warning lights. If it comes on during your ascent, please, remain calm. You will hear a loud buzzing coming from the field generator. The field will shield you from harmful radiation. This week there are no indications of potential flares and . . . "

Flares? What flares? Solar flares? That's when I first realized, I mean, really *knew* we were about to do something not terribly natural for human beings. Borderline stupid, you know. Funny, I hadn't thought about that before. Hell, I knew people climbed into this thing every few days and that there had never been a problem during its service. A service that now spanned more than twenty years. But . . . but there's always a first time, isn't there? What if this turned out to be the first time? What if we were going to be the first twelve innocent men and women on somebody's list of statistics? I thought hard about that; so hard I missed the bulk of the presentation. I thought about dragging Meg out of the building, but I didn't. I don't know why. I should have. Then I wouldn't be where I am now. Instincts are there for a reason, aren't they?

Anyway, after the presentation, they ran us single file through a little room where we were stripped stark naked. Instructions? "Raise your arms over your head, spread your legs, close your eyes hard, and don't open them until you hear the gong. Then move to the next room where you will be . . . " Yeah, stuffed into a little silver suit with hood to match. I was slicker than warm, uncooked bacon. Not a single hair remained on my body. I could have left my shaving kit at home and brought something else more important. The crinkly suit scratched at my recently raw, red skin and I felt like a foil-wrapped sausage. I'd never seen Meg without eyebrows and lashes. Not a hair on her head. It made her slightly tilted gray-green eyes stand out in stark contrast. She has a nicely shaped skull. Not all bumpy like mine. I did a double take and she kicked me in the shins. Okay, she had become a violent Little Hairless Silver Riding Hood.

"They didn't say anything about us being bald in the brochures," she whined.

I just smiled and said, "Eh, you look kind of cute and your eyes . . ."

She planted another toe in my shins. I suppose I shouldn't have said anything and just smiled. Maybe I should have said something soothing. You know, like, "You look so smooth, Meg." No, that wouldn't have been good, either. She would have kicked me somewhere worse.

They herded us aboard a tram with barely standing room so we all crinkled together in a moving ad for aluminum foil wrapped sausages. The tram-cum-sardine can whooshed out of the main terminal and headed away at a speed no sane person would drive. From my spot in the car, I could just make out what appeared to be a gargantuan tower on the horizon. I'd never seen a picture of the tower. The El, I thought. What else could it be? How the hell did they ever build an island this big?

***

The El's car was something to behold—as in overwhelming. It was nothing less than huge. It hadn't dawned on me how big it would have to be. Not like a cruise ship . . . but it was big. Then, as if a revelation had exploded in my brain, I realized that we were going to be in that car for three days. That's how long it takes to get to the shuttle level, which is something else I hadn't thought of. There would be twelve of us lucky winners and the six members of the crew. Three days. That meant meals, sleeping, lounging, and all that for three days. It made sense. I was proud of myself. I was beginning to think like a spaceman. Of course, a spaceman I am not, but I was still proud of my landlubber's reasoning.

The trip up was as comfortable as it could be, again considering. I had a small problem with the acceleration at first, not that it was horrible. Less than the elevator at work, really. My problems arrived when the acceleration began to go away and I got light. I mean, really light. Not quite weightless, but light. I kept getting lighter. It's a good thing somebody thought to make the soles of our suits with something that stuck to the carpet or walking would have been a major and hazardous project.

The food . . . was a surprise. It was good and it was plentiful. The opposite of what I imagined it would be. I was prepared for freeze-dried Chicken à la King and stuff like that. Drinking martinis through a straw and all. They had not held back any effort. I could only wish I could eat at home like that. Meg is wonderful in all womanly ways, but a cook she is not.

Meg and I spent a lot of time goggling in amazement through the few view ports available. They even had a small area with a see-through floor. I avoided that one after the first look. We watched all the presentation vids on how to handle ourselves in null-g. Like, if you push off to some other location, remember that you may feel weightless but mass was still there and moving too fast could really hurt when you got where you were going.

The actual transition to what felt like weightlessness was slow and gentle. I knew that because my guts stayed where they belonged and the sensation was not as weird as I had thought it would be. I guess that was because of how much time it took to get there. But it was . . . weird. Ever swallowed and had your whole body move? Weird.

The scream? Patience, I'm getting to that. Just hold on. Anyway, we made the transition from the El to the shuttle through a flexible, pressurized tube and they ferried us to ES-1. Again, no problems. It was fun, actually. I've never floated before. That's not what they called it, but that's what it felt like.

The trouble that got me where I am started when a group from TUMBLEWEED (The Union for Mitigating BLemishes / World Economy and Ecology Division) burst into the passage on our way to the dressing rooms. Okay, I exaggerated a little. It was more like they came in at a fast drift. I knew who they were because they were wearing uniforms with stylized, gold tumbleweeds with a big "T" in the middle emblazoned on their chest plates. They were brandishing nasty looking weapons and shouting TUMBLEWEED slogans at everybody.

"Phil," Meg muttered. "What are they doing?"

"I don't know, but I think we'd better do whatever they tell us. They look super serious to me," I said—quiet like so as not to draw any unwanted attention.

The leader, I guessed that because his uniform was a different color from the rest, floated into the center of the tube leading to the hub of ES-1 and drifted until he was within arm's length of our little band. He shot the ES-1 orderly, who was accompanying us, with some sort of dart on a long wire. The orderly's body doubled up and drifted toward the hub doors. He was out of control and bouncing off the walls of the passage. He wasn't moving, but I don't think he was dead. They'd lose a lot of points with the people who supported them by killing an innocent, you know. Then he forcefully gave us orders.

"Women to the left. Men to the right. Grab the rails and stay tight. Real tight." The words came out in a threatening growl and it was obvious by his tone that he was serious about what he was telling us.

Meg grabbed my arm.

"Phil?" she cried.

I told her as softly as I could that we needed to do as we were told. I wanted to shout, but I didn't want to make things worse for us. She loosened her grip and slowly drifted away. She was crying. I grabbed the rail on my right. Everybody reluctantly complied with the order, but not too reluctantly. Two TUMBLEWEED women floated over to the left and took our ladies in tow. Same for our side of the passage, except we got ape/human mutants. One stayed in front and latched onto my body suit and the other went to the end of the line to push. I heard Meg calling my name as they drifted away toward the hub entry. There was nothing . . . nothing any of us could do. Despite the six men from the El and our two captors, I felt very much alone and helpless. I remember thinking that this was turning out to be some vacation. Why the hell didn't I refuse to go on this nightmare? Well, because I didn't know it was going to be a nightmare, I suppose. I mean, there was nothing in the promotional material suggesting we might be attacked.

Attacked for what? I can only guess, but ES-1 is central control for all international and interplanetary communications. If you want to get your message out to a lot of folks, I suppose controlling the place that controls all communications in the system is a good place to start. Another moment of pride for me. Now I was thinking like a terrorist.

    ***

In the hub cylinder, we were each shoved into six separate doors that looked a lot like the airlock doors we entered when we arrived at the station on the shuttle. The guy doing the shoving was a cross between King Kong and Godzilla, and you don't argue with that blend. He said it was for our own good. You know, like no innocents would get caught in the crossfire. I could sympathize with that, but now I was really alone. I wondered about the women and worried about Meg. Had they received the same treatment? Each in their own little cell? I thought about what Kingzilla said and I felt better. Not good. Just better. An obviously computerized voice came from somewhere.

"You are to proceed to the outer door for transfer to Ptolemy maintenance bay. All human crew members except the maintenance exec are to debark in five minutes for separation maneuvers."

What did all that mean? I had no idea, but they were giving the orders so I figured it would be best to do what they said. Hey, I'm no spaceman and I sure as hell am no hero. I floated over to the outer door. There was a hiss as the door opened and air pressures balanced. That I understood. You know. I've watched the vids and knew that hiss and click business. I moved through the door and found myself in a garden. Garden? A small robot rolled out from behind some tall grass. Well, it looked like grass, and it wasn't really rolling. There were small tracks recessed into the floor. Otherwise, it would have been floating like I was.

"Are you the new Biological Maintenance Exec?" it asked.

"Uh, no. No, I'm not. I'm, um, Phil Bosworth. I'm a passenger on the station. We won tickets. We . . . "

"Curious. If you are not the BME, then why are you here? I have no Phil Bosworth in my files."

Another hiss and click sounded in my ear as the door behind me closed. Closed. There I was in a garden with a little machine that looked like a small tank with arms and it was talking to me. Nothing unusual in that. I talk to my home bots all the time. But I was trapped with no place to go. Tingles raced over my body at the thought. Why? Not why the tingles, but why was I in that garden . . . alone? Okay, not alone exactly. There was the bot.

"I don't . . . know."

"We are separating in thirty seconds. You should go."

"Separating? What does that mean?"

"The Ptolemy is leaving the station."

"Leaving? What do you mean, leaving?"

"Our mission schedule requires we depart."

"Depart? Depart for where?"

"The programmed destination for this mission is Drexler 21B"

"What . . . what's that, dammit?"

"It is not a dammit, it is Drexler 21B. Drexler Mining's asteroid 21B."

"This thing is getting ready to go to an asteroid?"

"Drexler 21B is an asteroid, yes."

There was a clank and a whir. I'd heard that sound in a recent Science Fiction vid. Real mechanical, you know.

"That would be the clamps releasing. We have separated. Prepare yourself for acceleration."

"Oh, my God. Oh, my God," I mumbled. I don't believe in that stuff, but I couldn't think of anything else to say. We were moving. I could see the tall grass in the garden moving, vibrating, and waving in response to the motion. I didn't feel it since I was still drifting in null-g, but it seemed like the garden was moving away from me. Then I contacted the bulkhead. No, that's not true. The bulkhead contacted me. See, I can figure things out. That's when I realized the damned thing was actually moving. That I wasn't hallucinating. That thought wasn't the worst of it. It was moving away from the station. Moving away from Meg and the El and home and my stuff and my lousy job that I suddenly wanted to go back to. Going somewhere and I was going with it—alone. Well, okay, there was the bot, so technically I guess I wasn't alone. All my stuff was back on ES-1 and all the comfort giving stuff was at home. I may not have been alone, but dammit, I didn't have any of my stuff and that's almost as bad as being alone.

"Stop this thing. Get me off this ship." I had never panicked before, but that seemed like an appropriate time, so I did. Did you know you can taste panic? Sort of metallic on the tongue.

"Ship operations are automated. I cannot interfere with ship functions. I am not qualified. I am a Gardener, Model 12A. They call me a Pot Bot."

The bot rolled over on his little tracks to where I was firmly glued to the bulkhead. I felt as if I was made of lead and I was sure my face was on its way to the back of my head.

"It is too late to debark, sir. The next opportunity to debark will occur in eight hundred twelve days. Would you like me to help you down—and do you play chess?"

I screamed. I screamed so loud it hurt my throat. I never scream.

J. Richard Jacobs is an award-winning author of science fiction novels (6). He has also published anthologies (11) and round robins (3), and written a couple thousand short stories, published in numerous publications. Recently he is concentrating on **Perihelion Science Fiction**, *which he considers the best hard science fiction magazine around. He also writes nonfiction science articles.*

7. THE CLIMB

Jon Ricson

Lysa looked out the window of the jumper jet at Indianapolis Prime and found herself wondering if she would ever return. She had been born there, went to primary, secondary, and late training there. She met Marcus and married there. Most every friend and relationship she had ever met could be traced back to Indy.

But this was a new start. She'd lucked into passage on The Climb. The recent horrifying space plane crash in Chicago had grounded all flights to high orbit, so the only way up was to take the space elevator, or as the world knew it The Climb. From Aries she would take the cruise she and Marcus had bought months ago and see where that led her (other than away from him.)

She had heard a lot about life in the colonies. Both Luna and Mars had growing communities, and even the mining colonies on the moons of Jupiter were interesting frontiers to her.

As the jet ascended to low orbit for the remainder of the hour-long flight and Indy shrank away, she leaned back in her cubicle and into her seat. In a few minutes, the cabin would stabilize and she could move around. She wasn't exactly one for small spaces. *Great thing for a person about to take a cruise through the solar system in a confined ship for six months*, she thought and shook her head. This was

67

so out of character for her. But something in her finally felt free. Free of Marcus and his infidelity. Free from her friends and family and their expectations. And now, free to move about the cabin.

The tone sounded and the vid played softly. "You may now exit your cubicle if you wish, but please be aware that gravity is low. You'll find refreshments in the common areas between sections. Thank you for soaring with us today."

She had only flown on jumper jets a few times, mostly for vacation getaways with Marcus, but had always enjoyed the gravity difference. It was just fun to bounce around. She bounced right for the bar.

***

He watched the lithe woman bound from her cubicle and towards the open area. However, he would not be mingling. He had a job to do, and could not risk any interaction that might interfere with that.

Turning on some news vids, he stopped at a report of the space plane disaster. His recently established leader, Derric Hayes, had been aboard that fateful flight. When it crashed, so did the hopes of many of his compatriots. They had planned for almost a year to meet on Aries Station and to begin the first large-scale phase of their blessed work.

"Excuse me, Mr. Diaz," an attendant voiced into his cubicle. "May we get you anything? A beverage or snack, perhaps?"

Diaz was not his name, but for the purposes of this trip, he would use it. "No thank you," he said, and switched off further audio.

He looked out the window onto the Earth, now visible as a large sphere from low orbit. Derric may have died, but the man known as Diaz would still carry out this mission in Derric's honor. Perhaps it was not too late for their plans to come to fruition after all.

"*Reorganize the Worlds!*" he whispered to the window.

***

As the last jumper jet descended vertically onto the pad, Jana Keller was happy it was finally time to get this underway. It had been a tiring few weeks. From chasing Derric Hayes through, under, and over Indianapolis Prime, to following him to Chicago, to the crazy adventure with

Peter and the horrifying crash, she barely knew which end was up.

All she knew was that before a well-deserved furlough, she had one more job: look for a possible Reorganizer faction member, while making sure everyone got safely to Aries station.

Another IP officer handed her the manifest for this last group of passengers. The Climb was usually for freight, instruments, supplies, and mostly non-human cargo that needed to get to space without delay and without waiting for a space plane flight. But with the massive disaster a few days ago, the space-going elevator had been opened temporarily for passenger travel.

Reading the manifest, she fingered the holodisplay, name-by-name, looking for her suspect, and instead saw a name from her past.

"Lysa?" she said to herself, even though the noise from the jumper jet drowned everything out completely and the wind pushed the sound all around on this small man-made island off the coast of Britain. She double-checked the iDent, matching it to the photo. It was indeed her old late training buddy, Lysa Cooper, or Lysa Harrington, as her married name read here. She had always liked Lysa, but never thought of her as the adventurous kind, more the type to find a guy and settle into a comfy Prime life.

The passengers disembarked the jumper jet and boarded a hoverbus. Jana watched from afar and followed the bus on foot to the prep building, taking a moment to trace the giant thick strand that rose out of the ship and into the heavens. She had not been to Climb Island before, but had seen pics. They didn't do it justice.

Checking the manifest again, she didn't see any obvious names. But she was sure the operative wouldn't use a name they knew and were looking for. That meant she'd need to visually inspect everyone. At some point that meant a reunion for her and Lysa, which would be fine. *Even though I kind of stole her boyfriend,* Jana thought, cringing a bit.

***

Lysa settled into the makeshift passenger section in the second level of the elevator. She had thought from the outside the ship kind of looked like a five-section ant, with bulbous sections stacked on top of each other. She had read that the middle three sections would protect against much of the radiation, but passengers were prepped extensively anyway.

The suits weren't necessarily bulky, although she wouldn't have chosen them for style, or for basketball. Not that she had played much lately, anyway. Her dainty Indy friends had never been into sports.

She briefly considered what to do with the helmet. They said the helmets would only be needed once they got to low orbit, and that would be a few hours from now.

The layout of the room in Section Two was unique. It was round and the middle of the room was a clear section that the cord ran through. Although the fiberglass (she supposed it was fiberglass) was at least three feet thick, she could clearly see the cable inside. It both impressed and horrified her to think that was all the ship had holding it.

"Attention all passengers. Please strap into your seats, as we will begin the final countdown for ascension in five minutes. Once the ship is moving up and has reached a consistent climb, we will inform you when movement is possible. A lavatory is available on every floor; however, please be patient as you will need to share with others . . ."

Lysa looked around at the two or three dozen others in the large section, and hoped she didn't have to go too badly. Could be quite a line.

"While we don't have amenities like food service, there are provisions under every seat including snacks and drinking water. Please see one of the section leaders for any other needs. Thank you and enjoy this special voyage aboard *The Climb*."

She was lucky and had a beautiful view out the small but well placed windows. Even though it was a gray day, she looked forward to watching as they rose above the ocean.

***

He strapped in as the message droned on about the specifics of *The Climb*. The protective suit chafed him, but he didn't think it would change the mission. He had anticipated that they'd have to wear something like this.

70

Looking around the section, he saw the woman from the jumper jet. A typical Prime. Enjoying a luxurious life, probably heading to a cruise or similar vacation spot. Her blonde hair flowed around her shoulders. But he wasn't interested. His calling was greater. His cause was purer.

He watched the cable inside the fiberglass tube start to turn as the ship prepared to lift from the ground. The friction from the rotation would soon pull the multi-section ship up towards space. It was only a matter of time now.

***

Jana finished a brief conversation with the captain of the ship, who had started the countdown to ascension. She told him of her mission and what she suspected, and he wasn't too pleased. Of course, none of the crew seemed pleased about having commercial passengers, or Interplanetary Police, here in the first place. This was supposed to be a scientific vessel, and they weren't used to ferrying space-going guests or cops.

She went to her seat near some other crew in the third section. As usual, she took the furthest seat from the window. If she had hated Earth to orbit at space plane speeds, she would *really* hate the ride in slow motion!

The captain had mentioned it would be at least an hour before the ascension would be steady enough to allow movement, and even then wanted to minimize it, as they had never before had more than a dozen passengers on board, much less the hundred they had now. So, as the countdown ended and the ship quietly lurched off the ground, she closed her eyes.

***

The man not named Diaz stared relentlessly out the window as the Earth slowly fell away. He had tried to sleep, and had briefly dreamed of Derric Hayes, his mentor . . . his hero. Part memory and part fantasy, they had been having a conversation in his semi-dream.

"You understand what we are trying to do Juarez?" Derric asked. They were sitting on the top of an old structure just below the Indianapolis Prime slaveways— under the world, as usual.

"Yes." Juan Juarez nodded and looked up at the Prime hovercars whizzing by overhead. "They must fall."

71

"And why must they fall?"

"Because they are greedy. Because they keep us underfoot like insects. The Prime world must fall. We must Reorganize the Worlds." Juan looked at Derric for acknowledgement, for acceptance, but Derric only stared out into space.

"All the worlds must fall, Juarez, not just on the Prime cities of Earth. We must pull it all down, and give the people the opportunity to rise." Derric's eyes blazed, and Juan swelled with pride in his association with the Reorganizers. No longer just a Strag from a poor Hispanic slum, but a soldier, fighting for a cause.

We must pull it all down . . .

With those words echoing in his head, Juan Juarez looked at the altimeter that logged the miles on the holodisplay above their heads. It read 25 miles. He sighed, and sat back . . . waiting.

***

Lysa curled her lip looking at the time. It had seemed like hours, but only had been 64 minutes since they gently lifted off the ground and began ascending. She briefly thought about getting up, but it seemed to be frowned upon by the unfriendly crew. This wasn't exactly a pleasure cruise.

So she just sat, periodically looking out the window, although there was really nothing to see but a blanket of clouds below, as they were much higher now than the 20,000 or so feet from where the highest clouds sat. Just a big blue sky and the warm mid-afternoon sun.

She was so lost in her stare that she didn't notice someone standing next to her seat. Looking up, her face turned incredulous.

"Hey, stranger," Jana Keller said, smiling.

"Jana?" Lysa hadn't seen her old friend since late training, even though they had tried to get together a few times over the years. "What are you . . ." then quieter, "are you on duty?" Jana put a finger to her lips, and pointed to the empty seat next to her.

Lysa looked around. "Go ahead, that guy got up a while ago for the bathroom. He must not be feeling well."

Jana looked around carefully and kept her voice low even though, with the sound of the elevator cord sliding through the tube in the middle of the room, as well as wind outside, the noise floor was high and it would be hard to eavesdrop. "Actually, I am working. I'm kind of looking for a passenger, and saw you on the list. So what are you going up for? And where's Marcus?"

Lysa sighed. "Long story. Let's put it this way, he's an ass, and it's over. And I am taking myself on a cruise."

"Wow, look at you! *Miss Space Explorer!*" Jana laughed. They both did, and easily fell back into comfortable step as they always had.

"So what about you, *Miss Secret Mission,* can you tell me what's up, or would you have to term me right here, officer?"

Jana shook her head, weary. "IP has been chasing these Strag members of something called The Reorganizers . . . ."

"Right, I've heard about them. Aren't they terrorists?"

"They think they are freedom fighters, but they are more a pain in my behind." And my gut, and my jaw, she thought thinking of her last run in with Derric Hayes. "So really, I just wanted to say hello, and should keep checking everyone."

Lysa touched her hand. "So . . . have you seen Peter?"

Jana lost her breath for a moment, the events of the last few days still very fresh.

"You know, I just ran into him a few days ago." That was literally the truth. She left out the parts about helping Peter on his mission, about the crash, and the sex.

"How is he?" Lysa asked. "I often wonder if he has found the life he was looking for."

Jana smiled. "He's at peace doing what he always knew he would. He's a great officer." She wondered if she should apologize, after all it was years ago, and then decided to just cut and run. "Oh well, duty calls."

"Right," Lysa said nodding. "It was really great to see you, Jana."

"Me too. Maybe we can get a drink on Aries when we get there," Jana said, knowing full well they wouldn't.

"That would be great." Lysa said. Jana waved and walked towards the next section of seats.

***

A woman had come by asking questions, but he smiled and shrugged as if he didn't understand her Prime, Standard English. Of course, he did. She was probably a member of the meddlesome and no nonsense crew, and he had tried his best to stay out of their way and anonymous.

Juarez looked at the altimeter, and then trying to be inconspicuous, reached for his pack at his feet. Of course, IP had searched the contents of all bags and cases going up, but security was more lax that even he would have expected. Still, the idea of a taking a holodisc player, and a few other innocuous items, that together could produce a tight laser, was ingenious.

He carefully assembled the small tools at his feet. He then gently slid it back under his seat, and looked back at the altimeter. Just a few more minutes . . .

***

Jana was getting concerned. She had narrowed the list to three. A strange, and quite rude, woman complaining unnecessarily. *What am I a flight attendant?* Jana thought. Then the quiet, unassuming Diaz, who feigned that he didn't understand her. Finally, a mysterious crewmember who kept staring at her when he thought she wasn't looking, although she had a feeling that guy was more likely just a perv and dismissed him.

The vessel swayed and a few passengers near her in Section Three moaned. The wind had picked up and the captain had announced it could get choppy as they approached low orbit.

"You might want to strap in," the first mate told Jana. "We're past the point of no return and this is where things get interesting."

She pulled the harness close. Soon they would need the helmets, and that didn't excite her at all.

***

Lysa was getting a bit sick to her stomach when someone behind her gasped. She turned to see what was happening, and a man had stood from his seat, and was holding something in his arms. He seemed perfectly at

74

peace with himself, but something was definitely off about him.

"Everyone stay seated," he smiled. "We will be at our destination very soon." And then the bright light sprang from the tool in his arms.

***

Jana felt the ship rock violently. Crew began to scurry, unharnessing themselves, and checking holodisplays. She heard a screeching sound, and saw a light erupt from the cord chamber. It was coming from Section Two below them.

"Captain, we have a report of a passenger holding some kind of laser!" the first mate screamed. Between the high noise that already existed on board, plus the new whine of the laser, and the rising commotion from the three dozen or so passengers in this section, it was cacophony.

She quickly unbuckled and pulled out her pulse gun, then bolted for the access ladder to Section Two. The captain yelled at her to sit back down, but that wasn't going to happen. They had crew aboard, but no one trained for this.

The damn Reorganizers were trying to take down *The Climb*.

***

Screams, shouts, and cries sounded all around him, but to Jaurez it was like a symphony. The laser was beginning to cut through the thick clear casing and soon would make contact with the 15-foot thick cord that hoisted the ship upward. Once the cord was severed even a little, the stress would blow apart the ship and the famed League of Sol Planets space elevator, *The Climb*, would instead plummet to the Earth below. The Primes would be stranded without a way into their precious solar system.

To his right, a man attempted to approach him. Juarez quickly turned the laser and it ripped cleanly through the soft flesh of the man's midsection, even the spine didn't slow the beam. The horrified passengers around him shrieked as the crewmember slid apart into two halves.

Then Juarez simply returned the beam to the fiberglass. He was almost through carving out a whole wall of the fiberglass protecting the cord.

***

Lysa was frozen in her seat. The blood of the slain crewmember was changing direction on the floor. Maybe it was the ship bobbing due to wind or whatever he was doing with the laser thing, but all she could see was the blood.

The terrorist stayed deadly calm, even as he had sliced the crewmember in half. Many seemed to join her in shock, which had temporarily stopped the screaming and wailing. Then she saw Jana.

***

Jana tried her best not to attract attention as she let herself down the ladder that, as luck would have it, was directly behind the man using a laser to sear off an entire side of the protective fiberglass for the cord.

She gently took a step towards him, trying not to alarm passengers so they wouldn't alarm him. Then her eyes met Lysa's. She was in shock like many of the other frightened people in the room, all with a horrifying front row seat of their impending death.

Someone on the opposite side of the room turned their head to look at Jana and that was all it took. The man whipped his head around, and Jana ducked as he swung the laser toward her. She fired a pulse towards his feet from under the seats, but it ricocheted off the metal seat supports.

The laser ripped up the floor as it got closer to her legs. Passengers began panicking. She could see the crewmember on the floor, or at least half of him.

She dove out from behind the passenger section, and fired two blasts at his chest. One hit home and he dropped the laser weapon. Rolling from the dive, she got to her feet. He rolled over reaching for the laser, but she was there.

For the second time in three days, Jana struggled with a member of the Reorganizers, taking blows while trying to wrest the weapon from him. Beyond him, air was whipping up from the cord, which was now fully exposed from deck to ceiling. She pushed him towards it.

The sound of the rushing wind emanating from the cord, that was still pulling the huge five-section ship towards space, turned what was already loud into madness. Jana didn't hear the shrieks and cries of the passengers anymore. She didn't think about the blood slick deck that they struggled on. All she knew was that the cord was her only chance.

***

He should have known she was IP. She was obviously trained and strong for a woman. They both gripped the laser, but he couldn't fire it. He was so close. All he had to do was get one more clean shot at the cord, and he would accomplish what he was made for.

Stupidly, she was pushing him backward. In a moment, he would feign losing momentum, and she would slip on the blood and fall. Then he would slice her with the laser, as well.

Behind him, the wind howled off the cord. He pretended to fall, and her momentum pushed her over him, and onto the floor. Juan Jaurez stood up and aimed the laser at her head.

***

Lysa watched in horror as Jana fell over the crazed man, who then took great delight in aiming the laser at Jana's head. Lysa suddenly looked at her hands, which were grasping the silly helmet the captain was preparing them to don. The killer's face looked strangely familiar, and suddenly she saw Marcus as he had looked telling her about his lover. How angry and crazed he had been.

Without thinking, Lysa hurled the helmet at him, striking him in the head, and dazing him momentarily. He staggered and shook his head.

***

Looking up, Jana saw the helmet bounce off the head of the Reorganizer. She desperately looked around for her pulse gun and saw it a few feet away. He shook off the effects of the helmet, and turned the laser back towards her. But she was faster. In one motion, she grabbed the gun with her left hand, and fired towards him. The pulse hit him directly dead center in the chest and he was blown backward through the hole he had carved in the fiberglass. His back hit the cord and his body was sucked against it instantly. Within seconds the spinning, rushing cord pulled his body into the foot wide crevice between the melted sides of the fiberglass. Blood soaked the clear tube as the

77

churning cord disintegrated his body, drawing it down the shaft.

***

Lysa ran to Jana, even as the captain was trying to reassure passengers the ship was still functional and climbing, and urging them to put on their helmets.

Jana was sitting up, dazed. She looked up at Lysa. "Nice throw, Lys."

"I was wondering what to do with that stupid helmet," Lysa smiled. "Good shot, yourself."

Jana smiled. "Not bad, and I'm not even a lefty."

***

Two hours later, crew worked around Section Two trying to clean the damage, as weary passengers departed the section for Aries Station. Jana came back down from talking with the captain and filing a quick report to IP, still feeling the most recent of her bruises. Lysa was the last to leave the section.

"I was only half serious about that drink," Jana laughed. "But now it's imperative. What do you say, *Miss Fast Ball?*"

"Right there with you, *Miss Quick Draw,*" Lysa smiled back.

And they both happily walked out of *The Climb.*

Jon Ricson has been writing since he found an old ledger book of stories and plays written by his father as a young man. Jon started adding his own stories of giant uncontrollable monsters, silly spies, and even comic musicals to the weather bound book. In high school, he invented a smart aleck Chicago detective he still writes about, and near future stories of our solar system. With his first full novels in both genres almost complete, Jon still finds offshoots of these universes for smaller stories, as is the case with "The Climb", a story from the near future about an adventure on the world's only space elevator. For more on Jon Ricson, including the latest news on releases and publishings, check out http://www.JonRicson.com.

8. R & R

D C Mills

I really didn't want to be here. Taking a tourist trip, particularly a round trip on, of all things, a commercial space elevator, was not exactly on my list of things to do before I died. Which could be any time, given my day job.

But Division HQ had decided in their wisdom that the civilian population of the Empire needed to see their friendly neighbourhood legionaries in the flesh, to be reassured that we were not all trigger happy psychos bent on killing and/or raping everything that moved. To that end, a number of us grunts and junior officers, including my fireteam, had been appointed to put on the pretty uniforms and go play tourists for a few days.

Hearts and minds, they reminded us once again. Hearts and minds.

So, here I was—here we were—in our clean, newly pressed parade ground uniforms that chafed in all the wrong places from being practically never worn, politely queuing up amongst honeymooners, excited kids, equally excited old people. Waiting to start the great adventure that was a round trip into Outer Space. Yee frogging haw.

Snafu seemed excited, for whatever reason, but then he was always excited, no matter if he was polishing boots or clearing a minefield. Snafu had a singular ability to focus on the task at hand. Maybe that was something to learn, to enjoy the moment.

The week before, we had been doing exactly that, clearing minefields around and in a small town where the locals had a hard time deciding whether to hate us for intruding into their private war or be reluctantly pleased that we were keeping them from being blown up on the way to the market.

Next week, we would probably deploy to some other outpost to defend another corner of the Empire against who knew what. But for now, we were back on good old Terra, on leave — except we had to comport ourselves in a dignified manner in order to boost the public opinion of the armed forces. So, no R & R after all: no drinking, no getting into fistfights, no whoring. Instead, a tourist trip on a commercial space elevator.

By the way, next week, instead of deploying somewhere interesting, we would still be on the commercial space elevator. At no more than 200 kph, it was going to take us eight frogging days to even reach the docking station in geostat orbit that was our temporary goal.

***

'Remember last time we rode in one of these things?' Jock put in quietly.

Did I remember? Frog, yeah.

The previous year, we had been stationed in orbit around Mars waiting for — and, they hoped, preventing — the outbreak of a war between two colonies. When the leader of one colony was nevertheless assassinated, we were sent in to clean up the mess. The swiftest means of deployment was the newly installed elevator, with climbers going at maximum speed downward — 328 kph, and we were on the surface in less than 48 hours.

We stepped out of the climber directly into heavy fire. Coming down a fixed cable isn't exactly sneaking up on someone, and the perimeter that was supposed to be around the anchor site hadn't been all that effective. It didn't help, of course, that the anchor had to be mobile to avoid the hyperactive moon, Phobos, snapping the cable twice a day. Securing an LZ that is constantly on the move is a frogging thankless job. So, you can't really blame the guys who were on it. Or not, as it were. Still, we lost too many men that day, before we broke through the hostile perimeter.

Yeah, I remembered.

**

Finally, we were all on board and being herded into a non-descript but comfortable lounge by a chronically cheerful flight hostess, who introduced herself as Julie and immediately launched into her prepared speech. Something about the duration of the flight, safety regulations, the view, the construction of the whole thing, opportunities for access to the outside in a secure suit, yada yada yada.

I knew that my mates were longing for a drink as much as I was, while calculating our chances with the various females in the group.

I caught myself counting everybody present, assessing his or her abilities and potential merits in a crisis. Habits persist, and even when I reminded myself that this was not a squad of recruits I had to keep alive through combat, I ran them through in my head. Less boring than listening to safety regulations, anyway.

Apart from the five of us, there were the staff of three women and three men, and the civilian passengers: a family with two small kids; a pair of honeymooners; a group of four twenty-somethings, who did not seem to be paired up on any permanent basis; an old couple; a middle-aged couple with a lonely-looking daughter; three plasto-surgically enhanced women who looked like a matching set of Barbie dolls — blonde, brunette, and redhead; and a man travelling alone. Thirty persons in all, the maximum number for this type of climber.

Julie was still prattling on about carbon nanotubes and how the climber car had two parts, A-sphere and B-sphere. Nice legs, though.

We were given numbers and key cards to our pre-assigned cabins, our homes for the duration. My team were placed in two adjoining cabins with not quite bunks, but sufficiently economy class to remind us that we were still grunts on duty.

Sledge had, to the delight of all, smuggled a couple of bottles in. At least we could drink the first night. The rest

81

would take care of themselves—after all, anything could happen. Maybe Julie the flight hostess and her colleagues were longing to party with the boys in uniform.

***

After a bit, everybody settled in to enjoy the flight. Well, everybody else. It was something like a cruise on a ship— not that I'd ever done that—with a number of passengers contained in a transport vehicle, passing time and admiring the view, while knowing that their true destination was home, and the docking station only a mid-way point featuring new experiences, in this case, zero gravity.

There was entertainment planned along the way, of course: your usual music, dancing, food, games. No swimming pools or tennis courts, as you might find on the deck of a cruise ship, rather, less spatially demanding activities. A couple of exercise rooms with weights, bikes, treadmills. Better than nothing.

Those who wanted the Full Experience could choose to go on a space walk. Dressed for safety in a real space suit, securely tethered, and accompanied by a Professional Guide (in this case the second pilot, Jeff), anyone could go outside into Outer Space. Photo opportunities were included.

***

Day four, Amanda approached me, her professional smile brittle. 'Sir, I'm sorry to have to ask you to get your man off the treadmill. It's not built for sustained activity over extended periods of time.'

'Why? How long has he been on it?'

'Well,' she hesitated, 'it's coming up on five hours now.'

I hurried to the exercise room, Amanda's heels clicking in my wake. Jock was steadily huffing along, face set in grim determination. Of course, it was him; he didn't get his call sign just for being Caledonian.

'Jock,' I said, 'enough now. You need to give the machine a rest, man.'

He looked at me in surprise. 'Bob? But I've only been here . . .'

'Five hours, man. Look at the display. You've done eighty kilometres. That should settle you for one day.'

82

'I'm sorry,' I said to Amanda. 'We're not used to being inactive.'

'Don't you guys ever relax?' she said.

'Sure, of course we do,' I said. 'That's what R & R stands for. Rest and Relaxation.'

'So, what do you usually do to rest and relax?' For a moment there, I almost thought she was flirting with me.

'Um, we go bathing.' *Swimming with sharks.* 'We play golf.' *Using live hand grenades for balls.* 'We go nature walking.' *Like the time on Mt. McKinley, or across the Bay of Rainbows.* 'And we, well, we party and have fun,' I finished lamely. Gods, I hate PR. Being a poster boy isn't as easy as it looks.

On the fifth day out, the new husband tried to pick a fight with one of us. He had already, ever since we embarked, been dropping hints about our perceived lack of social skills. According to him, anyone who had volunteered for the Army did it because they were incapable of being around regular people — 'normal' people. Oh, and we were probably all gay, too, which was why we'd chosen to live in an all-male environment. Plus, we were trying to steal his wife. Yup, logic.

At first, we ignored him and steered well away from the wife—not that she wasn't a nice person and easy on the eye, at that — but no need to fuel the paranoia. It all became too much for Sledge, who had been taking the brunt of the insults. Served him well for being the best looking of us.

'One punch, chief, just one punch.'

'Yeah, and who do you think he'll call first, the media or his lawyer? You'll be court-martialled — hell, we'll all be court-martialled. He's not worth it. He's just a damn soft civilian who's pissing himself that his pretty new wife won't see him as a real man anymore, compared to us.'

The next day was apparently going to take care of that.

***

The new husband suited up under the supervision of the pilot, Jeff, doubling as space walk guide, to go outside into Real Outer Space. The rest of us were gathered in the lounge, watching the live feed on big screens, the new wife oscillating between pride and fear. Airlocks hissed, and then they were out there. New husband's voice sounded over the comm system.

'This is amazing! I mean, look! It's all around . . . just amazing.'

A true poet, that one.

Snafu looked at Sledge. 'Wanna go?'

'Really?'

'Yeah, it'll be fun.'

Sledge shrugged. 'Yeah, sure, why not. Might as well . . .'

A thunk shook the lounge, dislodging the mood. Drinks spilled, one of the kids started crying, and the red-haired Barbie actually toppled off her bar stool this time.

'What the . . .?'

'Frog, we're under attack!'

'Where did that come from?'

A bomb! Was that a bomb?'

'Mummy, what's happening?'

I ducked and reached for my rifle before I remembered it wasn't there. I could see the others doing the same and shared a glance with Snafu. He was feeling as naked as I was.

An alarm started blaring, orange lights blinking, adding to the confusion. I smelled acrid smoke from somewhere. Something that wasn't meant to burn was on fire. The climber car shook again, this time with a series of smaller thuds — blast doors slamming shut between the damaged area and the rest.

'Snafu, Jock,' I shouted over the din. 'See if anybody's hurt. Sledge, Lucky, on me. We're finding out what's going on.'

I had, as always, done my automatic head count. All were present in the lounge to watch the space walk, apart, of course, from Jeff the guide and the new husband, whom we watched, and Barry, the first pilot, who was on the bridge, assisted by Julie the flight hostess. Everybody who was supposed to be here was still here. If it was a bomb from inside, it had to have been on a timer.

The new wife started screaming.

'She hurt?' I yelled.

'Nope. Look outside,' came the reply.

I looked. Gently thudding against the large pane of ceramic glass, separating the lounge from the emptiness, was a mangled body dressed in most of a space suit. The helmet was cracked and halfway gone, the face — what was left of it — bloody. One arm flopped about at an unnatural angle.

The new husband had found out what it means to put your life on the line.

'Right, Snafu,' I said, 'you get your wish. Come with me, we'll find suits. Can't leave him hanging out there, and we need to see if the guide can be retrieved.' The new wife was still screaming. I turned to the civilians, the women in particular. 'Somebody calm her down. We're going out to get him.'

Blonde Barbie hurried over to her, which surprised me momentarily. I would have expected one of the older women to take on the mothering role, rather than this shallow party girl. You never can tell.

The suits on this commercial flight were lighter than the ones we had been trained for, but rarely used, but they seemed able to do the job. They had all the requirements: air rebreather system, reenforced body glove, anti-radiation outer layer. The comm system in the helmets was familiar, too.

I could feel the pulse in my temples, a floating sensation beneath my sternum. Deploying via a space elevator is one thing, going out with only a suit between you and open space is another. I suddenly wondered what the new husband had felt to make him do this.

We suited up quickly and were ready to go, when flight hostess Julie called me. 'Sir, there seems to be a problem with the control systems.'

Did she just call me sir? 'What do you mean? And why are you telling me this?'

'Um, Barry was knocked on the head, and Jeff went outside, so there's no pilot, really.'

I groaned inwardly. Show the tiniest bit of initiative, and people look to you to lead them. Lucky was the most tech savvy of us, so I called him up.

'Lucky, get to the cockpit and see if you can work out what the problem is. Snafu and I are going out. Jock and Sledge can look after the civilians.'

'Yes, sir,' Lucky's voice crackled through. I have to say this for my team: no matter how hard we party or how much crap we dish out among ourselves, when it comes down to it, there's no hesitation, no slur in the carrying out of commands. We all know I'm in charge when it counts.

Which was why, of course, I had to lead the trip outside to retrieve the body of the new husband and find out what had become of Jeff, the guide. It was the most dangerous place to go right now.

The damaged part of the climber car was sealed off and could burn or not, as it pleased, without the rest of the vehicle taking any notice of it. The civilian passengers were all gathered in the lounge, being taken care of; Jock and Sledge had their emergency medical training, and the flight hostesses presumably had theirs, too. Julie and Lucky would see to Barry as well as to the piloting.

The galley had not been hit, so even if the controls were gone and we had to wait here, on the cable, for a rescue party, there would be food and water enough for several days.

So. Airlock. Stepping outside. Not quite zero gravity, but close enough. Lines tethering us to the hull, just like the new husband, poor sod.

The trick now was to get hold of him and manoeuvre him back towards the airlock and inside without getting the lines tangled, or cut, or getting him bashed up even more. I hoped the new wife wasn't watching, in case it got ugly.

We moved along the side of the car, towards the spot where the lines of the tourist and his guide were secured. Or had been; the remains of a broken snap hook still stuck to the cable running along the guideline on the hull. There was no sign of Jeff the guide.

The sudden jerking of the climber car would have yanked the cables the two men were tethered to, snapping the guide's line and whipping the new husband against the hull.

'Seems like the guide is gone for good.'

'What a fate — he'll fall towards the surface and burn up in the atmosphere.'

The new husband hadn't fared any better. At least, though, there was a body for the family to bury.

The outsideness became gradually less daunting, as we had a job to do. We moved to either side of the dead man and grabbed hold of him. I got the busted arm and had to remind myself I wasn't hurting him by tugging it. We managed to steer him gently back towards the airlock.

I called up Jock. 'Get inside the airlock to receive the dead guy,' I told him. 'We're going to assess the damage from out here.'

Once he was safely inside, Snafu and I let ourselves float away from the hull to survey the exterior damage. There was a large hole at one side of B-sphere, the one with the cabins and the lounge we had been gathered in. There was no fire, because there was no oxygen anymore; the smoke I had smelled earlier must have come from something burning briefly right after the impact. Or explosion.

'What do you think, Snafu?' I asked. 'Impact or explosion?'

'Definitely a hit from outside, sir,' he said without hesitation. 'Look at the edges of the gap.'

'Agreed,' I said. 'So we can rule out sabotage from inside. An attack isn't likely, either — that would have been followed up.'

'So, just an accident, sir?'

'Looks like it. We were probably hit by some random chunk of debris coming this way.'

'Had to've been one hell of a chunk to make that kind of damage,' Snafu commented. 'I mean, these things are built to take a beating, right?'

'Right. Something big — or fast. Maybe a meteorite.'

'And right when those two were outside. What are the odds?'

***

Back inside the lounge, I noticed at once the tension in the room. Everyone was very still, even the new wife who had collapsed into stunned silence.

'What's going on?' I asked.

87

Sledge gestured at the twenty-something men who were sitting side by side on a sofa, looking somewhat ruffled, but defiant. 'Those two decided that our companionless friend here was a terrorist bent on a suicide sabotage mission.'

'Makes sense,' one of them insisted. 'He's alone. He could have brought a bomb with him.'

'Or made one,' the other one added. 'From, like, kitchen stuff.'

'Idiots,' I muttered. Louder, I said to all assembled, 'The damage was done from the outside. The climber was hit by debris, or maybe a meteorite. It was an accident.'

'So, bad luck, then?'

'Just bad luck.'

The new widow began sobbing.

***

The controls had been only temporarily stunned, shutting down automatically on a time lock when the impact happened.

'Frogging stupid system,' Lucky complained. 'What are they supposed to do in an emergency — just sit there?'

'So,' I said, 'what next? Can we turn around and head back?'

'That's probably what most people'll want,' Lucky agreed.

Barry shook his head and immediately looked like he regretted it. 'We can't turn around,' he said. 'There's another climber on the cable, three days below us. We have to go on up to the docking station to switch.'

'All right, frog it,' I said. 'Let's make the best of it.'

It turned out that what had been hit and was now sealed off were two sleeping cabins and one exercise room. With a bit of re-shuffling, everybody had a place to sleep. The new widow moved in with the Barbies, and somebody else got the former honeymoon suite, though it wasn't a suite, of course, but a regular cabin like all the others.

The flight hostesses showed their worth, not once betraying fear or dismay in front of the civilians. They served meals, found extra bedding and temporary clothing for the unfortunate who had lost theirs, initiated games and entertainment, and smiled, smiled, smiled.

A call came through from Division HQ. 'I hear you and your men handled yourselves well, Sergeant.'

'Thank you, sir.'

'A blessing in disguise, this accident. Showed the civilians they can rely on Army personnel.'

'Two men died, sir. A young woman was widowed on her honeymoon.'

'Yes, well, unfortunate, that. But these things happen. It would have been a lot worse if you fellows hadn't been there.'

'Yes, sir. Thank you, sir.'

'Report to my office immediately, when you are back down again.'

'Yes, sir.'

And that was that. I really didn't want to be here.

D C Mills (a.k.a. Dorthe Møller Christensen) is a word nerd, both professionally and in her spare time. She teaches Latin to unsuspecting undergraduates and writes short stories in a variety of genres. Several of these stories are published in anthologies, so far The Future Is Short: Science Fiction in a Flash; World of Pirates; *and* Dangerous Days. *She lives in a small house in the middle of Denmark with three tall sons and a cat that doesn't steal the knitting. And she is, of course, working on a novel.*

9. MURPHY'S RIDE

Gary Hanson

TransCargo Flight 7603 left Perth Australia at 03:00 Australian Western Standard Time (AWST), with Flight Commander Lory Narja in the main chair. Lory smiled at the thought, because the cutbacks in 2054, and advances in automated avionics, had made him little more than a flight attendant. Lory watched the controls closely as the autopilot guided the 767 cargo jet into the sky, just clearing the cactus and brush at the end of the runway. The poorly maintained GE CF6 engines, combined with the heavy fuel load for the transpacific flight and the overload of bulk 3D printer cartridges made it far closer than it should have been. It simply did not pay to ship manufactured goods across country, and certainly not internationally. Since the development of 3D production printers 40 years earlier, you could make anything you wanted, even works of art, identical to an original. The only air cargo being shipped now was the specialty raw material cartridges for the 3D printers; there just wasn't much profit in anything else.

As the craft strained to gain altitude, Lory was wondering which would have given out first, one of these TransCargo flying coffins or his rapidly failing health. Not that it mattered much to Lory anymore. The Autodoc medical computer back in Hanger 33 had confirmed his suspicion of stage IV brain cancer—he only had a few weeks to live anyway. He wondered, though, how the radical group Jazera Qaida had known to approach him for this mission. He had been very careful to keep secret his discontent and conversion to the Salafism sect. It never occurred to Lory that the radical thinking and anger were likely symptoms of his brain cancer or, maybe, he simply had not been as secretive as he had thought. The real reason Lory and many others like him were the pawns of any number of groups, was this driving need to be remembered. Most of them had little talent and less creativity, so not having the ability to create, they were driven to destroy.

Lory reached for his IPod12c and connected to the Net3 public services for the latest news feeds. As he expected, the news was mainly talk of the USA President and other world leaders attending the 2055 G3+1 Summit at Gamma Moon Base. Upon returning to Earth, they would be making the rounds of the Pacific Rim countries. The entire delegation was returning on the South Indian orbital elevator from the Earth Geostationary platform.

The South Indian elevator was anchored at one end to the L3 Point above the earth and at the other end to the South Indian platform. TransCargo 7603's flight plan called for the aircraft to divert around the South Indian exclusion zone by 50 km to the south, before coming back north toward Madagascar. The elevator was on its way down to the South Indian platform and the timing appeared to be perfect for him to intercept it near the 767's absolute ceiling at 12,000 meters. If the other Jazera Qaida operatives could get the elevator defenses to chase their decoys to the northwest, and if the moles at the South Indian platform disabled the particle beams, Lory would have a free path to the elevator—his target.

To the northwest, Lory could see the South Indian platform—although, none of the platform's six carbon fiber ribbons would be visible until moments before he took out the elevator's Maglev Pod containing the President and the entire delegation. His timing had to be perfect. Only the Pod was vulnerable to attack. He would have needed a nuclear warhead to damage the nanotube fiber ribbons or the anchoring towers.

**

Leaving Earth

Secret Service Agent Gary Murphy was enjoying the trip back to Earth with the President, even though his stomach was still a little queasy from the low gravity he had been under during the entire trip. The view out the windows of the cloud tops and deep blue ocean was stunning, but for Murphy the curvature of the Earth against the deep black of space was a view he would not trade for anything. Even the corona discharge, from radiation flux around the Moon Base's magnetic shields, paled in comparison. Once they entered low Earth orbit the elevator was protected by the Earth's magnetic field. All the power generated by the carbon nanotubes as they passed through Earth's magnetic field was captured, in order to power the magnetic shields for the Elevator and Base. From where Murphy sat, he saw a flurry of activity around the communications station. He was just making his way over to the station as the alert message came in.

The American station operator, David Jones, looked Murphy's way and said, "Looks like we have some activity out to the northwest. A group of six Sal Lanki fighter jets are not answering our radio challenges."

"Yeah, I can see some of our escorts going to afterburners below us. I better inform our diplomatic passengers that we might be in for some excitement," said Murphy.

"Flash Alert," said the voice over the loudspeaker system. "South Indi defenses are under attack. Radar indicates a number of missiles are incoming. Suggest Maglev Pod 1 return to 90,000 feet."

"Roger, returning to 90,000 feet. Maglev Pod 1 out," replied Jones.

Murphy staggered under the increased gravity as the Maglev Pod slowed to a stop. Within seconds, the Pod was moving back toward space.

"I wonder what those guys were thinking; those missiles don't stand a chance. Most of them are going wide of the platform and the particle guns are not even bothering with them. Well, so much for that excitement," said Jones, taping on the radar screen. "Looks like the Sal Lanki jets have broken off and are hightailing it for home."

Murphy knew that the particle beam weapons were first developed during the Reagan era, in the late twentieth century, as part of the Star Wars defense systems. He also understood that the systems had come a very long way during the last seven decades. However, their biggest drawback remained line of sight targeting. Basically, if you can't see it, you can't shoot it down.

"Maglev Pod 1, this is South Indi Platform. All clear. You may resume your descent."

"South Indi platform, this is Maglev Pod 1 restarting descent. We are at 53,240 feet. ETA is now 05:32 AWST. Maglev Pod 1 out." This time Murphy felt himself go weightless as the Pod braked and then began the descent.

Aboard TC 7603, Lory looked out toward the South Indian platform and saw the missiles falling into the ocean, just below his position.

"Mayday, . . .day, this is TC 7603 heavy, have . . . hit . . . missile. Mayday. Mayday. Any sta. . .on please res. . .ond." Throughout the transmission, Lory keyed the mike to simulate radio problems.

"Ah, crap, the press is going to love this. South Indi let those missiles go, without shooting them down, and they take out a cargo plane. By tomorrow, this will all be the President's fault. Well, at least it's not a passenger jet," said Jones.

Murphy searched the sky to the east for any sign of the plane. "Do you think the runway at South Indi is long enough to handle a heavy jet? Would they even allow it to try with Marine One down there?"

"TC 7603 heavy, this is South Indian Platform, about 65 miles west of you. What is the nature of your emergency? Our runway is Class B with a 9000-foot length; I doubt a damaged 767 heavy could safely land at sea level under current conditions. We are currently restricted airspace due to the arrival of the Maglev Pod 1. Again, we are currently restricted airspace, TC 7603 what is your intention?"

Lory thought for a moment, than transmitted. "South . . . ian Plat . . . m . . . think . . . might be ab . . . return to Perth but need a direct vector, through y . . .

. . . airspace." Lory continued to simulate radio problems, while increasing power and climbing.

"TC 7603, we cannot grant you permission to enter restricted airspace," replied the platform.

Lory keyed his mike several times sending a grabbled message of "please retransmit." He then listened to South Indian try to raise him again for about a minute before turning back toward them. He could see the Maglev pod descending and about 5 minutes out. Lory expected them to try a warning shot, but that was one of the problems with particle beam weapons, the beam was almost invisible. The fighters were out of position and couldn't chance a missile with the Maglev in his shadow. All he could do was hope that Jazera Qaida took out all of the particle beam weapons before the platform got serious about shooting him down.

As Murphy returned to his seat, Jones was on the link with South Indi trying to find out what they were going to do. South Indi was being careful not to transmit on an open channel. If they were going to shoot the plane down with the particle beam weapons, they could claim it went down because a missile accidentally hit it.

The loudspeaker system announced "Flash Alert," and Jones heard over his headphones, "Maglev Pod 1, someone just took out the transformers that power our particle beams. Looks like it was sabotage. Assume TC 7603 is hostile; recommend you prepare for accelerated avoidance protocols."

Jones quickly gave the alert over the loudspeaker system. "Everyone, please take your seats and strap in. Emergency maneuvers in fifteen seconds. We are going to pull some gees, folks."

Lory was about 20 seconds away from the Maglev pod, descending from above, when the Maglev Pod suddenly dropped like a rock. He still had them, pushing forward to full power. When the Maglev did an emergency stop on the ribbon, it caught Lory off guard and, even though he tried to pull up, it was too late. He overshot his target, hitting dead on the ribbon just below the Maglev. The carbon fiber ribbon twisted to the side of the 767 fuselage, shearing through the left wing like a knife through butter. The explosion destroyed what was left of TC 7603 and splashed burning jet fuel up the ribbon, crystallizing the surface of the carbon nanotube fibers. The Maglev brakes released and they were in freefall. The pilot quickly initiated the drive to slow them down and within seconds, they were descending at their previous rate, but with a slight yaw, back and forth.

Murphy went forward again to check with the pilot, John Lewallan. As soon as he entered the command center, he could see the pilot was not happy. "John, how is it going?" asked Murphy.

"Not so good," said Lewallan, "the Maglev drive is slowing us, but some of the debris must be keeping the electro-magnetic brakes from closing enough on the ribbon. Our real problem is this damn yaw dragging us back and forth across the ribbon. I'm not sure, but I think it's increasing and we still have 22 minutes to touchdown."

"How bad is the yaw and what is the worst case?" said Murphy.

"Ever play with a guitar and slide you fingers down the strings on a note. If you watched the string in slow motion, you could see the vibration tighten as you move down the fret board. The vibration increases in both degree and frequency the closer to the bottom you get. Currently we are at 6 degrees with a 34-second frequency; I'm not sure which is going to be worse the degrees of yaw or the frequency. If it gets bad enough, it could cause the ribbon fibers to abrade."

"Better let Jones know. I'll inform the President, the Premier of the Euro Union, and the Asian Chairman of what's going on, and that we might need to evacuate," said Murphy. Evacuation meant only one thing—once they were low enough, they would escape by parachute.

By the time Murphy reached the President's suite, the yaw was getting worse. He told the delegation that as soon as they got to 5000 feet, they would begin the evacuation. The President would go first, then the other world leaders, and then their spouses. The Euro Union Premier objected about leaving without her husband, but Murphy explained that time was short and the evacuation was according to the required UN protocols. It was going to be tough enough for the recovery boats and choppers to rescue that many people from the waters, even near the platform.

"What about everyone else on board?" asked the President.

"Sir, the rest of the people are likely to be safe enough, just a little banged up after a very rough ride. But, sir, we simply cannot take the chance with you and the other leaders," said Murphy.

By the time they got the President and his jump buddy suited up, the yaw had increased to 8 degrees with a 23-second frequency, and the peak sideways thrust was about a 10th of a G. With everyone but the jumpers strapped into their seats, they opened the left airlock and timed the President's jump for the next cycle. The first group went out smoothly, at the absolute peak of the yaw. The other leaders went without any problems, but when the Euro Union's spouse went, there was a loud ping sound and, as Murphy watched in horror, something cut through the left arms of the paired skydivers. The arms separated from the divers and the two began to tumble, then were lost from sight.

"What the hell was that?" yelled Murphy, as the First Lady began screaming hysterically.

"Carbon fibers are beginning to snap. We can't risk any more jumps; that was the last one." The sound of more pings echoed through the pod.

"So much for it being safer on the platform—not with nanotube fibers falling out of the sky," said Murphy. "Jones, let the platform know the danger and warn the rescue boats to steer clear of the platform and the waters nearby," he yelled.

It took a few minutes to calm the First Lady and get her strapped into a seat. With everyone secure, they approached the last 100 feet toward touchdown; the yaw increasing to 36 degrees with a frequency of 9 seconds, producing a sideways G force of 1.6 gravities. Even with the Maglev drive at maximum, they were still going to hit hard, at about 9 mph.

The Pod cracked open on contact with the platform, dropping Murphy, and a couple of other seats, into an area below the tower anchors. Somehow, they missed all the loose strands of carbon fibers that had broken during their descent. Murphy was just lying there, stunned, when the tower anchors finally gave way. The sound of ripping steel screamed in his ears as the remains of the carbon fiber ribbon jerked what was left of the Maglev pod up and into space. The ground base no longer anchored the counter weight on the space end of the elevator and with the Maglev Pod breached; the remaining people onboard never stood a chance.

World popular outcry demanded the dangerous recovery effort, through all the jumbled and tangled individual carbon nanotube fibers. It took 8 months and two additional lives. The final death toll was thirty-seven, including the TC 7603 pilot. Based on Murphy's recommendations, Jones and Lewallan were given posthumous awards for valor.

Unfortunately, Agent Gary Murphy was no longer useful to the Secret Service, because someone in the media dug up his name and personal history. But, due to the loss of the First Lady, the wife of the Euro Union Premier, and the others, and all the things that had gone wrong during his watch, he did become famous. They named the entire incident "The Murphy's Law Ride."

As a first time sci-fi author (for a paid published work), I enjoyed the challenges of writing this story. My few past writing forays had been technical product documents and science articles.

My background is as a new product development engineer, currently working on designing automation equipment for the wholesale bakery industry. I live near Somerset, a small town in west central Wisconsin, about 10 miles from the border with Minnesota, near the Twin Cities.

I had always wanted to try my hand at fiction writing but never quite found the opportunity, until I noticed a science fiction micro-story writing challenge on Linked In. After submitting a few micro-stories to the monthly contest, Carrol Fix encouraged me to submit a little longer work on the topic of a space elevator disaster. I am a strong believer in Sci-Fi stories based on hard science, with plot line twists. I hope you enjoy my take on the Leaving Earth theme.

Gary Hanson

10. Retribution

Harry Alexiou

Marty Williams was excited. He kept telling his neighbours that he was "over the moon" at getting his ticket for the Space Elevator trip. Nobody laughed; they'd just wished him luck as he rattled off technical space details, without being asked. Today, he didn't care what people thought of him. He was a single guy and lived in a small house left to him by his mother. Having no loan on the house allowed him to save hard for his trip.

Marty had recently connected with an old friend on a social networking site. During their catch-up "chats", she'd expressed an interest in joining him on the trip, when he asked her. She loved tennis, he loved tennis; she hated golf, he hated golf. Science fiction movies were their favourites; it was a match made in heaven, he'd told himself. He threw his luggage onto the back seat and settled in for the journey, a journey which would be the peak of his much travelled past, and the start of an exciting relationship. He had good reasons to be excited as he gunned his all-electric Jeep south.

***

Orville viewed the parched landscape spread out before him, just half a mile from Interstate 505. A single tumbleweed was the only sign of life as it rolled along, stopping and starting, on a journey to nowhere. He

98

squinted back at the shack, where he'd held the girl since last night. It was ten in the morning and he was expecting the call from his accomplice, who would soon be receiving the money back in Sacramento. Orville's only job was to keep her locked up and blindfolded until he got the call from Jerry to get the hell out and meet at the pre-arranged rendezvous point. He smiled as he thought about his share of the ransom money.

"2.5 mill," he whispered.

The five million wasn't much to ask from the wealthiest landowner in the whole of the US. His phone rang, vibrating against his leg. He wrestled it from his pocket and answered the call.

"Yeah?"

"Hope you still got the girl, Orv."

"Course. You got the money?"

"Ain't got no money yet."

"But it's gone ten, Jerry."

"You think I ain't got no watch? I seen the time."

"Call me when you got it."

Orville hung up and walked lazily back to the shack, kicking dirt as he went. He opened the door and made his way to the girl tied to the wooden post in the far corner.

"Please let me go!" she sobbed, her face streaked with tears. "My parents'll be worried sick."

"Shut up kid! Your pa's paying the ransom right now." He leaned down and stroked her cheek. She pulled away.

"Leave me alone!"

"Don't worry missy, all I want is my money . . . you're not my type anyhow." Orville turned away from the girl and walked to the small partially glazed window, clutching his phone. He looked at his car with disdain. *First thing I'm gonna do is buy me a brand new Corvette.* Orville didn't hear the approaching attacker as he daydreamed.

The sudden whack to the side of his head left him screaming in agony as he turned to see the girl running for the door. He gave chase, head pounding, and lunged toward her, cut rope dangling from her wrists. Orville landed heavily and grabbed her left ankle, bringing her down. She lay there motionless as he picked himself up, holding his head.

"Damn it! You stupid . . ."

Orville realised she wasn't moving. The redness staining the floor caused him to cover his mouth, his stomach knotting at the sight of blood. He bent down to check her pulse, but couldn't find it.

"No no no! Wake up! You can't be dead."

The phone rang, vibrating on the floor. Orville checked the caller ID. It was Jerry. *No explanation would be acceptable to Jerry*, thought Orville, as he watched the phone ringing. His trembling digit touched "*Accept.*"

"H-h-hey" said Orville.

"He wants to speak with the girl before he hands over the money," Jerry said.

Orville felt sick to the core as the request was processed, ever so slowly, in his distraught mind. He couldn't respond and dropped the phone to the floor, his partner's voice still faintly audible as he stood and exited the shack. He sat in his car and calmly turned the key in the ignition; it whirred uncooperatively.

Orville rested his head on the steering wheel. "Come on baby! Help me out here!" he screamed, turning the key once more, simultaneously pumping the gas pedal. He exhaled forcefully, welcoming the throaty sound of the engine as he turned the vehicle towards the 505. He made it onto the highway unsure where he was going, his mind doing cartwheels with Jerry's last words resounding in his ears and the image of the girl lying dead on the floor.

Orville punched the dashboard repeatedly as the car spluttered to a halt at the side of the road, after only a mile or so. He stepped out and kicked the door, steam escaping violently from under the hood. He slid down the side of the car and held his head in his hands; defeated, realising he would probably spend the rest of his life in jail.

After five minutes sitting on the roadside against the car door, Orville stood up and cranked open the hood. As he inspected the damage, a car approached and slowed to a stop beside him. A bespectacled man rolled down the window of the Jeep.

"Hi there! Trouble?"

"Yeah . . . she's dead . . . 'bout as useful as a porcupine in a balloon factory."

"Yeah, looks bad . . . geez, that's a hell-of-a bruise you got there."

Orville felt the side of his head. "No airbags on this old girl, hit my head pretty hard."

"Where you headed?"

"Same as you, due South, I hope."

"Okay, then. Hop in."

Orville didn't have a clue where he was going as he settled in next to the talkative stranger.

"I'm Marty," he said, extending a hand to Orville.

"Or . . . Rob."

"Orrob?"

"No, just Rob . . . too much of being out in the sun, I guess."

"Huh. You see that sign, Rob, that's where I'm going. Trip of a lifetime."

The sign read, "SPACE ELEVATOR TERMINAL-85 MILES."

Orville had heard of the space elevator and had never given it much thought. Space had been turned into some kind of holiday getaway and the only way up was in a space elevator. Faced with the thought of life in prison, it started to sound like a desirable destination. He wanted to know more from the stranger.

"So, what is this 'Space Elevator' contraption?" said Orville, a plan already forming in his mind.

"Well, the Space Elevator is something many people thought impossible, at least in the 21st century. It's an amazing feat of engineering, starting at the brand spanking new Space Port Terminal. When passengers arrive at the terminal, a high-speed, sea skimmer ferry whisks them to the launch platform out in the Pacific, right on the equator line. With my ticket, I get to sit in a pod with 49 other lucky travelers. We hurtle into space at 120 miles per hour on a cable—an extremely strong cable constructed out of carbon nanotubes. When we get to the top, 100,000 miles up, we can spend time at the huge space station paradise, before returning the next day, or the next week, if you can afford the accommodation. At $400 per pound of weight it's not cheap, but I've been dieting and saving money for a year . . . in fact the two things go hand in hand!" Marty laughed at his own joke.

Orville had listened with interest, but had no desire to hear any more, geeky, scientific facts. It was the perfect time to make his move.

"Oooh, stop the car, Marty. I think I'm gonna vomit!"

Orville exited the vehicle holding his stomach with one hand and his mouth with the other. He moved to the rear of the vehicle and crouched low, feigning sickness, producing throaty guttural noises as he waited for his moment. He could hear Marty asking if he was okay, calling his name repeatedly, but silence was his only response.

The car door opened and Orville watched through the windows as the helpful stranger made his way to the rear of the vehicle. Crouching low, Orville picked up a small rock and walked around the car to sneak up behind Marty.

"Sorry!"

The crushing blow sent Marty spinning into the roadside ditch. Orville was sickened by his own actions. There was no going back; he'd crossed the line. Jerry had asked him to babysit the girl, "easy money" he'd said, but he'd screwed it up and now he'd killed someone else. Two days ago, he was a supermarket employee with no criminal record, aside from petty theft—now he was a double killer on the run. Orville sat in the front driver's seat and looked in the back, grabbing at the sports bag nestled on the floor. He pulled it onto the passenger seat and rummaged around for the "ticket to space" and anything else of use.

Orville found the Space Elevator ticket, along with money, credit cards, and personal belongings. He put the bag beside him and accelerated hard from the roadside showering his unlikely savior with dirt.

The journey to the terminal had taken more than an hour and he followed the signs to the check-in parking zone. Once inside the building he followed signs to the check-in desk. Holding the bag, he fidgeted as he observed the other passengers ahead of him. His body tensed as he could see the photo ID of passengers being checked. Beads of sweat broke out on his forehead, while he rummaged around in the bag looking for the ID.

"The queue's moving," said a voice behind him.

"What?" snapped Orville, turning around.

"Err, the queue, are you going?"

"No . . . go ahead."

Orville left the queue, sat down, and continued hunting for the photo ID. In his haste to find it, he'd overlooked the zipper compartment at one end of the rectangular sports bag. He prayed as he unzipped it and put his hand inside. The relief was so strong that it almost brought tears to his eyes. He studied the photo of Marty Williams. Fortunately, Marty wasn't wearing glasses in the photo, but neither did he have a moustache. This could work in his favour. Orville had the same straight mousey hair as Williams, but he decided to refashion it to appear similar, at least. He entered the men's room, grabbed a grooming kit from Marty's bag, and proceeded to attempt a makeover.

The queue had all but gone with only one other traveler in front of him. He was next in line and smiled widely at the female check-in clerk. He presented his ticket and photo ID to the clerk. She scanned the ticket and looked at Orville then at the ID, then back again to him. She looked at the photo once more, taking her time to decide. Orville, still smiling, hoped to confuse the identification process.

"Have a good trip, Mr. Williams," beamed the clerk.

"Much obliged."

Orville dabbed away the sweat as he boarded the *Sea Skimmer* and sat with the bag across his lap. He watched the others, listening to their excited chatter.

He noticed a woman passenger frantically looking around, a permanent frown creasing her forehead. She was looking for somebody. Orville felt his pulse quicken as paranoia set in. He fixed his gaze out of the window across the bay, avoiding eye contact. The curious woman eventually settled down as they sped off to the platform, a short ten minute journey.

They approached in choppy seas and Orville could see the tethered space elevator, a long, clear, pod-like vessel with rows of seats visible. The light tap on his arm made him jump.

"Your first time into space?" asked the passenger.

"Uhuh, yeah."

"A space virgin, eh. Thought you seemed nervous. Don't worry you're not the only one."

Orville didn't want conversation; he just wanted to be left alone as they pulled up to the platform.

The public address system burst into life. "Please ensure that you take all belongings with you, as any unclaimed items will be destroyed."

They manoeuvered into position beneath the towering platform, the sheer size of it dwarfing the *Sea Skimmer*. Cushioned hydraulic arms gently moved into position to hold the craft. Orville exited with the other passengers.

The assembled group received some brief pre-ride advice before they were ushered into the gleaming glass pod of the space elevator. Seat belts fastened, the elevator moved off slowly at first then accelerated towards the upper atmosphere.

The woman next to Orville turned with a frown and spoke to him.

"Excuse me. Do you mind if I see your ticket?"

"What? Why?"

"I think I may be in the wrong seat."

"Why would you think that?" he said.

"Well, I was supposed to be sitting next to an old school friend, Marty Williams."

Orville's insides screwed up as he looked blankly at her, then out into space.

"Okay, listen," he said, turning back to face her, "I don't want any trouble."

"So, tell me how you got Marty's ticket."

The beads of sweat forming on his forehead were telling, as the woman watched him closely, waiting for his answer.

"Marty and I are golfing buddies, and when his ma got sick he didn't want to waste the ticket, so he gave it to me for a hefty discount."

The woman sat back and stared ahead of her, drumming her fingers on the arm rests. She turned sharply to Orville and spoke calmly, a cynical look in her eye.

"I hope he told you about the anti-radiation inoculations," she said.

"The . . . the what?"

"You have no idea what you've gotten into. Without those jabs you're gonna start with a headache. Do you have a headache?" she said, eyes narrowing. "And then, after a couple of hours nausea, vomiting, then it's downhill all the way . . . death will be a relief," she said through gritted teeth. "Hope you enjoy the ride." She stood and made her way to the back of the pod.

Orville felt the heat of his panicked state as he sweated profusely. His head felt hot. *Is that a headache coming on?* He placed an open palm against his stomach, as he searched his body for symptoms. He removed his jacket and flapped his t-shirt against his skin—he was suffocating, his breathing laboured. A space steward appeared next to him.

"Can I get you some water, sir?" She smiled.

"Err . . . yes . . . please."

Within seconds the water appeared, but the nice space steward was nowhere to be seen. Instead, a heavily built, uniformed man offered him the tumbler. Orville didn't care too much, as he gulped down the water.

"Headache coming on, sir?" he asked, a similarly dressed man joining him.

Orville touched his head and glanced at the pair, a frown creasing his forehead.

"What's going on, are you medical staff?"

"No, sir. We're Space Elevator Security. We need to ask you a few questions."

Orville leapt up. "You gotta help me, I'm frikkin' dying! I need a doctor . . . the space radiation, it's killing me!"

The security guards grabbed him from both sides and frog-marched him to the rear of the pod.

"We'll get you help, alright," the guard growled, "just as soon as you're settled in at the Lunar Penitentiary."

***

Back on Interstate 505, Jerry was chained to his new friend, an FBI agent. He directed the father, more FBI, and two paramedics along the dirt road to the shack, unsure what they'd find. As the FBI opened the door, none of them expected to see the scene before them. The girl was sitting up, somewhat dazed, her head bandaged with a ripped off section of her dress. The paramedics rushed to her side, laying a stretcher on the floor.

Leaving Earth

"Her pulse is very weak."

"That's okay," said the father, as he held his daughter in his arms, "It's a genetic anomaly — she always gives the doctors a fright."

Jerry looked out across the arid landscape.

Where in the world was Orv?

Harry Alexiou has been a short story writer for a writing group on LinkedIn since April 2012. This has led to a collection of e-published anthologies of 3 minute, 750 to 1000-word short stories in various genres. Harry has collaborated on a crime novel with four other writers, which is due for release in late 2014. This face-to-face group is led and organized by published author, Eve Makis, whose credits include Eat, Drink And Be Married, The Mother-in Law, *and* Land Of The Golden Apple. *Not one to sit on his hands, Harry has self-published his debut solo work, a 40,000 word novella entitled* The Tower, *a techno-thriller set in the year 2040, now available online:* http://goo.gl/emqBvM.

Like the Page at https://www.facebook.com/1400mtower. *Revisions on a full-length novel are also awaiting a gap in his busy schedule.*

11. NO MAN LEFT BEHIND

Karl Morgan

Interstate 10 cut across the East Texas landscape and stretched to the horizon. Even at this distance, Tom Drake could see the silver line to his right rising from the ground and reaching to the heavens. The Starlight Industries shuttle bus took the newly constructed exit ramp and headed south. He had flown in from the West Coast early this morning, landing in San Antonio only an hour ago. His destination was that silver line, the first space elevator ever constructed. Several unmanned test runs had already been successful, but now it would be his turn, as a recently awarded Congressional Medal of Honor recipient, to be one of the dignitaries on the first trip with passengers.

A middle-aged man sitting behind Tom rose and took the seat next to him. "You're Tom Drake, aren't you?"

"Yes, sir, Senator Martinez," he replied.

"Please call me Jaime. I want to thank you for your service, son. Your story is an inspiration to us all."

Tom blushed. Media coverage had made him easily recognizable. "Back in your day, you were quite the war hero, too, Jaime."

"Well, we all do what we can, don't we?"

Tom nodded and smiled.

"So, what do you think of our little elevator?" The senator nodded toward the distant structure.

A gust of wind from the west caused the bus to shudder.

"It's a technological miracle. I can't image that thing is going to take us into space. It wasn't that long ago we were using Apollo capsules and Space Shuttles to send folks into orbit."

Another gust of wind pushed the bus close to the shoulder of the road. The driver slowed, pulled off the highway, and came to a stop.

"Is something wrong?" the Senator called out.

A sea of tumbleweeds rolled toward the road. The driver walked down the aisle telling the passengers they would wait here until the high wind subsided and reassuring them that this was normal for the time of year. In minutes, the weeds began to cross the road like a wave. Dozens more were trapped against the side of the bus and along a small shed, just off the road to the west.

"Looks like a tsunami," Tom commented.

The wind speed increased, pushing the bus back toward the road, which was now blanketed in rolling weeds. The passengers clung to the seats, some shouting, or screaming with fear. One last heavy gust pushed the bus further across the road causing the small shed to collapse. Then it became eerily quiet.

"I guess that's it," Martinez said.

"Look over there!" shouted a woman, two seats ahead of them. She was pointing toward the broken shed, where a person could be seen lying within the boards and shingles.

"Let's go, soldier," Martinez said as he headed down the aisle. Tom was on his heels. A pile of tumbleweeds blocked the door, but they pushed their way through. They hurried down the embankment and over the remains of an old fence and started removing the rubble. Other passengers now joined them, clearing the weeds and helping to get to the victim. The driver was on his radio calling for help.

When the last of the debris was cleared, they all knew they were looking at a corpse. Blood was everywhere and a bullet wound was in the back of the man's head. He was wearing an Army dress uniform with the three stars of a Lieutenant General. The wail of a siren pierced the silence of the scene.

"That's General Wainwright," Martinez sighed. "I knew him very well."

"He's the one who got me the invite for this trip," Tom noted. "He also personally shepherded my Congressional Medal of Honor through the process. Who would do such a thing?"

A Texas Ranger vehicle pulled up behind the bus and the two Rangers approached.

"What happened here?"

After Senator Martinez told the officers everything that happened, the bus continued toward the Starlight Industries compound a few miles down the road. Martinez returned to his original seat and began calling his office and others in Washington, to relay the news about the general's death.

Tom was glad to be alone with his thoughts, remembering how Wainwright had called him a week ago with the opportunity to ride the space elevator. At the time, Tom was just happy for the chance and did not even think about Wainwright's prior opposition to the elevator plan. Now, it was all he could think about.

After passing through the heavy security at the main gate, the shuttle followed a squad car through the array of buildings. Starlight Industries had started as a private enterprise in the San Francisco Bay Area. When Henry Starlight presented his technology to the world at a symposium four years ago, all of that changed. Now the company was a government agency, and Henry Starlight retired on the fifty billion dollars he earned by selling his company. While that played out, Tom Drake had been fighting in Kirghizstan, Pakistan, and the Sinai Peninsula of Egypt.

No one could have foreseen the rapid growth and fervor of modern Al Qaeda. The loosely assembled groups the world fought while Jaime Martinez was in Iraq and Afghanistan were now a tight and cohesive force. Tom knew from experience most of the regional governments in those areas were puppet regimes secretly supporting the terrorists. Only drastic changes in battle tactics enabled the destruction of the terrorist entity. Tom had been there, deep in the Sinai, when he and his squad came under withering fire while on a routine patrol. They retreated toward a ditch they had crossed, to find cover. As he ran, Tom called for reinforcements. Minutes later, he and his men crouched down in the ditch, while fighter jets screamed over their heads, firing missiles at the enemy. After a series of large explosions, Tom peeked out of the gully to see plumes of black smoke and fire in the distance. It was deathly quiet when Tom called his men to follow him to reconnoiter the area.

They moved quickly and found dozens of bodies near four destroyed tanks and several trucks. And then, there they were. Near one of the trucks were ten bodies, most of them he recognized, from briefing photos, as the Al Qaeda leadership. The rest of the bodies were too disfigured to recognize. He knelt down next to the bodies to pray for their families. Despite their reputation as ruthless murderers, he knew they were people too. When he opened his eyes, he saw one of the bodies was not dead, and had an Uzi pointed at him. Before he could speak, the man fired, hitting Tom in the chest and both arms in a spray of bullets. Tom rolled on the ground leveling his rifle. The man had grenades in each hand, preparing to throw them at Tom and his men. He fired, hitting the man in the wrist, causing one grenade to drop. The man swung his arm to hurl the other grenade at him. He fired again, striking the man in the forehead, and the half toss rolled the grenade toward Tom. Then they exploded.

That was his last memory until he awoke at Walter Reed three months later. He had been in a medically induced coma since his injuries. His arms and lungs were now bionic replacements. He had to remain in the hospital another six months to adapt to his new appendages. Finally, he was allowed to return home to San Diego. That was already two years ago, and his next adventure was about to begin.

After breakfast the following day, the group assembled in a vast hangar in the compound. A simulator of the elevator vehicle was there, and the Mission Specialist, Cybil Brewster, showed them around and explained the systems. She told them this was nothing like the space travel of a few decades ago, when people had been strapped into capsules or shuttles and blasted through the atmosphere. While there were spacesuits available, they were only for emergencies. New coatings and materials developed by NASA and Starlight protected the capsule from radiation. This first elevator was a prototype. Future versions would have much larger cabins for higher capacity. The Texas Lifter, as it was nicknamed, was to test the concept and usher in a new age of space travel.

The group of ten rode the shuttle over the last hill before the ground station. As they crested the hill, the base of the elevator came into view. What looked like one cable from a distance was actually three. The cables rose from inside a large terminal building and disappeared into the Texas sky. Once inside the building, the cabin was finally visible. It was triangular with couplings at each corner connecting it to the cables. To reach it, they had to pass between a line of photographers and the workers who were eager to see their dream come to life. After a few awkward moments, Tom was finally inside. To get to the passenger area, they had to walk through two antechambers that protected the interior from the vacuum of space. Ten large seats, similar to first class seating on transoceanic airliners, awaited them. Each seat faced the windows that filled the external walls.

While the others were taking their seats, Martinez pulled Tom aside. When they were out of earshot, Jaime said, "Tom, I don't have a good feeling about this."

"I don't understand."

"Wainwright being found dead here is too much of a coincidence. Clearly, he was assassinated. You saw how they killed him." Tom nodded. "I asked the President to delay this trip, but he says I'm overreacting. Please help keep an eye on things, too, okay?"

"Of course, but did you hear anything else?"

"You know Washington. It will take months for them to say anything—if they ever do." He smiled and added. "I'm probably just reading too much into this, but let's keep our eyes open." He turned to find his seat.

Tom went to the last open chair, which faced the operator seat. Cybil was standing in front of her station, making sure everyone was strapped in safely. When satisfied, she said, "It looks like we're set in here. Okay, just relax and enjoy the ride. The first few miles can be a bit disconcerting as we pass through the densest part of the atmosphere. After we reach fifty thousand feet, our speed will accelerate quickly. Starlight One, the station on the far end of the tether, is more than twenty two thousand miles above our heads in a geostationary orbit. The whole trip should take four hours. When we arrive, Commander Jepson will show you around and explain our future plans, and then he will join us as we return here in time for dinner. Please just sit back and enjoy it." She sat and strapped herself in.

Suddenly, the elevator shot through the opening in the roof and headed skyward, pressing Tom down into his chair. His stomach was churning and he had difficulty moving at all. He watched Cybil calmly tapping controls and speaking to the terminal as the cloud layer shot past them. A second later, he could see the curvature of the Earth as the sky above grew darker. He was becoming accustomed to the speed and looked around.

"This is quite a ride, Ms. Brewster."

Her seat pivoted and she smiled, "Isn't it the best? You might as well nap or get some rest. It's going to be deadly dull for a while." She turned around again to manage the controls. Tom took her advice and closed his eyes.

He was shocked awake by violent shaking. The cabin was whipping around, as the three cables seemed to be swaying in a breeze—unlikely in outer space. Cybil was working several levers, trying to regain control. After a few minutes, the capsule slowed to a stop and became still again. Cybil removed her straps and turned to face the passengers.

"I'm sorry about this," she told them. "I thought the trembling was an imbalance in the gyroscopes, but it isn't. Ground control has informed me that alleged Al Qaeda forces have sabotaged the elevator. A small explosion on the Cable C coupling caused the shaking. The terrorists say that is our only warning and that, if their demands aren't met, they will detonate a second bomb which will cut one of the cables."

"And then what happens?" a passenger asked.

Cybil looked down and thought for a moment. She looked up and replied, "Then we slide down the other two cables, out of control."

"There has to be something we can do?" Jaime asked. He had already left his seat and approached her.

"I've been told the demands were outrageous, Senator, although they are still negotiating. I've been asked to go outside for an EVA, to find anything I can."

"Tom and I are going with you," Jaime said. "We're both soldiers."

Cybil agreed and a few seconds later the three entered the first chamber, sealed the door, and began pulling on their suits and helmets. After checking each other's suits, they opened the next door and sealed the one behind them. They clipped tethers from the wall to their suits, and opened the external door. The rush of air outward lifted them from their feet for a moment. Earth lay fifteen thousand miles below them, Texas baking in the midday heat. Cybil clipped her tether to a rail next to a metal ladder and began to climb up on the outside of the capsule. Tom and Jaime followed her lead.

On top of the capsule, she unhooked her tether and connected it to another rail that led to the center of the craft. When all three were together and tethered to the rail, she pointed to the right coupling and said, "You can see that's the damaged one. I will check it out and see if the cable has been compromised. I doubt the second bomb will be there because the first one would have detonated it. You two check out the others and let me know." They each let out enough slack in their tethers to reach the corners of the structure.

Jaime was still ten feet from his corner when he realized he had hit the jackpot. The bearing that provided separation between the coupling and the cable had been replaced. He wondered how the ground crew had missed what he could see from here.

"It's here," the senator said into his microphone. Seconds later the others arrived and reported their corners were in working condition.

"What do we do now?" he asked. "I'm sure that thing is set to go off, if we so much as touch it."

113

"If all the jostling and friction on the ride up here didn't set it off, it's not booby trapped," Tom replied. He knew that, with his enhanced arms, he was the best one to do this. "I'll get rid of it, Jaime. But, you two should go inside, just in case."

Jaime thought about arguing, but then saluted him and followed Cybil back to the edge of the structure. When they had disappeared over the side, Tom moved forward. He got on his knees at the edge of the capsule, where two girders connected the coupling to the main structure. Looking down, he saw the Earth floating serenely beneath him and gasped at the view. The cables streamed downward out of sight. He shimmied along the girder to the coupling, which was a ten-foot long, four-foot diameter cylinder. He tried to pull himself on top of the cylinder, but he was literally at the end of his rope.

Tom unhooked the tether and attached it as best he could to the girder, and then climbed on top of the coupling. The bomb was pressed into a caulk like substance that had to be some kind of plastic explosive. There was no visible detonator, so he surmised it was buried inside or on the bottom.

"How is it going?" Jaime's voice said over the helmet speaker.

"Have Cybil tell ground control this is a plastic explosive, and find out why they didn't detect it. This wasn't disguised at all."

"I'm on it," Cybil's voice said.

"What are you going to do, son?"

"I can't see a detonator, so I'm just going to rip it out fast," he replied. "You might have everyone pray for us, Jaime."

Tom was positive he was about to die. Al Qaeda would have their revenge. He took a deep breath, grabbed the plastic, and pulled on it. It seemed glued to the coupling, but he kept pulling. After a few seconds that seemed endless, it suddenly came free and he flew backward with the bomb stuck on his hands. His tether jerked loose and he was tumbling out of control across the top of the capsule. He finally pulled one hand free, and reached down to grab anything. He caught a railing and slammed down on the ship. Without thinking, he jumped up, tore the bomb from his other hand, ran to the edge of the ship, and hurled it out into open space. "It's gone! Take us down fast!" he screamed as he ran toward the ladder.

The elevator began to drop causing Tom to float upward. He was able to hook one foot under a rail at the last second. The bomb detonated several hundred feet away. As Tom headed back toward the ladder, the concussion of the explosion hit him, knocking him off his feet. He was flying toward the edge of the capsule, frantically trying to grab anything he could. He passed over the edge with his fingers inches from the ladder. This is it, he thought.

A hand reached out of the open chamber and grabbed his hand, pulling him safely inside. When he stopped gasping for air, he stood and found Martinez next to him, still in his suit. Martinez closed the outer door and began pumping air into the room.

"Thanks, Senator," Tom said, knowing he could never repay the debt.

Jaime smiled and replied, "We grunts have to watch each other's backs, Tom."

"No man left behind, right, Jaime?"

Karl J. Morgan is the author of the **Dave Brewster** *series of science fiction novels, the* **Heartstone** *series of fantasy novels, and the upcoming* **Modern Prophets** *series of suspense novels. The* **Hive** *received an honorable mention at the 2013 Southern California Book Festival. His stories are ultimately optimistic and present a positive view of life, our relationship to spirit and to each other. He lives and writes in Southern California.*

12. ODD ONE OUT

R M Pala

There were two escape suits.

There were three of us.

We were running out of time.

But, I'm getting ahead of myself. Let's go back to the beginning. The christening of earth's first space elevator was a media frenzy. The world watched as investors and politicians hailed it as the dawning of a new era of peace and prosperity. It took five years just to design it, and over 15,000 people to make it a reality. Despite best efforts, the program's top brass could not convince the person on the street that it would affect anyone's life. The average Joe didn't have an appreciation for the development of the carbon nanotubes composite ribbon. The regular Jane was unaware of the sophistication of the computer programs that made millions of adjustments every second.

So, some genius came up with the idea of sending regular folks on the ride of their lives. Everybody in the world got a vote. Less than 17% bothered, but that didn't stop promoters from seeing it as the way to put their clients in the spotlight.

Take, for example, the movie star Clara Carmichael. When she was known as Edith Ann Brown she ran away from Topeka at the age of fifteen, did the LA Hollywood scene; sex, drugs, booze and whatever else eats aspiring kids and spits them out. Clara got a break; at rock bottom she appeared in an indie film directed by one of her friends and was nominated for a Golden Globe. The publicity machine worked day and night touting her as the next blond bombshell. Her agent got her name on the list and don't you know it, she got the most votes.

Then there's the physicist, Jeffery Tambour, who's on all media all the time, trying to help the public understand the incomprehensible. He got the second slot and planned to make a number of 'casts from the elevator car explaining, well, everything. He even planned to do some experiments.

I was the last chosen. I didn't want to go. I'm nobody. But they concluded that they actually needed at least one real person, so they decided to pull a name out of a hat. Literally. I choked on my ham sandwich when my name was announced. My boss called, officially giving me time off. My wife just smiled.

They must have run that car up and down the nano-whatever flagpole a million times before they let humans ride it. One hundred percent guaranteed. Perfection and unprecedented accuracy and safety.

Why, then, am I on the floor feeling the oxygen being squeezed out of the air with each breath?

The whole adventure started out fine. It was a hot, humid day on the anchoring platform. We were on the equator and the sea state was zero. Besides, the platform was the size of several football fields. It hardly felt like we were at sea at all. A flotilla of small boats buzzed around us, mostly press trying to get pictures and relaying events real-time to their subscribers. Our handlers shepherded us to the podium and we pretended we actually listened to and cared about what was being said. We all wore the same cute outfit: white cotton polo shirts with the elevator logo on the left breast, slacks the blue-green color of Bahamian shallows, and brand-name color-coordinated running shoes with the logo. We each carried a shoulder bag; you guessed it, *logoized*. The two stars ignored me for the most part until the photographers yelled at us to get closer together; smile, wave, and we did, like well-trained animals. Good boy, here's a treat.

I kept looking at the car, the tin can that could, if we wanted, take us a quarter of the way to the moon and back. This trip would be shorter, only about 30 hours. The can was clad in radiation blocking materials sandwiched together, some of which hadn't even existed a few years ago. I can't say that I was afraid at that point, though I felt a stirring of anticipation in my gut. One of the handlers brought me water.

"When are we going to get on with this?" I asked. He grinned and rocked back on his heels.

"Relax. The trip out and back will take more than a day. This lot will be off on the next big story before you get back."

I wanted to wipe that self-righteous smirk off his face. All the people who worked for the company were so certain they knew what they were doing.

Two escape suits. Three people. Stuck 40 kilometers in the sky. What, you may ask, knocked out this testament to human arrogance? A short. A tiny spark of a mistake. Pushing buttons in just the wrong order brought the whole show to a stop. That burned out circuit meant we weren't going anywhere. No, let's get it right. Two of us were going to jump out leaving the third behind to die.

We were having trouble deciding who that would be.

The actual departure, the moment we were on our way, was anticlimactic. The handlers herded us into the tin can and strapped us down.

"Just a precaution," one said. "It's a real smooth ride. The G-forces change, but the computer will warn you if you should strap in. Your food and water is stowed under the big window and the toilet is over there. Close the curtain for privacy. Any questions?"

He was up and out before I could ask anything. The door was heavy. It took three technicians to close it. I must have looked worried, because the professor leaned over and patted my arm.

"There will be metallic sounds as we release the restraints and some bumping but it will settle down. You'll be fine."

He flashed his "Mr. DeMille, I'm ready for my close up" smile. I felt short of breath and my stomach flipped. I thought I was going to be sick, but I metaphorically shook myself by my lapels. The first clank sounded like it came from over my head.

I felt a bead of sweat make its way down the side of my face. The movie star crossed her legs and fished in her bag for lipstick. I turned to the physicist.

"Jeff, they said you plan to do some experiments for the masses . . . " He looked down his nose at me.

"Jeffery," he said.

I shook my head. "What?"

He cleared his throat. "I prefer Jeffery. Yes, I will have time for one or two little things once we're up there," and he pointed up and winked. I tried smiling but it wasn't worth the effort.

I unstrapped and when I stood, my right leg buckled at the knee. It was my first indication that we were going up at more than one G. I grabbed the handrail and went over to the big window. I also wanted to check out the food. I couldn't see the cable above or below, but the view of the horizon from even this modest height was breathtaking. I looked at the control touchscreens and was struck by the lack of labeling.

"They don't want their customers to be uncomfortable, which is why it will take half a day to reach our highest point. Their plan eventually is to extend to 100,000 kilometers. There's room on the base for three more." Jeffery got out of his chair and stood next to me. "If you have any questions, I'll be happy to answer them." I put on the kind of smile used to cover the discomfort of someone dumping a drink on you.

"Thanks, Jeffery. I'll keep that in mind. Why do you suppose they haven't labeled any of the buttons?"

"Oh, that's to keep amateurs from making mistakes."

I opened the storage compartment and removed one of the food bags. It was what is referred to as a 'gourmet' lunch, meaning that the ingredients were unpronounceable and the portions tiny. There was fruit juice in soda bottles from Jordan and "gourmet" cookies, which I must admit really are tasty. They'd fed us a good breakfast so I put the bag away for now.

Miss Carmichael remained aloof. She continued to work on beautifying her face. I thought a trowel would have been more efficient. She examined her handiwork, sweeping the mirror in the compact in even rows like searching with a metal detector. Nope, nothing there.

Hours passed. Jeffery appeared to know his way around the tin can. He pushed a button, which released a cot. He caught me staring.

"Tired?" he asked. "There's another one over there," he added.

That there were only two bunks should have been a warning. Before I could move, bombshell was pushing buttons like crazy until the other cot unfolded. She collapsed on it and turned her face to the wall. I decided to pull her chain, just a bit.

"Ahem," I said. She didn't move. "You know there are cameras sending down a constant stream of whatever we're doing. During the whole thirty or so hours we're together. People will be watching, dissecting . . ." I paused for dramatic effect, "judging? Every little thing we do." I snapped my fingers. "Like that!"

She sat up, swinging her legs over the side of the cot and stood up, all in one motion. "Yes, but there's no sound unless we open the mikes." Her voice was breathy and childlike. "I can say whatever I want. There is a teensy weensy space over there," she pointed to where she had done her makeup, "that's partially blocked from view."

Jeffery frowned and put his reader down. "Now, you two need to get along. This is supposed to be a happy trip. Clara, you haven't even looked out once . . . ."

It started as a shudder no stronger than a cat's purr. It got louder and rougher. Things got bad real fast. I was thrown across the floor and ended up with my back against the wall. Clara went down on her knees after making contact with the windowsill and Jeffery was thrown out of the cot. It sounded like a train engine was running over an empty tractor-trailer and loud as standing on the flight deck of an aircraft carrier. I covered my ears. I think I was screaming.

Then there was silence. Everything was still. I lay on the floor, my back hurting where I had hit the wall. My ears were ringing. Clara moaned. I saw blood on the edge of the window where the side of her head hit it. Jeffery, his face gone white, struggled to get up on the cot.

"What happened?" I didn't sound right. I coughed. "Jeffery, what happened?"

He must have been in shock. He sat on the bed, his eyes scanning the room, not saying a word. Lights on control panels lit up red, some flashing. I crawled over to the communications panel and after punching lit buttons, opened a channel.

". . . come in. Do you read? Come in." There was fear in the voice on the speaker.

"We are here and we are hurt," I shouted. Silence. I keyed the mike. "What happened?" Silence. "Come on you idiots, I want some answers. What the hell is going on?" I slid to the floor, my back too sore to stand.

"What is your condition?"

I stared at the mike, unbelieving. "The professor is missing in action, the starlet is unconscious on the floor, and I think I've broken my back." I tried to move but the pain was unlike anything I'd ever experienced.

The voice came back on, but it sounded different, more comforting. "We believe we know what happened," it said. "A short circuit has occurred due to an overabundance of activity. First, the emergency brakes have activated and you are in no danger of falling."

I breathed a sigh of relief. "Thank God," I answered. "When can you get a rescue team up here? The professor is not responding and the movie star seems to be coming around, but she's bleeding and I don't know . . ."

"We can't send a rescue party."

I could not have heard that right. "Say again."

"We can't send a rescue party."

I couldn't move. I felt my face flush with heat and the back of my head tingled.

"Well then," I started. "What . . . what are you . . .?" I tried to calm down. "What are you going to do? Leave us up here?" Tears welled up in my eyes and rolled down my cheeks. A pain in my chest felt like congestion from the worst cold ever. I ached all over.

"There is a leak. You are losing air."

I started to laugh. This had to be the most ridiculous thing ever. "Next you'll be telling me that we're going to get hit by an asteroid."

Silence.

I shook my head, trying to clear it. "What do you suggest?" I asked. I must have sounded reasonable because the voice came back more confident.

"There are two EVAC suits. You're at a point you can still use them. You free fall for about four and a half minutes, and then pull the parachute. If you black out, we can deploy the chutes remotely."

I looked at Clara and Jeffery. Clara was attempting to stand and Jeffery was curled up in the fetal position. I cupped my hand over the mike and turned the volume down low.

"We have two suits and three people. What do you suggest? Rock paper scissors?"

"Who are you talking to?" asked Clara. She moved her jaw with care and a cut below her left eye bled badly. I stalled.

"They're working on it. You should wash your face; you have a bad cut."

She looked in her mirror. "That's where all the blood is coming from," she grumbled. She hit Jeffery on the rump. "Come out of it, man."

I keyed the mike. "Are you there? Or is it your coffee break. I can wait . . ."

"That's not helping . . ."

"You're not helping!" I exploded.

Silence.

I thought I could stand a lot, but that voice had become important to me and I couldn't deal with silence.

"I'm sorry." I whimpered.

"That's all right," came the voice. "Now, let's take this one step at a time. We estimate you have one hour of air left. You are in charge. We will support whatever decision you make about who stays and who goes. How can we help you make that decision?"

They had to be nuts. I was supposed to make this life or death decision?

"I'll have to get back to you." I switched off the mike.

I tried to stand, but kept slipping back down to the floor. Clara was applying ice to her face. Jeffery was still hugging himself and rocking.

"Jeffery," I called. "Jeffery, can you understand me? We have to talk." He looked up, his eyes bloodshot, and nodded.

"What do we need to talk about?" Clara asked.

The cut had stopped bleeding, but that side of her face was badly swollen. Either she didn't appreciate our predicament or she was in shock. It never occurred to me that she just might be calm under fire.

"They can't send a rescue team," I said.

Jeffery moaned and started rocking again. Clara reached over and slapped him across the face. Stunned, he stopped rocking and shook his head.

"I'm sorry, yes, did you say something about no rescue team?" he asked.

"So what do the brains down there suggest?" asked Clara. "And do they know what happened?"

I took a deep breath. "First, you hit every button just to lower the cot and accidentally hit the jackpot. As to a solution, they suggest that two of us jump out of here. Oh, by the way, we have less than an hour of air left."

Imagine the look on the face of a hunter who has just been shot by a deer.

Clara recovered first. "Why two and not three?"

"Because there are only two suits."

"Can anyone here spell Titanic?" she said, her face twisted with disdain. She started to pace back and forth. "Well," she said, slapping her hips. "They always say women and children first. So how are you two going to decide who gets the suit?"

"Not so fast," said Jeffery, now fully engaged. "Equality makes that a ridiculous notion. We should examine our worth to humanity. What have we done in the past to improve the human condition and then extrapolate our value on into the future?"

"Nobody understands you." I knew where this was going. "She at least entertains people."

Jeffery got red in the face and puffed out his cheeks. "Can you imagine the scandal, the outrage, if an eminent scientist is abandoned in favor of a media whore and a nobody? By the way, just for giggles, what do you do?"

I grabbed a handhold and pulled myself more upright. "What I do is less important than what I represent. I'm here for the workers, the taxpayers, and the little guys. That makes me Everyman, you pompous idiot. You're so smart; find a way to get us out of here. And you have," I looked at the clock, "forty minutes before we run out of air."

Clara kneeled next to me. She squeezed the back of my leg, just above the shinbone. I felt a stab of pain and then nothing.

"Do you feel that?" she whispered. I couldn't but I didn't say anything.

"Can you feel this?" and she squeezed above the knee.

I shook my head, and the implications were not lost on anyone. Panic, like enveloping fog, rolled over me. "I have a family, a wife, a life . . ." My vision began to narrow down, my head was hot and spinning and sweat stung my eyes.

"It's not a bad way to die," I heard Jeffery say. "Asphyxiation, I mean."

"Shut up," snarled Clara. "Or I'll throw you out myself." She turned back to me. "You wouldn't survive the fall," she said, smoothing back my hair. "It seems the paralysis is spreading. Tell me, what makes sense?"

I nodded, my brain refusing to work. I heard rather than saw them don the suits. Clara retrieved the food and drinks.

"All for you," she said and kissed my forehead.

I heard the hiss as the inner door opened, and the harsh metallic click as it closed. I reached for a bag and opened a soda.

If I had to die, I'd die eating cookies. If I timed it right, I could make them last until the air ran out. My eyes closed.

The sound of ground control woke me. I looked at the clock and realized I'd been asleep at least ninety minutes. I slapped the buttons on the console until the mike turned on.

"What's going on?" I demanded. I grabbed my legs, which tingled with thousands of pins and needles.

"We've corrected the problem with the air. We've also taken care of the computer lockout. The technology is new . . ."

"You're kidding. You mean I get to come home in style? What do Clara and Jeffery say about that? Must be pretty pissed."

"Um, they didn't make it."

I was stunned. "What happened?"

Silence.

"Tell me, dammit!"

"They deployed their chutes too soon. They were caught in an upper level jet stream. We don't know when they're ever coming down. Their suits will run out of air long before they land."

What a rotten way to die. I felt sorry for the movie star. Toward the end, she was acting almost human.

"By the way, how are your legs?"

I stopped rubbing my calves. "I can feel them."

"It seems Miss Clara stuck you with a syringe filled with something she planned to use on herself during the trip. Some kind of sedative high. She confessed to us about it when she realized she wasn't going to make it. She really came unglued—ranting and raving. I think she was mad she gave you the good stuff."

I had nothing to say.

"Go ahead and strap in," said control. "We'll have you on the ground in a few hours. By the way, you're the lead in tonight's newscast."

Not bad for a nobody.

R M Pala grew up in Northern Virginia and spent many happy hours making up stories and running around "the creek." She is married and has two grown children. She lives with her husband on a small farm close to the Manassas Battle Field. She is the proud owner of Primadonna, a Frisian/Lipizzaner dressage show horse. She has written two novels: MarsFace, *hard science fiction, and* Hollywood and Wine, *a historic mystery, available online.*

RELATIONSHIPS

13. Cavia Porcellus

D.A. Couturier and Timothy Paul

"Fifty round trip tickets," the journal had announced, but Burke Lahr only saw four other people in the small windowless room, their eyes darting around the sparsely furnished waiting area as they smiled at one another. Sitting closest to him was a young woman with auburn hair.

"Burke," he said, extending his hand.

"Naomi," she replied, as her hand fell limply into his firm grasp.

"Where are the others?"

"I don't know," she shook her head. Her quiet, beguiling beauty drew his attention to her left hand. *Nothing,* he smiled to himself. Perhaps winning the ticket would produce more rewards than he'd anticipated.

"I'm Abe." A short bald man across from Burke held out his hand.

"Burke," he nodded. "What made you enter the lottery?"

The old man shrugged. "Retired. Lots of time to fill."

"And I'm Ming," a woman with hair the color of a starless night stood up.

Everyone followed suit, performing the ritual as if from a mental checklist.

"Rashid." The dark-skinned man greeted the others with obvious reserve. Burke noted the checkered turban and white robe.

Determined to lighten the somber mood in the room Burke clasped his hands together with a slight slap. "So, where you all from? I'm from Ypsilanti. It's in Michigan."

"Please take a seat," a stern voice instructed from an overhead speaker. "We will be with you shortly."

Falling back into an awkward silence, they complied. Five minutes passed before a door opened, drawing their attention. A thin man of medium height stepped in. Dark, rimmed glasses teetered low on his nose. Burke chuckled thinking the scientist was the epitome of his profession. Completing the picture, a white lab coat swayed just above black, Ralph Lauren wingtips.

"Welcome. Welcome. As you all know, you've been chosen for the manned mission on the Spatial Projectile and Centrifugal Elevator, otherwise known as the SPACE."

"Where are the others?" Abe asked. "Aren't there supposed to be . . ."

Dr. Lab Coat broke him off mid-sentence. "SPACE only holds five at a time. You are lucky to be in the first group."

"But there have been others?" Ming asked barely above a whisper, "I mean . . . it is safe right? Why did we have to sign all those waivers?"

He slid his glasses up the bridge of his nose and smiled. "There's been more than adequate testing. A number of specialists from the private sector have already . . . traveled. With any new advances in science, protestors and supporters line up at the doors. I'm sure you can imagine our attorneys' eagerness to cover all litigation angles."

Ming nodded, "Of course."

The man seemed to plug on a smile like a child thrusting the pink, bulgy lips into a Mr. Potato Head. "This is the first time we have allowed the general public . . ." his voice trailed off and he began again, "I heard one reporter liken it to the Golden Ticket from the Chocolate Factory."

Rashid stood and approached the scientist. "I am not entirely sure why I am here. I did not enter a contest nor did I apply for this endeavor." Looking at the badge hanging from a cord around the scientist's neck, he added, "Dr. Thornburg."

"Rashid Saffar. Thirty-three. Born in Bahrain. Received your Ph.D. at Cornell in Biomedical Engineering." Dr. Thornburg rattled off this information as if he had internet-stalked the Bahraini for years, "Yes, we know who you are Dr. Saffar. You may not have chosen us, but we chose you."

Dr. Thornburg clearly had Rashid's attention as well as the others. *Had they all been chosen?*

"This will be an opportunity of a life-time and, based on your current research project, we assumed you would not pass on a ride in the SPACE." Dr. Thornburg spoke to all but his gaze never left Rashid's face. "Think of the experiences you will gain. Papers you could publish. The fame you could achieve. This is only the first step."

Dr. Thornburg's arrow apparently landed dead center, for Rashid bowed slightly and said no more. Neither did anyone else.

"Now, if there are no more questions?"

Something in the man's inflection grabbed Burke's attention, but before he could form a question, Thornburg turned away.

"This way, please," Thornburg said.

They followed obediently. *Like a duck with ducklings,* Burke thought, *but to where?*

Numerous corridors intersected the long passage and the further they walked, the more troubled Burke became. He fought back a growing sense of confinement bordering on claustrophobia. Windowless doors adorned with ominous signage, such as "Private," "No Entry," and "Authorized Personnel Only" grew more dreadful as they went along—if that were possible. "Quarantine," "Isolation Area," and "Danger!" added to his discomfort. "Bio Hazard" and "Restricted Area—Deadly Force Authorized" seemed blatantly malicious.

"In here," Dr. Thornburg ushered them through a relatively benign door labeled, "No Smoking."

The entryway was more than six inches thick and built entirely of whitewashed cinder blocks and cement. This room was much larger with several tables and cots covered with crisp linens. Bottles and medical supplies lined the south side and a thick curtain separated the room into two sections. It reminded Burke of the military hospital during his tour in Japan. He'd spent two boring weeks stuck in bed with a bad case of pneumonia before being sent back to his unit.

"My assistant will administer your inoculations and complete a perfunctory medical examination. Just as a precaution, you see."

"When will we see our rooms, Doctor?" Naomi asked.

Burke winked. She looked away but not before he saw her pretty cheeks flush.

Ming added, "And our things?"

"All is prepared and your personal effects are secure."

Abe said, "We've heard it all before. Seven days to get there, three days at the Station, and then seven days back again. We should stop pestering the doctor with questions. We all signed the waivers and read the contract. Let's get on with it. I have grandkids waiting to see Grandpa Abe make history."

"We here at the Babel Institute have taken the utmost precautions to ensure your safety," Dr. Thornburg rattled the pre-scripted speech. "As previously mentioned, many private individuals have traveled in the SPACE, however this is the first time we have offered it to the general public. We are happy you will have this once-in-a-lifetime opportunity."

The curtain behind Dr. Thornburg fluttered and parted.

"Here is my assistant, Dr. Griffith. I will see you shortly. Have a safe trip." he disappeared behind the curtain, dismissing himself.

Dr. Griffith leaned over Burke checking his vitals.

"How do you feel?" She pulled the stethoscope from her ears.

"Fine. When do we leave?"

"Leave? You've already been there," she wrapped the blood pressure cuff around his arm and pressed the start button.

"I have?"

"And come back again. Don't you remember?" she asked above the sound of the air compressor tightening around his upper arm like a Boa constrictor.

Short bursts of air slowly released its grip. "Uh," he thought hard, "Yes, I remember now." Images of them leaving came to his mind.

"There now, you see? I knew you would. SPACE travel can cause lapses in memory but your mind will soon fill in all the pieces." She patted his arm and pulled at the Velcro. "You had me concerned for a moment." She wrapped the rubbery hose around the readout and pushed the whole apparatus away from his cot.

"What an adventure," he said. *And it had been.* Unimaginable, until one experienced it first-hand. Even he and Naomi had time for some "Spatial Projectiles" of their own. A contented smile crossed his lips. He had fallen in love with this one.

"You're vitals are good. You should be back home within the next 48 hours."

Dr. Griffith pulled at the curtain around the metal track on the ceiling and attached it to the wall behind his head. Casting her eyes to the right, "Why don't you say 'hi'? Mrs. Pao is awake." She disappeared behind the partition of the next bed.

Burke raised up on one arm and looked around. Ming stared intently into a small picture, tracing the object with her finger. If she noticed him, she gave no indication.

"What you got there?" he asked.

"Oh, this? A sonogram. Can you believe it?" she held it out for him to see.

He saw a black and white, shadowy form of a fetus in the middle of the photo, "That's great."

She beamed with happiness. "I'm going to have a baby. Dr. Thornburg scolded me for not telling them," she chuckled, "They said I could have miscarried on the trip, but all tests show the baby is fine."

"Why didn't you tell them?"

"I didn't know. My husband and I have been to every specialist in three states. Mortgaged everything we owned. All attempts failed. Until now. I can't wait to get home and tell Ca." She opened a small bible and tucked the picture inside.

"Congratulations," Burke offered, waited a moment, and then asked, "Where's Naomi?"

"Over there."

"Over where? Who is that?" Burke pointed to the bed next to Ming's, where an elderly lady who appeared to be in her late seventies or early eighties, slept.

"That's Naomi."

"Funny Ming," he laughed, "Cut it out. That woman must be part of the second group to travel in the SPACE."

They had all grown close over the days they had been together. Perhaps Naomi and Ming were playing a joke on him. Still, he had a nagging feeling something was terribly wrong.

Ming jerked her thumb. "That's her."

"No it's not. Naomi's twenty-five. Gorgeous with boobs out to here." He rolled his arms out with emphasis.

"Now who's being funny? Naomi is the oldest of the four of us. You, me, Rashid and Naomi."

There were five of us.

"That is NOT Naomi!" he said a little too loudly, causing the woman to stir.

There were five. What was his name? Where was Naomi?

Ming smiled at the older woman. "Good morning."

"Morning. I think I need a vacation from my vacation," the old woman chuckled and slipped from the bed into the large reclining chair by her bedside. Reaching into the nightstand, she pulled out a book and started reading. "Morning, Burke."

"Uh . . . hi," he stuttered out. Peering closer he could see a hint of auburn in her gray hair. Her hands were heavily veined and liver spotted, but Burke could still see a hint of former beauty. It was as if someone had water colored over an original picture, muting the entire person before him into this.

"Where's Rashid?" Burke asked noticing the empty bed at the far end of the room.

"Doctor said it was Space Sickness. It's severe enough that he had to be transferred to a facility better able to handle it," Naomi interjected, but didn't look up from her book. "What's wrong with you, Burke? You act like you've seen a ghost."

This is wrong. All wrong. Naomi is twenty-five. I remember now! The man's name is Abe. And he's a grandpa. Grandpa Abe. And I remember he went into the SPACE with us.

Burke sat back on his cot and listened to the frustratingly complacent interactions among the others. He looked across at the woman they said was Naomi. Dr. Griffith brought her a pill with some water and she set her book down. "Where are my things?" she asked. A few minutes later the doctor brought her a basket and Burke was not surprised to hear comments like, "These aren't mine," and "I had one of those once. Lost it when I was quite young." But it was the doctor's response that sent a chill down his spine.

"There must have been a mix-up. Why don't you keep the extra things safe until we find the owner?" Griffith was placating her. Proof of deception.

What happened to Naomi? He closed his eyes and concentrated. They had travelled in luxurious accommodations, each berth perfectly matched to the tastes of the individual. Seven days had been enough to strike up a serious romance with the young Naomi and the two of them had grown serious in their short time on the terra-formed asteroid. The spectacle of earth through the darkness of space led to romantic nights of intimacy. But there was no memory of a return trip. What happened to them between that last night and—now?

"I need to visit the head," Burke said to no one in particular. He waited until Griffith disappeared into a curtained cubicle and stepped out. Walking along the passageway, he noted the familiar signs of warning. He thought they'd been in a different order. And the lighting was different—or were the walls just a different shade of hospital gray?

Approaching voices echoed from an adjoining hallway. Burke turned away, down another corridor with more rooms on either side. Some were workshops or laboratories with strange equipment and tools unlike anything he'd ever seen. Other doors bore nameplates. *Dr. Anne Griffith, M.D., D.Sc., Ph.D.* was on the first one he looked at. *Damn!* he thought. *All that education and she's just an assistant.* She

135

was below Thornburg, and Burke knew he was little more than concierge for this enterprise.

Near the end of the hall, he found a modest-looking nameplate that struck an immediate chord: P. Hermann. Before entering the competition, Burke had read about the program. Dr. Peter Hermann, co-founder of SPACE was the pre-eminent physicist in all Europe. Inside the office, an animated conversation drew Burke's attention.

"A barren woman comes home pregnant—*there's* something we didn't anticipate." The voice was male, deep, and authoritative.

"Yes, but where did the barren version go?" a woman's voice responded with an equal level of confidence. "Each would have received the sonogram at the quantum hub's medical facility. Following their return, both will send ripples of discontinuity through their respective timelines. We may be able to devise a way to measure the impact."

"Perhaps. But this may well be the same Ming we sent through, in which case there will be nothing to measure. Remember, she's as surprised as anyone is. There may simply be residuals in the trans-dimensional pathway with regenerative properties. If she had intercourse shortly before departure this could be a natural result."

Burke stepped back from the door and caught his breath. That conversation belonged in a science-fiction movie. Yet here he stood in a well-funded—and secretive—complex operated by world-renowned scientists.

A faint noise wafted down the corridor and his special forces training kicked into gear. Two steps away he tested the door with Dr. Ito Hiro's name and found it open. He guessed this room belonged to the woman's voice next door and stepped inside. A well-ordered office with functional furnishings was, for the moment, unoccupied. Footsteps in the hallway came close, passed, and then paused before stepping into Hermann's office next door.

Burke leaned against the wall and found the voices nearly as clear as they had been in the hallway. He hoped to hear more of the debate over Ming's mysterious—*dare he call it miraculous?*—healing. Instead, a familiar, unmistakably sharp voice interrupted their discussion.

"Burke's missing," Thornburg announced.

"Nothing to worry about," the woman replied. "He's in my office next door."

"You may as well come over and join us, Captain Burke," said the deep voice he assumed was Hermann's. "We have a monitoring system that will track every move you make and you're not going to learn anything we don't wish you to know."

He looked around the office for security cameras, but saw none. An adjoining door between offices opened and Thornburg beckoned to him.

Towering a foot above his collaborator, Peter Hermann was an imposing figure. His square jaw, broad shoulders, and perfectly proportioned frame would have inspired a Greek sculptor. Only the horseshoe ring of fine, white hair wrapped around his head gave any indication of age. By contrast, Ito had a slight frame and soft demeanor. Yet the conversation he'd overheard revealed confidence and strength along with the fantastic ideas of a visionary.

"What is it you're doing here?" Burke demanded.

"Something of an audacious question, from a man skulking about in restricted hallways."

"Call it what you like. I prefer the term investigating. You're going to have some hard questions to answer about this operation of yours, Dr. Hermann."

"I'm sorry to disappoint you, Captain, but any questions of consequence have already been answered to the people who matter."

"We are funded by a coalition of sixteen different governments," Ito added. "Do you imagine there's anything you could challenge that hasn't already been addressed?"

"You may have sold this to governments, but there will be an outcry when the general population learns what you're doing."

"And exactly what do you postulate is happening here?" asked Thornburg.

"You're inviting people to an experience of a lifetime, hand-selecting the ones you want, and then experimenting with them like guinea pigs."

Dr. Ito stepped close to Burke. "Our research has implications for humanity far beyond your comprehension, soldier," she said coldly. "Have you ever looked into the cosmos and realized you're no more consequential than a speck of dust? Suppose you could know that your life impacts an infinite number of dimensional timelines. Guinea pigs? In many ways that's exactly what you are."

Undaunted, Burke shot back, "Beautiful, Doctor. I'll quote you directly when I address the media."

"That's not going to happen," Dr. Hermann interjected. "In any dimensional plane. As part of your preparation for the SPACE, we inserted the tracking device in your ankle. We also implanted a failsafe next to your heart. A fast-acting poison. If we find it necessary, I will push a button and then call in a team to care for your remains."

Burke studied the three academics in front of him. He could immobilize all three in a matter of seconds. But he would have to kill them all and then reach a medical facility before anyone else with knowledge of the poison discovered his escape. He was a soldier. Highly trained. And he had no doubt he could succeed, but what would it matter? The woman he had fallen in love with was gone.

"Stalemate Captain Lahr?" Ito asked.

"What happened to Naomi?"

"We're not sure anything out of the ordinary happened," Dr. Hermann answered. "She may simply not be the same Naomi that traveled with you in the SPACE."

"That makes no sense. How can there be a different Naomi?"

Thornburg and Ito looked at each other and raised their eyebrows as if to say, *what the hell.* Hermann stared at Burke for a long moment and finally said, "According to your dossier, you attended a high-school ROTC program and completed a college education at West Point. Have you ever read anything about quantum mechanics?"

"I read a few Philip K. Dick novels. Does that count?"

"Do you know anything of parallel worlds or multiverse theories?"

Burke furrowed his brow, growing impatient at the misdirection from his question. "I've heard people talk about things like all possible realities happen, somewhere. That doesn't tell me what happened to Naomi."

"If you were as accomplished in your mind as you are in combat, it should." Hermann turned away, apparently finished with his response.

Dr. Ito explained. "It's probable that the woman you went to the asteroid with is now in a different—or parallel—world. A different time stream. We're not yet sure how closely different timelines match. The Naomi who came back with your group has identical DNA with the young one you left with. She also has the full memories of a seventy-eight year old woman, which your twenty-five year old would not have. Our conclusion is that Naomi has been returned to our time stream—our world—and the girl you knew before is now in another."

Burke's head reeled and he felt a sick, sinking feeling in the pit of his stomach. He was going to propose and now the woman he loved was beyond his reach. He took a breath to clear his head then asked, "Why don't the others remember her the way I do?"

Thornburg took up this answer. "You're the anomaly," he said. "We're not exactly sure what happens during the transportation phase. But with every other test we've done, the people who return share memories of each other and their time on the asteroid. Often, those who come back are altered in some way, such as Naomi and now Ming. You're the first person to remember the original group as they were."

"What happened to Abe?" Burked asked. He was getting angry again and that was good. Better than the depression that brought him to this place to begin with. Despair would likely get him killed.

"Abe came back the same age he left," Thornburg said. "But with the mental capacity of a three year old. He has no memories at all, which may be related to the fact that none of your other companions remembers him, either."

This has to stop, thought Burke. He stepped back into a defensive posture. "And what about Rashid? Space sickness?"

Hermann responded, "Rashid is on a ventilator. A dormant virus common in Bahrain merged with a new class of spores in the SPACE. They're multiplying in every organ in his body. An unforeseen, but noteworthy casualty."

139

"Collateral damage?" Burke asked ironically. He only had to lure Ito a few steps closer to the others. He looked at her and asked, "So what happens now? To me? To them?"

"Captain," she replied. "It's clear enough that you're preparing to engage us in a physical assault. That would be a foolish gesture since the button that would end your life is at my fingertips."

"My life may as well be over anyhow," he snapped.

"It doesn't have to be," Hermann said.

"What?"

"Would you like to go find your lover?"

"What?" Burke said again. He was caught off guard. Confused.

"You apparently have the ability to recall things as they were before you departed," Thornburg interjected. "You are unaffected by the group psyche interactions in the SPACE. Such a tool could shave years off our research."

"And you would be able to tell if you returned to this world," Hermann added. "You alone might know that you've gone to a parallel world running the same experiments we are. Eventually you might travel to the same world as your Naomi."

"Is that really possible?"

He understood what they were saying. *Possible, yes. Guaranteed? There was no promise.* But, for a retired soldier with no surviving family, the hope of finding a life partner was worth the journey.

D.A. Couturier
Author, editor, and finance manager for a marketing agency, Dee Ann has borne a love of writing since childhood. Her first novel is the story of a young girl's survival in backwoods Tennessee during prohibition. Her short stories range from traditional science fiction to speculative pieces on contemporary issues. Dee Ann lives in Washington State with her husband and three children.

Timothy Paul lives in Washington State with his wife and family. A former professor of Theatre Arts, he has worked as a freelance and professional writer, director, and educator. His first published speculative fiction story was included in a recent anthology. He is currently working on a second science fiction novel, while marketing his first. Other published works include profile pieces for a regional magazine, theatre reviews, book reviews, and articles for newsletters.

14. Drifting to the Moon

Clement Chow

Imagine a man who's gifted in math and science, but can't conform to the engineering job he's doing. Imagine the same person who can communicate well with most women, but stammers when talking with one he's attracted to. That guy was me, trying to cool down my resentment of my job by lifting weights four times a week—with 79 female friends and zero girlfriends.

While I stared at the space elevator, being constructed during my 26th birthday, I said to myself, "This elevator will tilt and fall down during construction, before its outer space counterweight can keep the whole structure upright." My previous engineering education (no matter how much I denied it) told me that the 10 by 10-foot elevator shaft was far too narrow, compared to the 375 miles it would extend from the lithosphere up to the thermosphere. Without mentioning the bending, shear, and torsional effects of wind on the structure, gravity itself will cause it to buckle during the ground-up construction.

They said the elevator was for future space travel, because propelling massive aircraft from the earth's surface was far too inefficient. Having a small elevator pierce through the sky and then having the space tourists enter a shuttle in near outer space was the logical solution to the cost-benefit formula. Funded by the aerospace giant United

Technologies, designed by the architect HOK, calculated by the engineer AECOM, and built by the contractor Bechtel, the elevator would be operational four years from this date, on my 30th birthday.

But I had no time to think about the space elevator, because later that day, on my 26th birthday, I did an earth-shattering thing. At least, it was considered so in my own private universe. I was studying for my Master of Finance at the time, because I figured I was more interested in money than engineering. Turned out I was equally disinterested in both. Anyway, the instructor at the time was the blazing hot Ava Haneda. She had tanned skin, the most unique voice, the tiniest nostrils, and the cutest round face.

I never possessed any ability to ask a woman out on a date, so I thought she would be no exception. But on that last lecture of the semester, some unknown source of courage told me to go for it, since I had nothing to lose. We only had two long conversations before this, which wasn't much.

I waited for half an hour after class, until the keen students exhausted their questions. Then I tried talking normally with her along the hallway, in the elevator, and in the lobby, until we were about to exit the building. It was the absolute last chance I had to tell her how I felt. I looked through the glass doors and up into the night sky. It was, also, that night that Cassini 2 took off for a four-year journey to Uranus, my planet of love. If I couldn't ask her out that night, with a rocket going to my favorite planet and with her lavender breath brushing against my face, then I might as well become a biologist and do research into asexual reproduction.

"Ava," I stammered inside the building lobby.

"Yes?" she asked in a standard tone.

"I was thinking . . ."

She stared at me with the most intense eyes, which made me blush a little.

". . . thinking whether you . . ."

A lazy old man walked right past the narrow space between us. After walking a few more steps, he turned to look into my eyes and snorted, as if looking down on me, thinking that I could never ask a girl out. I wanted to prove him wrong, and I asked, "Do you want to go out with me sometime?" To Ava, not the lazy old man.

She blinked at me for a few seconds, while the small pores in my face acted as ventilation to remove the exhaust from my system. The next few words she spoke were totally unexpected from a finance person, much less an instructor of finance.

"Only if you can take me into outer space in two years," she said, with her unique voice. "Well before the launch of the space elevator."

***

And, so, there I was, for the next two years, trying my best to get into outer space. Having both mechanical engineering and MBA degrees, going into outer space seemed more or less doable. First of all, mechanical engineering branched out into fluids and machinery. Machinery branched out into immovable equipment and moveable vehicles. Vehicles branched out into land, sea, and air vehicles. You get the drift. What I'm saying is that the fact that I'm from fluids is actually a far fetch from aerospace engineering.

But she was always there for me. She would meet with me for coffee twice a week, discussing how we were getting closer to achieving the dream in two years. She would occasionally stop by my lab when she got off early from work. Days that you can get off work on time are hard to come by for a chartered financial analyst. I started to feel like I had already accomplished much, by having her constant support and by proving to myself that I could have a clear goal in mind and not be the usual drifter that I had been. I told myself that, no matter what the outcome, I would no longer be a drifter again. Even though, I was horrified by the mere thought of traveling on the space elevator.

***

It was my 28th birthday, two years after my promise to Ava. Yet, I was no closer to the goal I set out to achieve. My original plan to work in an aerospace engineering firm, designing aircraft hulls, so that fluids could glide past more smoothly during flight, ended up in 29 failed interviews. I could only go back to my old job. As the professional route was out, I turned to hobbies. With previous knowledge in the NATO phonetics, I luckily got my private pilot license (PPL). But with that, I could only watch rockets go up from a higher vantage point, and nothing else.

I turned to practicality. It cost $400,000 for two people to experience weightlessness with Virgin Galactic. My bank accounts originally amounted to $40,000. But after renting planes and taking classes for the PPL and instrument rating, I'm too embarrassed to reveal how much I have now. Meanwhile, rolling the Powerball in the Florida Lottery still hasn't paid off.

As the events had turned out bleakly in the end, perhaps without knowing it, I had once again reverted to my original self. That night, I was so depressed that I couldn't bear to call Ava. All I could do was to look up at the moon and, hopefully, catch a glimpse of a shooting star.

That was when my Galaxy S15 Smartphone rang, with my favorite Hummingbird Heartbeat song from back in 2010. Smartphones were getting very smart. The surface five-inch screen could unfold two times to reveal a concealed 10-inch screen. That was where the quirky face of Ava popped up, with her quirkiest expression to date. Somehow, her cheerfulness reinforced the shamefulness inside me. "I'm sorry, Ava. I tried my best already. I can't take you into space."

Her face displayed a gleam of hope. Was it because I had told her the truth, even though it was tough to admit? Or was there something I wasn't getting? Suddenly, two tickets appeared between her Smartphone screen and her face. The words on the ticket read Space Elevator: A Slingshot Trip Around the Moon.

Tears rained down my cheeks. It was worth it in the end. Even if it wasn't me bringing us into outer space, it didn't matter. Our dream to venture towards the lunar sphere paid off. "How did you get the tickets?"

"I played the Fantasy 5 from the Florida Lottery. Guess I was quite lucky. It really does feel like a fantasy!"

I could only sigh in relief. Since the time we met, 28 months ago, there were days when I didn't quite understand her, when I felt like she was a complete stranger. Sometimes I would question what I actually saw in her—whether my imagination was so vivid that it created a picture of pure fiction. Then, I would silently congratulate myself for holding out this long, to make new discoveries. The fact that we both unknowingly chose Florida lottery meant we were quite compatible after all.

"I guess we leave in two years."

Living on the 10th floor of my low-rise apartment, I stretched my hand, with the Smartphone, as far out of my bedside window as possible. The moon was as glorious as usual, but now there was also the space elevator undergoing construction from the ground to the sky. From where I lived, the elevator was right underneath the moon. Only four fingers of space separated the two objects.

"It's a little weird," Ava said, looking through her device at what I was seeing.

"What is?"

"Oh, it's nothing. Looking at the sky just got me thinking. People from different parts of the world are dealing with different problems every day. Some may be struggling to start life in a new country, while others may be undergoing the loss of someone special. Yet every night, we all look at the same beautiful moon. Isn't it strange? How we're all connected by the moon?"

"Sure is strange." I looked up at the yellow moon with its round sphere of imperfections. Sure is magical, too.

***

Thursday, May 2nd, 2026. A clear night with almost no clouds. My 30th birthday. It was after dinner and past 21:00 when I took Ava to the nearby suburbs where we strolled along a lakeside boulevard. In the backdrop behind the lake was the Miami Four Seasons Hotel, with its huge LED facade, that normally displayed advertising messages. But on this night, there weren't any words, making the building tower almost pitch black. After making a phone call, I hung up and asked Ava to try her best to look at the pitch black building.

"What is there to see?" she complained. "Is this another one of your games again? Because I'm not li . . ."

Individual words were displayed in a set pattern, at a set frequency, on the formerly pitch black facade of the building. The first word was "Ava." The second word was

"Will." The third word was "You." The fourth word was "Marry." And the last word was "Me." I knelt down in the standard position and looked up into her eyes, which filled with a look of kindness, making my decision to propose even clearer. She said yes.

It took half an hour to drive her home; time that I personally thought was well spent. I stopped the car downstairs of her apartment and turned off the ignition. Before we kissed and said goodbye to each other, I asked her a very important question, one almost as important as the previous question two hours beforehand.

"The space elevator that we're both very much looking forward to go to . . . Do you still want to go? Into sp . . . space, I mean."

She looked into my eyes and said, "Looks like someone's got the jitters!"

"Se . . . seriously, this is no joke. Aren't you even scared in the slightest? I know you're used to watching horror movies, but this space elevator is another story."

"Nothing scares me. Whether they'd be horror movies or rollercoasters."

"I may not be from civil engineering, but the construction of the space elevator seemed rushed at best. Nobody knows what will happen. We may be riding up the elevator to the mesosphere, where it malfunctions and we plummet hundreds of miles down to our death."

"Don't say anymore."

"Dying in a confined box and being squashed at high speeds is quite miserable."

Ava scratched her neck. "Oh, Max, why do you have to do this?" She held her hands behind the small of her back and kicked her shoe against the padded interior. "Why today of all days?" She stared up into my eyes. "You were so thoughtful of me, giving me the best proposal ever. And now you want to ruin everything. Why?"

I closed my mouth.

"What? Nothing to say now? You were full of talk earlier."

I often didn't know how to talk back when Ava went berserk. This time was no exception.

147

"Was this dream of going into outer space mine only? In that case, I don't want to force you to plummet to your death. I won't want you to be miserable."

My words really sunk into her head. "No Ava, it's my dream too, more than you'll ever know . . ."

"The more I think about it, the more I want to ride the elevator, even more than going into space itself." She opened the car door, got out, sat on the hood, and motioned for me to do the same. "Just look at the space elevator, a line of neon white piercing through the night sky. Isn't it magical? It's like it's splitting the left side of the sky from the right." She placed her hand on my thigh. "Even if it's for a short time, I want to share the sky with you."

***

30th birthday +3 days: We drove over to Cape Canaveral to meet with our tour guides. Maverick was the mission captain, pilot-in-command, and the last air force F-22 veteran. Hornet was his capable assistant and first officer. Dangerfield was the space elevator specialist; if anything were to go wrong in the elevator, he would be the one to turn to.

As the five of us stood in close proximity to the elevator, I realized that my previous worries were naive as a kindergartener. Staring from a distance, the structure really did seem flimsy and feeble. But from this vantage point, one could say the structure was sabotage-proof, even if a meteoroid were to hit it head on. The first reason was the carbon nanotube material. Known as the material stronger than diamond-reinforced steel, lighter and clearer than glass, and artificially manufactured at a hundredth the cost of real diamonds, it was required to withstand the immense tension between earth's gravity and the opposite force of the space-bound counterweight. This material comprised the bulk of the elevator shaft walls and the surrounding four-tier pyramidal defensive cladding. If a meteoroid were to strike the leading edge of this triangular cladding, the meteoroid would no doubt split like butter on a knife. The construction was that sophisticated and convincing, withstanding the test of time, space, and the evolutionary passage of prowess.

"What are those hovering black dots?" Ava pointed up a couple hundred yards in the area near the space elevator.

Dangerfield gave out an audible snort with the sound waves directed in her trajectory. He then turned to me and said, "I'm sure you know what this is about, Max?"

I nodded, eager to display my knowledge. "First-class security system. The first and last line of defense of the aviation wing of the Marine Corps. The anti-personnel and anti-armor armament of the most capable fighter helo, the CH-46 Apache."

She held on tighter to me. "Fire and forget?"

The space elevator specialist stared at my fiancée with amazed eyes. "Say again?"

"Fire-and-forget. Hellfire missiles. One of the Apache helicopter's strongest weapons for any threat, such as, sabotage or terrorism."

Dangerfield cleared his throat. "Well, . . . y. . .yes, ma'am. Affirmative. Not that we have to worry, but having the security patrol is better for public relations, giving our investors and customers greater peace-of-mind. But if you were to ask me, I'd say it's a waste of money. Even if a 125,000-tonne oil tanker were to fly, somehow, and then crash into our structure and explode, there wouldn't be a single splinter or scratch."

Ava eased up instantly. "Well, that's good to hear. My hubby has been anxious since Day 1 about how the elevator will fall down from a meteor strike."

Dangerfield snorted again. "Ain't gonna happen. Even if all else fails, we still have loads of satellites."

"This is new to me," Hornet questioned. "What about the satellites?"

Dangerfield once again had a chance to snort and to boast his military knowledge. But he was beaten this time by the mission captain, who had chosen to stay silent until now.

"N2 projectiles," Maverick replied. "In case all else fails, 51% of all GPS satellites can fire N2 projectiles from the thermosphere to the lithosphere, each one capable of eradicating an area of 5000 square kilometers, the size of metro Tokyo. Using the sheer force of gravity and a little bit of kick, these 20-tonne bullets strike down with the impact of two nuclear warheads, hence the term N2, non-nuclear."

"Funny how the space elevator goes from the lithosphere to the thermosphere, while the N2 goes the other way around," I couldn't help but say.

"Hey, guys," Ava said. "Not trying to intrude into your insider conversation, but I think we need to get going." She pointed forward toward the opening elevator door.

Even though the elevator shaft was mostly transparent carbon nanotubes, the bottom pit, foundations, and door were all marine-grade 316 stainless steel with matte finish. A large key-like object in the center of the door popped out four inches from its socket, emitting some industrial dust in the process. It then proceeded to rotate 180 degrees counter-clockwise before going back into the socket. The strange door then split open horizontally, resembling tapered teeth as the two landing doors rolled up to the top and bottom respectively.

The 10 by 10 foot interior was initially in darkness before the interior neon lights turned on and transformed it into a light box. The hazy figure of a person was revealed to be a blazing hot elevator operator.

"Welcome, guests and crew," she said. Her conservative navy-blue flight attendant attire wasn't enough to prevent her bosoms from exploding outwards. But even that asset was inferior to the perfect proportion of hips and thighs.

A sharp, piercing, breath-taking numbness infiltrated the outer portion of my foot. A high-pitched thump was audible from the epicenter of this pain, until the heel of someone's shoe finally lifted away. "Ava?"

"It's about *time* you quit staring at the young lady," she said with the most indifferent voice she could muster.

The six people on board ventured through the atmosphere at 250 miles an hour. To the outside observer, it was like a black spot riding up the bright, neon gas light tube.

Inside the elevator, I looked at my foot and imagined how bruised it would be with the shoe removed. Ava was now standing between the elevator operator and me, with her arms crossed and jaw locked. Seeking to be the mediator, as I always wanted to be, I attempted to clear the air with a question. "What's that trapezoidal box with the words Biozone Buozoil written on it?" A blue light emitted from the center.

"Why don't you address his query, Ms. Angelina?" Dangerfield suddenly spoke in a polite manner. Perhaps the elevator specialist was also affected by the attractive woman who also sported an attractive name.

We were already traveling through the mesosphere when she answered. "Why, thank you Mr. Drift for the question and Mr. Dangerfield for the permission to answer." She raised her left hand to point towards the machine, revealing an engagement ring very much similar to the one I gave Ava. "This box is the reason for the breathable air in this air-tight chamber. It splits the carbon atoms from carbon dioxide to produce oxygen. The carbon atoms are then split at the sub-atomic level into protons and neutrons, which combine with the nitrogen to form oxygen when necessary. Argon and neon are regulated to stay at three percent during emergencies, for lighting purposes."

Ava looked up at the operator. "If all this sub-atomic collision is happening in the little box, is it safe to be standing next to it?" That was my Ava, she always had a way of getting straight to the point.

Before she could answer, a loud screeching sound, which seemingly came from all directions, enveloped the entire space elevator lattice. In a blink of an eye, Angelina's expression transformed from carefree to weapons-free. She stared out the small window on the side of the subatomic gas transfer machine. Her whole body literally vibrated. She headed for the other three windows on the other sides of the cubic elevator. Looking out windows number one, two, and three, as counted in a clockwise direction, she vibrated, wiped sweat from her forehead, and stayed calm respectively.

I stood there, unable to move my muscles. Was my worst fear of dying in confined space about to come true? Only my eyes and ears had the capability of movement, so I used them to the maximum. Based on the chaos and conversation that was happening around me, the north-facing window next to the Biozone box had a burning meteoroid flying directly in our direction. A blazing meteoroid impact was also imminent for the east-facing wall. An F-35B Lightning II was coming from the south to blast apart the meteors, while the west was generally free of debris with only mesosphere skies.

We all stared at Dangerfield, the space elevator specialist, hoping he would come up with a master plan to disintegrate the meteors. But his non-verbal communication showed that he was no meteoroid specialist.

Having fired all 180 rounds from its 25mm Gatling gun with no effect to the eastern meteoroid, the fighter jet opened its bottom hatch and released the safety on its MBDA Meteor beyond-visual-range air-to-air missile (BVRAAM) to strike at the core of the eastern meteoroid. Before releasing the weapon, two objects fell from the sky. Both of them were N2 projectiles as previously mentioned by Maverick. The first impact disintegrated the northern meteoroid, while the space elevator only shook less than an inch.

However, the second impact with the N2 projectile didn't occur because the BVRAAM already split the eastern meteoroid into two portions. The non-nuclear projectile traveled through the center space between both meteoroid halves and headed straight down in the direction of gravity. The resulting explosion vaporized the lithosphere and its inhabitants within a 25-mile radius and released the earth-bound counterweight of the space elevator. No longer affixed to earth, the whole structure floated up and into outer space at an accelerated pace, and would eventually drift to the moon.

Ava wrapped her body around mine as our elevator continued going up into the thermosphere. "What do we do now?"

"Everything will be all right," I told her. But in my mind, I knew our chance of survival was less than 10 percent. With Dangerfield kneeling and under extreme distress, that percentage dwindled down to two.

"Aren't those the shuttles we were supposed to fly on?" Hornet pointed at the two vehicles as they were blown off course, never to return to us.

Maverick could only pat his shoulders. "Have I ever told you how comfortable I felt every time I knew you were the co-pilot?"

Hearing those words, I looked down at the woman next to me and gestured for her to loosen her arms around me. I picked her up by the hips until our eyes met. "We've been through a lot, haven't we? That time when I said I liked you, that time when I proposed next to the lake, and the times in between when we would share the same ice cream cone." I hesitated before saying the rest. "I think we've lived long enough to know each other well, don't you think? There's just one thing I'm not quite sure about. It's whether I've been a good boyfriend." I looked into her brown eyes. "Please tell me I've been a good boyfriend."

Born in Hong Kong and raised for six years in Toronto, Canada, Clement Chow has been interested in science and the inner workings of the universe since a young age. This interest drove him to complete a degree in civil engineering, which explains some of the structural engineering terms used throughout the story. Although he has forgotten how to do calculations, because his second degree in landscape architecture nearly brainwashed him, he maintains his devotion to science and science fiction. "Drifting to the Moon" is his second published short story.
His blog is at https://cthchow.wordpress.com/.

15. Godzilla and Icarus

Amos Parker

"Welcome, honored and excited guests!"

One of the ten, young Japanese hostesses smiled. In the year 2050, she spoke in singsong to the 50 tourists who'd just stepped onto the space elevator platform floating in the Pacific. At the platform edge, metallic spider arms clasped and held the tourists' ship *Kodiak*.

The year before, and nine months early, Japan had birthed its promised scientific child.

All the beautiful Japanese girls stood resplendent in costumes—half-Hawaiian flower dance and half-Japanese kimono—waiting to greet the guests and be of service. They wore their leis in the elegant way they wore their beauty, both waving and blooming.

"Would you look at that?" Cosgrove sighed, believing he meant only Japan's invention. "What a wonderful creation for Mankind."

"It does look that way," his wife Elaine replied, crossing her arms and sensing in him the emotions he hid from himself.

He'd bought round trip tickets for that innovative, ocean-anchored Japanese creation. They would soon leave Earth below and rise up to the stars in a house of an elevator that clutched a 100,000-kilometer carbon nanotube ribbon. At the top floated station *Godzilla*.

Cosgrove had said the trip was a fifth anniversary gift to her, and not just for him. Elaine had not bought the tickets, and did not buy the reason that he gave for their purchase, either. But the gift's message about their marriage left a void in her, or expanded it, and magnified the one already between them.

They had no children for her to fall back on. His wealth had not bought children the way it had bought the rarified, round-trip passes.

Yet she'd consented at last, for his love of science, and in the spirit of compromise. She tried.

"But remember, it's 'Humankind'," she said, feeling too conscious of her natural look, in the light of the handfuls of hostesses. "'Mankind' is just half of a compromise."

On the platform deck, the other 48 passengers stood quiet and attentive. The hostess who'd spoken before spoke again, gesturing at the dark void of a doorway behind her.

"Yes. Soon you come. Pleasure awaits!"

The other nine bright Japanese girls nodded and gave small bows. Elaine felt clumsy and awkward in the light of their grace. She stroked her frazzled hair, fretting.

We can't save the world with our feet off it, or our heads above the clouds.

Elaine taught ecology and wore a tee shirt with a world globe on both sides. The front showed the Eastern Hemisphere and the back the Western. She tasted memories of pollution—much of it from the voyage of the *Kodiak*. She seemed to hold the innards of the Earth inside her, organs blending beneath the surfaces her tee pictured.

She looked unwell. Often she did. Her husband knew what she believed God would write on Mankind's gravestone. She often spoke it aloud.

I gave talent. I forgot wisdom. Whoops.

Cosgrove did not look unwell. He never did. He worked as a freelance corporate physicist. He loved science. He loved innovative, beautiful, new technology even more, in part because it comforted. So he loved Japan's pleasure platform much more than he did the old, tired, and mediocre *Kodiak*.

And for the same reasons, Elaine had grown almost sexless to him. But he knew she tried.

"Soon you come inside and get high!" said the leading hostess, in the warm, salty air. "Your turn, like other tickled groups before. We experienced professionals."

She spoke standing, fronting the other nine, and from underneath her white and red geisha makeup. By no means old, Cosgrove could tell she still was the oldest of the ten. She radiated seniority. All 50 of the rustling passengers, who would soon elevate, paid her rapt attention. The platform arms handled the luggage, drawing it from *Kodiak* to storage with delicate swoops.

"We welcome you to the *Smiling Icarus* with relish! We will climb you. We will join with you. Please feel free to take advantage of us!"

The 48 murmured. Cosgrove swelled, in general and with distinct geography. What a new way to ride.

"Please follow and massage your excitement, everyone and all. We have white, flushing thrones for excreting before we buckle and rise."

Cosgrove smiled at her, without acquiring her attention. With theatricality and arms almost dancing, she turned, entering the portal past her underlings. The 48 began moving.

At the back, Elaine and Cosgrove waited, watching.

To Elaine, the lead hostess vanished like a beautiful fish sliding away through water. She turned, looking through the complex of metal arms that held, replenished, and unburdened the *Kodiak*. Sprays and brushes cleaned it. Seeing, she thought of trips to spas she'd refused, places of greater beauty than hers. Like the spider arms, spas held with comfort, replenished physical wellness, and pulled out money.

But where she had refused, the *Kodiak* consented. Now a practical part of the platform, it began to look special and even new. And it would wait for their return, with innocent faith, as though they had not betrayed its terrestrial nature.

Elaine looked at Cosgrove as the nine other hostesses entered the dark portal and the 48 drifted after. With an innocent smile, he looked back to sea. What goes on while comfort, wellness, and money work to pamper Humankind?

And what is customer service when leaving the earth behind?

Cosgrove saw that his wife looked even more out of sorts than usual.

"Attitude, sweetie."

"I know, honey. I know."

"If you don't mind, I'll stand and look at this marvel for a minute."

"Sure."

The 48 thinned to 40, 25, and then to a skinny 10. Voices chattered. Excitement percolated. Odors of bodies and perfume mixed with scents of salty air in the gentle breeze. Small waves slapped the hull.

Elaine looked up at the elevator, resting at the base of the ribbon and so much like a house. It reeked of superior comfort.

Rise. Rise. Rise.

Long. Fast. Hard.

Weightless.

Elaine heard creaking joints. An elderly woman, with milky white eyes and a rickety hunch, touched her arm. Elaine looked down at the upturned face. The old woman smiled an out-of-place, too-white denture smile. Her curly, grey hair grew with uniform thinness.

"Is it time to go up to Heaven now?"

Elaine moved her lower jaw hard to the left. She felt the dwindling crowd's discomfort with, and indifference to, the elderly woman. She melted.

"Almost."

"Good. I'm so tired of being alone. Albert's waiting up there. He told me what he'd learned in life would matter in Heaven, at least. Or it wouldn't be Heaven."

Elaine looked around. She felt lighter.

Cosgrove felt heavier without the crowd and the hostesses. He wanted all the 58 to stay, to drink in the sight of the ribbon, elevator and platform with him. He wanted very much to share his love. The achievement inflamed him, yet he shivered.

Elaine thought of something.

"Are any of your children with you, grandmother? Grandchildren?"

Cosgrove clicked his teeth. Elaine knelt. The old lady's eyelids fluttered.

Leaving Earth

"No. Why? They should stay here and live."
Elaine smiled.
"Wise, grandmother. Honey?" Elaine stood and turned
to her husband. "Help her along. Give her your arm. You
have energy.
Perplexed by his strange chill, Cosgrove nodded.
"We're being left behind anyway."
The elderly woman took his muscular forearm. They
walked inside, the last three to leave the sea. He might've
been guiding the imitation of a woman, done in origami and
brought to frail life. And the platform had begun to seem as
insulating as paper.
He wanted more. Reality called to him.

***

"Five to one and samurai balance!"
The lead hostess spread her arms, light on her
bouncing toes. The rainbow flowers in her lei flounced and
rustled.
"We service you now, money payers."
The younger nine shifted in their places. Cosgrove had
the sense of them as compressing springs gathering energy.
They looked just beyond high school, in age, yet disciplined.
Everyone, 10 exotic hostesses and 50 passengers, stood
in the central, circular room of the lift house. Fifty seats
occupied the outer rim. Wide, high, thick windows occupied
the entire 360 degrees, revealing endless oceanic blue. A fat
pillar took up the room's center. Up against it pressed 10
more seats. All 60 seats displayed fine, pink plush over a
floor layered thick with baby blue carpet.
The hostess beckoned, pointing to her underlings and
the passengers.
"You take advantage of us."
The ten hostesses broke apart like a disintegrating
human fabric. Each of them gathered together five
passengers.
The leader came to Cosgrove, Elaine, and the old lady.
Completion came in a teenaged couple with four wide eyes,
the bloom of extreme youth, and groping virginal courtship.
"I'm Teddy. This is Julia. Do you have roses?"
The hostess gave a musical laugh. Cosgrove melted.
The hostess put her hands together and bowed to Teddy.

158

"Please feel free to take advantage of our beautiful freeze dried foliage."

"It's just that, you know, we'll be hitting Valentine's Day on this trip."

The hostess beamed, hands brushing the flowers around her neck.

"Oh yes. It is the day of clubs! We are prepared."

"Huh?" said Teddy, scratching his head and drinking in his girlfriend's blank expression. "Clubs? This isn't caveman love."

The hostess laughed. She touched a soft hand to her left breast.

"Man cave? No. Cards for playing. Hearts. Diamonds. Spades. Clubs. To hit Valentine's Day, yes?"

She turned to Cosgrove and Elaine.

"Yes? Valentine's Day and the beating club?"

She blinked with large brown eyes at Cosgrove, her smile radiant.

"Hearts," Cosgrove said, touching her breasted hand with a forward fingertip. "But spades and clubs might work better, sometimes, on Valentine's Day."

All around, beautiful Japanese women assisted murmuring passengers. Formal brightness and sunshine reigned. Some hostesses windmilled their arms for nodding passengers. Laughter filled the sealed structure's air.

It occurred to Cosgrove that he hadn't introduced anyone.

"Cosgrove. This is my wife Elaine."

"As you wish. Is this your own family grandmother elder?"

Elaine shook her head.

"No. She came alone."

"I'm Eleanor," said the old lady, "and I would like to sit down now."

She blinked, bleary.

"What will you do with my body in Heaven?"

"I am Akahana," began the hostess. "I am special with shiatsu and if you approve me only I will rub it well."

Cosgrove seemed to rise. Eleanor sat down.

"I'm not a raw fish. No one eats me. Cremate me and release my ashes into space."

159

"So sorry, no smoking. Patch or gum?"

But Eleanor slept, already. Akahana smiled.

"You will tell her when she wakes to not burn? I must give advantage. *Smiling Icarus* will accelerate for many hours and you will be seat buckled. Carrier ribbon . . ."

Elaine imagined the elevator falling, crashing and burning as Akahana gestured at the room's central pillar.

". . . will support us. When accelerate ends, you will unbuckle and explore home we have joyfully made without kindly abusing anything. Steady ride. Food supplied. Pleasure wide."

Akahana chuckled at the scripted rhyme.

"Sake, cold or hot. Television. Much fine rubbings for a happy ending. No radiation for *Shining Icarus* penetration. Only Earth and galaxy view penetrates. Please take advantage of penetration."

Cosgrove's owl eyes bulged. With fewer people to look at, Akahana grinned back at Cosgrove with perfect white and real teeth. He pressed his hands and bowed. She pressed her hands and bowed back.

"We last one week toward high satisfaction?"

Elaine frowned. Julia blushed.

Cosgrove, his mind off on its own carbon track, contemplated his endurance. Week? Weak. He looked at Teddy and Julia. They hugged like love would last forever. Being their age felt interminable.

"After one week," continued Akahana, pointing up toward space, "we reach *Godzilla*. You will disembowel high over Earth, and then–"

"Disembark," said Elaine. "Not disembowel."

"Of course!" replied Akahana. "Humble apologies. Disembark. In shielded station you will enjoy Earth from distance and float free with organs rised like featherless birds, unless you accept our play costumes. Counterweight is far enough for blue planet to still be beautiful. In some years we may add kilometers to ribbon as Earth dirties much."

Elaine coughed.

"Organized. Not organs rised."

Teddy spoke.

"Why don't the ribbon and *Godzilla* fall?"

160

"Staying up," replied Akahana with vigorous nodding, "is hard. But old Japanese men do it. We love with science. Lead to perfect samurai balance!"

Cosgrove's organs swooned. He envied and spoke.

"He's asking about the specific science. I can tell him. I'm an old scientist. Take advantage of me."

Akahana laughed and shook her head.

"I do. I do. Swing arm!"

Teddy blinked and frowned.

"What?"

"Earth spins so swing arm! Like this!"

Akahana whirled her arms like windmills, in opposite directions.

"Spin arm and feel hand pull!"

Teddy and Julia did. After several seconds they began to laugh and nod, dropping arms.

"We're no good in school," Teddy said as Julia nodded in agreement. "Especially in science class. We don't love science. But we get it. So . . ."

His eyes lost focus. At last he spoke again, kissing Julia's ear.

"Why doesn't the ocean platform fly off the Earth? My shoulder joint—"

Akahana cut him off.

"Gravity, I say to you! Science and perfect compromise."

"Oh."

Teddy looked at the Eastern Hemisphere on Elaine's tee. He looked too long, and as if he'd looked too long at the Sun, Julia glared at him like the Sun.

Cosgrove spoke, questioning.

"Compromise . . .?"

He brightened.

"Perfect samurai balance?"

Akahana's eyes widened to what seemed like saucer size. She bowed as deep as the Mariana Trench."

"Hooray men!"

Cosgrove tingled.

"I . . . I really, really love science. And every real man loves a really long sword."

"We get it on fine!" Akahana cried. "I and we all here because of science love and fine swordplay!"

Leaving Earth

Elaine refused to uncross her arms, in case her husband needed catching.

And so it goes.

***

Elaine sighed and turned to look down at Eleanor and then out the window over her seat.

Sapphire hued ocean sparkled, mercury-poisoned and polluted beyond vision. She felt the machinery underneath her begin to hum. She looked down at Eleanor's seat belt and it looked to her like a single, well-engineered, and voluntary prison bar.

She heard Akahana.

"Now you will sit. We go! Equipment all penetrated."

Cosgrove, Elaine, Teddy, and Julia sat, joining Eleanor.

As if choreographed, all the other 46 sat too. In an excited minute, 50 paying customers sat around the outside rim while 10 paid employees sat along the inside rim, facing their 5.

Everyone fell silent. But in the silence, electric energy flowed. Akahana raised her hands with glee.

"Prepare! We explode!"

Some giggled, some squawked.

"Off to Heaven," Cosgrove whispered to Elaine after a glance at Eleanor. "No sushi in my Heaven. Shiatsu. Sushi. That's funny. I love humor."

He sighed, lay back, and closed his eyes.

"I don't even like *cooked* fish. We're not travelling to Mercury."

Elaine craned her neck to look out the ocean view window behind her husband. She thought of many kinds of cooking, much of it done wrong.

"It's just as well."

***

Akahana cheered as they lifted off without exploding.

"Yay!

Red lights turned on in a ring over the hostesses and all the way around the pillar. Acceleration felt gentle, slow, and well-engineered. Cosgrove nodded with a scientist's approval. Beauty and technology lifted them over Earth's filth.

"Good. Very good."

162

Many of the hostesses trembled with present, anticipated joy.

At 1.5 accelerating gravities, the pressure of the acceleration did not make Elaine feel like the apple in a cider press she'd anticipated. No pesticides or worms squeezed from her, out of this or that orifice, like jellied, meaty organs.

"We pleasure you all for being here!" Akahana said, many times. "Very!"

Silence otherwise prevailed, during acceleration. Hours passed by, gathering thought in 60 heads.

At last, over the head of each of the Japanese attendants, red lights turned green. Elaine thought of blood fertilizing vacated grass. The acceleration pressure ceased. Then Earth's gravitational pressure ceased. Blood soared in weightlessness, in everyone, over a bright lawn of baby blue carpet, pink chairs, and planet.

"Release!" Akahana cried, unbuckling and gesturing. "Joyful release!"

Elaine alone stayed buckled. Cosgrove called to her, with a question.

"Elaine! Would you look at this?"

He somersaulted, head over heels and then heels overhead. Eleanor held fast to her chair's armrests. Teddy and Julia, embracing and kissing, spun in a slow, counterclockwise, idling drill spiral.

Elaine looked past Cosgrove at the attendants, and in particular at Akahana, who spoke.

"Everyone be gentle to our weightlessness friend. Do not go heels over any globe head with too much fastness. That is like loving wrongly and clubbing, yes? It is easy to smash globes and contact is impolite."

She smiled.

Across the room, half obscured by the pillar, two middle-aged men bumped heads. One woman called out that she felt sick. Her attendant gave her a bag, which the sick woman filled.

Cosgrove somersaulted over Elaine, his spin stopped by a hand on the ceiling.

"Sweetie?"

She shook her head.

Leaving Earth

"Oh, Cosgrove. You look like a tumbleweed."

"*I was as God made me,*" he said, grinning. "That'll be on my gravestone."

He stopped smiling. "But really, sweetie. You're the tumbleweed."

She frowned.

"How?"

"Lost. Cut off. Out of samurai balance."

He looked away from her and at the view she'd turned on.

But she still didn't unbuckle. With a clumsy gripping of the back of her seat, she turned herself to look out at falling Earth. She'd seen, and loved, the famous 60s photograph from space. She caught her breath. It was quite a certain statement.

"Would you look at that."

"Happy to," her husband replied, not seeing Akahana drift near from behind. "The world looks fine without us. Don't you think so?"

Elaine looked back at him.

"Looks can be deceiving, honey."

Amos Parker has believed he should be a "real writer"' since high school in the early 90s. But it wasn't until getting fired from a job, in 2007, that he finally found (and flipped) the switch in his body/mind/soul necessary to become more than an email and journal writer. He got fired early on a Monday morning, 'round about September 3rd, on a lovely early fall day, and spent the day wandering around the nature paths in East Burke, Vermont. The first half of the day was spent wondering what the Hell to do next: the second half, after flipping the switch, was spent mentally hammering out a fantasy book plot, terrified that, if he didn't lock it in hard, the switch would un-flip. But in spite of some bumps along the way, it never has. Since then, a space currently of almost 8 years, he's written about 10 novel manuscripts, 6 books of short stories and novellas . . . and failed utterly to find the "switch" in his mind/body/soul necessary to care much about fighting to be published and make money off his writing.

16. FIVE DAYS AND NIGHTS

Douglas G. Clarke

1 – The Office
Sara sat in her leather chair, behind her large oak desk, straightening the stacks of paper sitting on it. She adjusted the lone picture of her black lab.

"You going to be okay without me, boy?" she thought. She reached behind her head and pulled out the pins from her tight bun, letting her silky black hair tumble down. She shook it out—enjoying the feeling—knowing it would be a long time before she would be able to do it again.

"Anything else I can do for you, Miss Davis?" came a voice from outside the office.

"No, Barbara. I'm ready to go. Sure wish you were coming, though."

Barbara peeked in the office. "You don't need me."

"Need? Maybe not, but it's going to take longer without you. Instead of four months, Henderson is estimating it'll take six months to be up and running. Six months! I wish I could get my hands on the person who bumped you."

"It's nobody's fault—things happen. You better get going, your plane leaves in two hours."

2 – Space Elevator Port

Seven hours later, a limo stopped at the entrance to the Hillary Clinton Space Elevator. While Sara waited for the driver, she touched up her makeup and smoothed out her skirt over her long slender legs.

When he opened the door, noise assaulted her like a slap across the face. A semi-circle of reporters faced away from her, yelling questions and flashing their cameras.

"This way," her driver said, as he headed towards a side door.

Sara ignored him and waded into the sea of reporters.

"Excuse me. Excuse me."

The sea parted at the command of her voice, and then the cameras were on her.

"You want a story? I'll give you a story. We're about to put into production a factory that will produce enough Cancerlite to eradicate the evils of cancer once and for all. And do you know what is standing in our way—every 20 seconds allowing another person to die of this now curable disease?"

Sara paused as every reporter leaned closer.

"A seat on the space elevator. My associate got bumped because someone with a lot of money wants to go on a joy ride. This will delay our success by weeks."

"Mr. Harris, is that true?" one of the reporters asked. As one, all the cameras swung back to the well-groomed man in the three-piece suit.

"This is the first I've heard of it, I assure you. I have no intention of getting in the way of science." Mr. Davis paused and looked over at Sara. "If your associate can get here before we leave, I will gladly give him, or her, my seat."

"Lucky for you it's a five hour flight to get here, or I'd take you up on that offer." Sara spun around and marched away, leaving Mr. Davis to fend off the reporters.

3 – Departure

Sara sat in her chair, practicing hooking and unhooking her five-point harness, and becoming annoyed with the perky young woman who was drilling her.

"I've think I've got it."

"One more time, Miss Davis. Can you do it for me with your eyes closed this time?"

166

An exasperated sigh escaped her, as she pulled the two straps across her chest and deftly snapped them in place.

"I believe you're right, Miss Davis. You do seem to have it."

Sara thanked heaven as the smug little stewardess with her tight little skirt across her taut little rear went to help the next passenger. Sara got up and walked around the inside of the tiny elevator. It was like a donut with the bundle of carbon nano-tubes stretching through its middle from the Earth up to the Rock. There were three pairs of chairs set around the inner core, with two bathrooms and a galley separating them. Across from each pair of chairs was a window revealing the busy port beyond. Between the windows, along the outer wall were three doors; one was marked "exit", which Sara knew lead to the air lock she had entered through. The other two were simply marked "storage"

As she walked, she greeted four of the other passengers, who were more as she would expect on a trip like this; two technicians, a project manager, and a system engineer like herself. It was Mr. Harris, who was sitting in the chair next to hers, who was the odd man out.

"How are you doing, Sara?" he said as she returned to her seat. "I don't think we've been properly introduced. My name's Andrew Harris, but you can just call me Andy."

Sara shot him a cold look. "The name is Miss Davis, if you don't mind, Mr. Harris.

"Pardon me, Miss Davis, I didn't mean to offend you. I just figured since we're going to be sitting next to each other for five days, we should be a little less formal."

"Well, you figured wrong."

Sara pulled out her tablet and started reviewing the figures on the plants latest test runs.

"I see you're all buckled in," said the stewardess, "so it's time for me to wish you a safe and comfortable trip. The automated computer system will be your guide on this trip to low orbit, and thank you once again for choosing to ride with Otis, the name you can trust."

4 – Take off

The acceleration was only one-tenth of a G and only lasted for eighty-six seconds, but that, added to the one G of Earth pulling her down, was enough to make Sara light headed as she sank into her seat. The only sound was the rushing of the air outside as they shot upward. The indicator below the window showed their progress. As they passed 11,000 feet, the rushing of the air decreased and then the acceleration stopped. They were cruising at 185 miles per hour with 22,234 miles to go.

"Now, was that a rush, or what?" came Andrew's voice from beside her.

"A rush, I guess. I'm feeling a little woozy."

Andrew unfastened his belts and made his way across the cabin. He returned with a squeeze-bottle of water and two white pills.

"These are for the wooziness."

Sara took them and then looked into his eyes—his bright blue eyes. "You don't need to be nice to me."

"Is it a crime to be nice to someone? I think the world would be a much better place if we were all a little nicer to each other."

5 – Dinner

Sara was feeling better, but she still sat in her seat with her belts fastened. The aroma of beef gravy filled the cabin and her stomach growled in response.

"I hope you don't mind, but I took the liberty of making your dinner. Of course, I'd rather be cookin' for you over an open fire, but that darn microwave is the only thing we've got.

Sara took the offered plate and the accompanying squeeze-bottle of wine.

"Thank you, Mr. Harris. That was very kind of you."

6 – Midnight

The cabin was dark. The only sounds were that of the ventilation system, the electric motors that drew them upward, and the snoring of Mr. Hernandes in the seat around the corner. Sara sat, still buckled into her chair, her face illuminated by the pale glow of her tablet.

"You really should try to get some rest," came Andrew's soft voice. "You won't be able to cure cancer, if you're dead tired when you get up there."

"I'll be fine. I'm just not used to sleeping in a chair."

"You should come look outside then. It's quite a view."

Sara reflexively put a hand across her chest, grabbing the belts.

"You'll have to get up at some point or you'll burst." Andrew got up and stood next to her. "Give me your hand and I'll help steady you."

Sara hesitated, but she knew he was right. She set down her tablet and unfastened the belts. She tried to get up by herself, but found that ten hours of sitting didn't make that practical. She placed her hand in his. The warmth of his hand sent a chill through her body. She started to sit again, but he put his other arm around her waist and got her to her feet. She could feel his strength, his control.

"You're freezing! Why didn't you say something?" He steadied her against the wall and removed his jacket, slipping it across her shoulders. The warmth of it caressed her—then his arm was around her again. After a quick stop at the bathroom, he guided her to one of the far windows.

"Mexico City."

Sara looked out the window at the lights far below, but her thoughts were on the arm that still held her up. It felt good to be held. How many years had it been since a man had held her? She shook at the thought.

"I'll be right back," came his gentle voice, and then the hand was gone. She thought she might fall, but she managed to keep standing. Soon she felt a blanket being wrapped around her and then the arm around her waist again. She laid her head against his chest and was asleep.

7 – Morning

Sara woke, finding herself strapped into her chair—toasty warm under three blankets. She could hear the other passengers eating breakfast.

"Orange juice?"

Leaving Earth

She looked over to see Andrew with a bottle in his hand. He looked much "softer" in the cardigan sweater, but the day's worth of stubble on his face added roughness.

She smiled. "Thank you, Andrew."

"You're quite welcome, Miss Davis."

"Sara. I'm sorry I was such a bitch yesterday."

"Not a problem, Sara. We all have our bad days. Squeeze toast?"

Sara made a funny face at the bottle. They both laughed.

8 – Evening

"Why are you here?" Sara asked.

Andrew smiled, lost in thought for a moment. "I want to help others experience this. I want to make it possible for people to come up here just for the joy of it."

"You mean rich people. Don't you think there are more important ways to use these limited resources than to make a playground for the rich?"

"Quite the contrary. If my plans succeed, and I open a hotel on the Rock, those rich people will help pay for many more resources for you scientists to use. You're a businesswoman. How much does your company want to pay to be up here?"

"Not much, but it still feels wrong."

9 – Sunrise

Sara and Andrew stood by the window and watched the sun rising over the rim of the world. The window's built-in filters protected their eyes from the damaging rays.

"I still can't get over how beautiful the earth looks from up here," Sara said in a whisper, not wanting to wake anyone.

"Yeah, it pales compared to anything men can make."

Andrew's left hand hung at his side, and she slipped her right hand into his, intertwining their fingers. She reached her left hand across and pulled his arm against her, resting her head on his broad shoulder.

"Hum, Miss Davis. I think you've misunderstood my intentions."

Sara dropped her hands and took a step back.

"It's not that I don't think you're a beautiful woman. Or smart. Or capable. It's just . . . I'm not looking for a relationship right now."

Sara turned to stomp away, but realized there was nowhere to go. She balled her hands into fists and hit them against her thighs. She turned and looked at him. She could see sadness in his eyes, which just made her feel worse.

"I knew I should hate you, and all your rich buddies, but, no, I let my guard down for a few days."

Sara turned and tried to stomp away the best she could in the stupid slippers she had to wear on the way-too-soft carpet. She marched across the room and into one of the two restrooms, shutting the door behind her.

10 – Waiting

Every minute she stayed in the restroom made it that much harder to come out. She replayed their conversation in her head, over and over again. She chastised herself for feeling anything. She imagined what the other passengers were saying.

Several hours passed, the exact number lost to her, when the knock came. It was a quiet knock, timid. When she didn't respond, it came again.

"Miss Davis. I feel I owe you an explanation. Won't you come out, so we can talk?"

"So everyone can laugh at me?"

"No one knows. I told them that dinner wasn't agreeing with you."

Sara sat in silence.

"Please, Sara. I already feel terrible about this."

"Good," was her only reply.

11 – Dinner

In the end, it was hunger that brought Sara out of the bathroom.

"How are you feeling?" Andrew said and it seemed there was real concern in his voice.

"Why are you being nice to me? Why can't you just be a stuck-up rich guy?"

Leaving Earth

"Because I really do care about you. Let me get you some dinner."

"Fine." Sara collapsed into her chair and stared at her feet.

Andrew was back in a few minutes; ham, pea paste, and apple sauce in hand. He handed Sara the plate, then reached down to pull up her table, before sitting in his seat.

"Well."

"You think I'm doing all of this because I want to make money or give my friends gifts."

"Sure. That sounds reasonable."

"I'm not. I don't need any more money, and, honestly, I don't really have any friends."

"So, why are you here?"

"I'm trying to find some peace for my soul. I'm trying to fulfill a promise I made."

Sara rolled her eyes. "Okay, I'll bite. What promise?"

Andrew looked away from her. Sara realized it was the first time he had broken eye contact with her in all their conversations.

"Is it really that bad?"

"Not bad," he said to the floor, "but hard."

Sara didn't mean to, but she found her hand on his shoulder.

"A year ago, someone asked me to make a promise—which wasn't anything new—I had been making her promises for 19 years. But this one was different. She asked me to promise her two things: First, to build a hotel on the Rock and name it after her; and, second, to release her ashes into orbit."

Sara's hand dropped from his shoulder to the table, sending her plate to the floor, but she didn't care. Her eyes were fixed on Andrew's face.

"Was she your wife?" she asked gently.

He nodded.

"Annabelle. My darling, sweet Annabelle. It was the night before the cancer took her. She made me promise. And now I'm taking her up to say goodbye for the last time. I'm so sorry you took my kindness for something more. You can understand, right? If this was a different time . . ."

Sara put her hand back on his shoulder and gave it a squeeze.

12 – Slowing down

"Attention," the computer voice blared. "In five minutes we will begin our deceleration. For twenty minutes after that point, the cabin will experience weightlessness, as it is rotated 180 degrees in preparation for our deceleration and arrival at the Rock. Will all passengers please take their seats?"

The six passengers hurried to their seats and they waited impatiently for the remaining four minutes. There was a slight change in the tone of the electric motors and then everything started to get lighter. Thirty seconds later, they had unbuckled their belts and were floating around the small room.

They tossed candies at each other and practiced their summersaults, looking like nothing more than a bunch of oversized six-year-olds.

"Are you having fun?" Sara asked Andrew.

"The time of my life. I just wish Annabelle were here. We used to dance a lot and had always wondered what it would be like to do the swing in space. I guess I'll just have to imagine it."

"Maybe not." Grinning, Sara held out her hand towards him. "I've done my share of rug-cutting."

Andrew took her long slender fingers and held them in his big hand. With a quick tug, and a tuck on her part, she spun into his arms. When they touched, their movements combined and sent them into a spin like a tumbleweed.

They laughed and held on to each other. The tighter they clung, the faster they spun, until Andrew broke the embrace and let her spin away, with just their hands touching.

Applause erupted from the other passengers. Someone found a swing song on the entertainment system and soon they were all trying to dance.

13 – Arrival

The rest of the trip went by quickly. Sara and Andrew spent a lot of time talking and laughing. Andrew shared about his life with Annabelle. Sara talked about her work and her black lab, Bert. Neither of them talked about what they were going to do when they stopped being together, but that time came anyway and they made their way out of the elevator.

"It was really nice meeting you. I hope you find some peace." Sara said with a smile on her lips.

Andrew smiled back. "And I hope you get your plant up and running quickly, so you can get home to Bert."

They reached the end of the walkway. Someone was waiting for Andrew. Sara went with the others to find her luggage.

14 – Goodbye

Andrew stood by the window as a thin trail of dust started to stretch away into space. "Goodbye, Annabelle." He placed a hand against the cold glass. "We had wonderful times."

"Do you mind if I say goodbye, too?" Sara said in a quiet voice—not threatening or intrusive.

"Not at all. I think Annabelle would have liked you." Andrew put an arm around Sara and pulled her close. They watched the dust escape from its container until the last sunlit sparkles faded away.

"Thank you," Andrew said.

Sara nodded her head.

"Would you like something to eat?" Andrew asked.

"Sure, that would be nice."

"Can we call this a first date? I'd really like to start over."

Sara took his hand. "I think it's too late for that," she said, and then pulled him closer. She pressed her lips to his. When she finished kissing him she said, "I never kiss on a first date."

"Well, how many does it take?"

"Let's call it five and count from there."

Andrew pulled her closer and returned her kiss, with interest.

174

Douglas G. Clarke is a Systems Engineer, Dutch oven cooker, Publisher, Game Developer, and, when he has time, a Writer of short stories—with two novels in the works. He lives in San Diego with his wife and two almost-grown children. You can find out more about Mr. Clarke at his website: http://douglasgclarke.com.

When asked about his writing he says:

If things had been different, I may have chosen writing as my primary career, but things weren't different. I was born with dyslexia and dysgraphia, which in simple terms meant that in seventh grade I was reading at a fourth grade level and writing (penmanship and spelling) at a second. My parents paid to have me tutored outside of school and by the time I was in 9th grade, I was an avid reader. The penmanship and spelling, along with what in the 1970's was high tech—typing—were still far below grade level.

To this day, I can't use cursive writing and my penmanship is something only a doctor, or my mother, could love. Check-as-you-type spelling and grammar checkers have helped a lot, but they still don't help much when I correctly spell the wrong word (on instead of one). Thanks to the computer, I can actually write a short story and even a novel. Thanks also must go to my very understanding editors, who probably roll their eyes at the kinds of mistakes I make.

I've heard it said, and I wish I knew the exact quote and who said it first, that all great artists create from the dark times they've gone through and their disabilities—that, somehow, if creating is not hard work that stirs up deep emotions, a masterpiece cannot be the result.

It's funny, because as I sit to write a chapter of my book, or a short story, I have some idea about what it is I'm going to write. But the effort required to type each word, (both finding the keys to hit and figuring out how to spell the word), and the effort to keep the sentence structures correct, doesn't give me much space left to think about what to write. Instead, as I finish each word, the next word seems to just be there waiting for me to write.

I've read about how characters in a story start talking and say things that the authors didn't know they were going to say, and lead the story in directions they hadn't planned. I have experience this not only in dialog, but in action and narrative as well.

I guess that my writing is very much right brained, or perhaps the Holy Spirit is whispering in my ear. In either case, my writing is very much from the heart and, at times, thought provoking.

My earnest prayer is that my writing will both entertain and inspire.

UNSEEN REALMS

17. BABEL ASCENSION

Ami Hart

"Good evening, Rabbi Freeman."

Seth ignored Miles' mischievous, tilted grin. Rabbi today, sheikh, or Father tomorrow. Seth actually disliked using the titles.

Meaningless, all was meaningless.

Seth put the shofar up on the shelf, and dragged his finger across the polished ram's horn, lost in morose thoughts. He shrugged them off then turned, catching a reflection of himself in the office window. His black hat sat at a jaunty angle; the dark robes could be mistaken as a western style overcoat from a distance. A smile tickled his lips.

I can spin Psalm 91 like a six-gun.

"Hard night?"

"Uhuh." They were on the wrong side of midnight and all Seth wanted was a large whisky, a soft bed, and someone to share it. His mouth twitched at the thought of calling up a dollar whore special. He knew a few not-so-nice ladies who owed him some special favours.

I like it simple.

"We have a good line-up tomorrow," Miles said.

Straight back to business, Seth thought, unenthusiastically.

Ever since the Vaporal alien invasion, exorcism services like his had been run off their feet. He shouldn't really complain, he needed the money.

"We have another standard Islamic Ruqya requested at Noon in San Jose. Get the holy water ready, they want the works, and it might take a little more than just the Throne Verse this time. It's a bad Jinn—they say."

The Vapours are all bad Jinn," Seth muttered dryly.

"It's been referred to us from Exo-Spectral Services."

"Huh, they couldn't get a club sandwich out of a paper bag," Seth groused. "Have you synthesised any more of our magic potion?"

"The monoamine doper cocktail is done, new and improved. Even a guy like you would see angels."

Seth grunted in amusement, *the only angels I see are the type who would take my creds and my* . . . . Something caught his eye, a flash of red outside the window, illuminated for a moment by the lights of a passing shuttle. The door opened slowly and the figure darkening their doorstep entered.

"I think I'm seeing one now," Miles murmured, none too discretely.

He wasn't wrong.

There she was, standing in the doorway, all fine long curves and the height of an Amazon. Her red hair tumbled around her shoulders in loose curls. Her storm-like blues scanned the office with a quiet, calm confidence. From first impressions, Seth had never seen someone so completely and utterly off limits. His stomach tightened and he could barely breathe. Then she spoke.

"Seth Cyrus Freeman," she said, looking straight at him. *She's not asking*, he thought. *She knows who I am, yet I have never seen her before. I'd certainly remember if I had.*

"Yeah, that's me." Seth pulled off his hat and raked his hand back through oily, black hair. *Damn*, he thought, trembling.

"Come with me now; we have a job for you."

"We? Are there more knockouts behind you?" No reaction. "Sorry, we're closing up shop for the night. Come back tomorrow and we'll see if you can fit us in . . . I mean, if we can fit you in," Seth drawled. He turned to Miles for backup, but he was just gawping like an idiot.

"We will triple your usual rate."

"Done and done," Miles chirped in thinly veiled delight.

Seth groaned and yanked the robes over his head, throwing them at Miles, along with a look that shouted, thanks a lot.

Unconcerned that he was parading around topless in front of their guest, he flicked open the belt of his pants on his way out, casting a supercilious glance over his shoulder. She showed no embarrassment at his undressed state . . . no reaction whatsoever.

What was she? A robot?

After pulling on some clean pants, he returned from the back room. She was just standing there, a picture of patience.

"What role do you want me to play?" Seth asked from between clenched teeth.

"Traditional Roman Catholic would be most appropriate. Are you familiar with Latin?"

"Am I familiar with Latin?" he scoffed. "This is what I do. I can moonlight as a Catholic priest with my eyes closed."

She seemed amused. An unladylike snort escaped her. "Is that so?"

The way she said it made him pause—as if she could see every dirty little thing he had ever done.

Very unsettling.

"Where's the job?"

"Olympus Orbital Platform."

Damn, damn, and . . . damn! "All the way up there?" The bottom dropped out of him for a moment. He cleared his throat hoping to dislodge the fear that swelled inside. "Are they believers or not?"

The Amazon cocked her head at him. "Why is that relevant?"

"Because knowing will make my job a whole lot easier, sweet-cheeks."

"A lapsed Catholic."

"I guess not then. Miles, get me the juice."

Miles scampered away to the cooler. He came back a short time later with the case, packed and ready to go.

Seth nodded in resignation and ambled past Miss Universe 2095. She smelled sinfully good, the aroma slightly reminiscent of ritualistic incense, but without the harsh choking cloud. He breathed it in with an audible sigh. His nimble fingers buttoned up the shirt quickly, as she cast a glance at the retro clock hanging on the wall. He collected a pouch of sacred artefacts and slipped them into his pocket.

"We must leave," she said.

So, Ice Queen was suddenly in a hurry.

"Make like a tree and leave, I know. Aren't you an eager beaver?"

Beavers like wood. Stop it, Seth! he reprimanded himself.

Miles waggled his eyebrows as Seth departed. Seth shook his head. *Not this one, Miles. She's trouble with a capital T. But the money, surely that was gonna be worth a little hot trouble.*

***

Her sleek Tropo-shuttle took them to Babel Cuatro, just south of Quito. The space tower loomed out of the moonlight sprinkled landscape, a big, black, blasphemous needle shafting the dark sky. Its sprawling base straddled Mount Chimborazo, an active volcano.

Seth often wondered whose bright idea that was. The South American republic president seemed most likely. *Idiot. Yes, a volcano is a perfectly reasonable place to build the stairway to heaven.* Seth shuddered. *If that mother ever opened up, the tower could just as easily become the stairway to hell.*

Chimborazo was known to be the most distant point from the centre of earth, so that probably had something to do with its selection. Seth wasn't familiar with the science.

The shuttle pilot parked. Even the boarding platform seemed too high. Seth set his jaw grimly and stared out across the night-shrouded landscape.

"Contact in 30 minutes, final call for boarding," came the announcement.

She led the way; Seth let her lead. The soft groove of elevator music drifted around the foyer. The officials cleared the way as she handed over two return tickets. There was no red tape, no papers needed—her beautiful form cut through it all like a hot knife through butter.

There's no backing out now.

They built the space elevator capsule with 30 small passenger cars and a cargo hold. She led Seth inside one car, and showed him to a window seat.

Just dandy.

At least it was dark—he wouldn't see the Earth rushing away in too much detail. She sat opposite.

Now there's a view I can appreciate.

The seat tried to autocorrect his bunched posture. He sank back and looked for the seat belts, but found none. He began to sweat; searching for a distraction, he turned his attention back to the beauty. Her lips were full, perfect, and damn kissable, but there was this look about her—an impenetrable barrier that screamed—do not cross.

His gaze travelled down her form leisurely; he couldn't touch, but he could have a good look. The swell of her chest was proportionate to her lean physique and he wondered if she was an athletic type. There was something about the width of her shoulders and the drape of her arms that suggested power.

Hard to tell.

The conservative navy blue suit served to conceal everything in an appropriate air of professionalism.

"Have you been doing exorcisms for long?" she asked, her tone light and conversational.

"10 years," Seth replied, holding her piercing blue gaze.

"What's in the case?" she asked, with what seemed like genuine curiosity.

"Haven't you ever been to an exorcism before?"

He was surprised, when she stated flatly, "Not one like this."

What other kind is there?

"Just some necessary ingredients to make the process seem real to the possessed."

"Drugs?" she inquired, her nose wrinkled up, as if she smelled week old gym socks.

183

"Yeah, that's right," he grumbled. "This stuff takes the whole 'you gotta believe' motto, and blows it out of the confessional. It can make even the most cynical humanist fall to his knees and begin rambling like a prophet of old." He stopped talking, but the thought kept running—*even men like me.*

She gave him a sympathetic look, as though she knew what he was thinking.

Only one person knew me like that. Now she's gone.

When the madness took over the planet, this alien invasion, they discovered the only ones free of it were the religious types. They did their little exorcisms and then everything fell into place, right as rain.

Some, like him, might argue the connection was made too late.

Nevertheless, folks began taking notice of the coincidence, especially when there was money to be made. Suddenly, you didn't have to live with blackouts and the lack of impulse control. You would call your local Bible-basher and pay him for a quickie exorcism. The trouble was, the possessed had to believe. If they didn't, the Vaporal was going to stick around. A successful cleansing was only possible in those who already had the VMAT2 Gene, or people who had been artificially mind shafted with the doper. It was simple—give the person a sensationally mystical mind-blow and the Vaporal would be expelled.

"Harnesses will now be engaged," chimed an automated announcement.

The straps snapped across his lap and chest, so tight he could barely breathe, or maybe it was just the sudden feeling of terror that overwhelmed him.

The countdown commenced and his companion locked him with her gaze. Those amazing eyes grounded him for a moment and then the ascension began.

"It is a climb of 45,000 feet," she said.

"I know how tall it is." Seth grumbled. His face felt cold and damp, as the fear seeped from his pores.

"You needn't be afraid; I won't let anything happen to you." Her mouth quirked into a half smile.

"How are you going to stop this thing from malfunctioning?"

"Seth, have a little faith, this structure will not fail. The only thing likely to fail is the humans running it."

Seth tried to suppress the panic. He squeezed his eyes shut tightly as the chamber hurtled skyward, like a bat outta hell, with an angel up its ass.

When he opened them again, he saw her looking out toward the curving eastern horizon where dawn blazed. Something hissed as they slowed.

'We have reached the top," she murmured.

The irritating music was interrupted by another grating announcement. "Thirty seconds to magnetisation."

The dull music started up again, as their capsule rotated at the top of the world.

A deep throb pulsed under his feet, as the massive electro magnet did its work. "Reversing polarisation . . . 3 . . . 2 . . . 1" came the disembodied announcement. Then the world became a blur and his insides seemed to drop into his legs. Through the torn visuals and jerky vibrations, he saw her watching him with unnerving calm. It would be damn embarrassing if his late beer and burger supper came back up. He gritted his teeth.

Their ascent slowed and the capsule shuddered as the thrusters intermittently engaged. He dared to look out the window. The deep black of the pacific stretched out beyond the pinpricks of light edging the coast of South America. Tiny beacons of civilisation amidst the darkness. Seth drew in a long and sweet breath; he'd held it for some time.

"Beginning docking procedures."

Olympus swallowed their view as the reverse thrusters slowed their ascent to a crawl. Seth felt a jolt as they mated with the station. When he stood, the buoyant artificial gravity made up for his jelly legs. With shaking hands, he retrieved his case from the luggage compartment.

"Follow me," she said.

I don't even know her name.

"What do I call you?"

She quirked a finely sculptured brow and those red lips curled upward. "Call me Mikaella."

Seth rolled the name around his mind as they left the dock. The bright lights and loud music of the pedestrian arena were mildly interesting. Lush looking food joints filled with beautiful-looking people, who basked beneath ambient lighting. They passed dance halls, shops, food marts, and those dime-a-dozen souvenir stores.

She led Seth away from it all—down dark alleys into the residential zone, until they stood outside an unremarkable grey door. She touched the E-lock, her slim fingers stroking the buttons. The door slid open. Inside, dimness pervaded, and Seth shivered.

A woman came out of the shadows. "Thank God, you are here," she sniffed, dabbing at her tear-weary eyes.

"I have brought someone to help your son," Mikaella replied, all silk and kindness.

Seth flicked the switch in his mind and became the Father. "Show me to the afflicted. I will do what I can." He stole a look at Mikaella and noticed the flicker of amusement in her eyes. He straightened his shirt and followed the weeping mother into the adjoining room.

Nothing prepared him for what greeted him. The smell. It stained the air. Either this place had bad plumbing, or the kid was in a really bad way. The stench was almost enough to put a dampener on his Mikaella-focused libido. Almost.

A young man lay on a bed, tossing and turning, his dark hair so saturated with sweat that it clung to his head like a helmet.

Seth paused, the kid looked sick. *Vaporals don't do this!*

Mikaella must have noticed his doubt, because she quickly ushered the mother out of the room and shut the door. Seth felt her hand rest lightly on his shoulder. "You must get started."

What? She still wants me to go through with this? The money. Think about the money.

A lurking fear chastised him. *The money won't do me any good, if the kid dies.*

Despite all the voices inside telling him not to, Seth opened up his case of tricks. He took the needle and measured out 0.5mls. He grappled with the kid to administer the drug. It was impossible. The possessed thrashed his head from side to side. Seth couldn't have the needle snapping off in the kid's brain.

186

"Hold him for me, damn it!"

Mikaella obliged, gripping the boy's head on either side with firm hands. The struggling ceased immediately. Seth forced the boy's right eye open and pushed the long needle in deep through the tear duct.

Now, let the juice do its work.

***

He checked his watch and picked up his book and the Benedict medal inscribed with *vade retro Satana*. The kid began to growl. An animalistic sound, from some deep primal place.

He began the ritual.

"In nómine Pátris, et Fílii, et Spíritus Sancti. Amen."

Things went to hell in an exorcist's hand basket. The boy gnashed his teeth so violently that a bloody foam began to trickle from the corner of his mouth. The kid spoke, and Seth came to the conclusion that something was extremely wrong. It wasn't the fact that the thing was speaking— Vaporals can speak through humans—no it was what it was saying, that put the wind up Seth's panties.

"You're no priest! Fraud! You say the words, but you are nothing! Nothing!"

Time to turn up the volume.

Sáncte Míchael Archángele, defénde nos in proélio, cóntra nequítiam et insídias diáboli ésto præsídium . . ."

Mikaella looked at Seth, eyes alight.

Was she enjoying this?

"Your words are empty, Cur. Just like your soul . . . after losing her. You believe in nothing, and nothing believes in you!"

Enraged, Seth grabbed the holy water and splashed the writhing youth.

What was this? Some kind of sick joke.

The harrowing screams that followed made Seth shrink away, the ritual temporarily forgotten.

Suddenly, Mikaella's hand clutched his, her fierce gaze pulled him back, and those perfect lips said the words he needed to hear, "I believe in you."

At least one of us does.

***

187

Leaving Earth

An hour later, the kid was sleeping peacefully. No Vaporal got expelled, yet despite that, Mikaella assured him, "It is finished."

Seth followed her outside, noticing how the foul smell had fled with whatever had been in that boy. He couldn't begin to explain what had just happened.

Mikaella turned to him in the quiet hallway. "You did well."

Seth ground his teeth, "What the hell was that? That's no Vaporal infestation and you know it!"

"No, it wasn't. We have work for you, Seth. More cases like that one." She reached into her pocket and gave him the gold credit chip. "And all of them as equally well paid."

"Why me? I'm not even a believer—you heard that *thing* in there."

She leaned forward; her hot breath tickled his ear. "You will be," she murmured in a husky tone. Those eyes flashed with promise. A tingling sensation crept down his body, and there was no avoiding its destination.

He shouldn't care enough to ask, but he did. "Who are you, really?"

"Certainly, Seth, I suppose it's time for formal introductions. I am known as the Archangel Michael . . . but you may continue to call me Mikaella."

Ami Hart is a writer, artist, and mother of two from Christchurch, New Zealand. She lives in two worlds: one being post-quake Christchurch and the other is a fantastical place where dragons and space ships soar, sometimes side-by-side.
Ami is a member of SpecficNZ and the Christchurch Writers Guild. She has had several short stories published in various anthologies and is currently writing a fantasy novel. She blogs about her writing adventures here, http://www.amilibertyhartwriter.com/
Publishing credits:
Reflections: An anthology by the Christchurch Writers' Guild, ("Ned's Hallelujah")
The Future Is Short: Science Fiction in a Flash ("Snap and Crackle", "Unwanted Gift")

18. After-Life

Randall Lemon

Merv had to get off-planet fast. The authorities were closing in. At the rate Merv was going, he would soon run out of places where he wasn't hunted.

Merv had been born on Moon colony. Of course, his name hadn't been Merv back then. In those carefree days, he had been Little Tommy Tucker, the apple of his Mother's eye and all-around choirboy. For thirteen years, Tommy had been quite the goody-goody. His Mom had made liberal use of a strap to his back to keep him that way. A lot of guys who turn bad claim it was because they fell in with bad companions. What a load! Merv knew that he *was* the bad companion. One day, little Tommy just turned a corner in his life and Black Tom was born.

Sure, his Mother's death probably had something to do with it. The fact that his father was a louse, who left Tom's mother before Tom was even born, was another reason. But all that was just window dressing. Merv knew he could have ended up a decent member of Earth-Space society—he just didn't want to.

Why work when stealing was so much easier? Why stay sober when getting high was so much more exhilarating? Why be the one who gets hurt when hurting others provided such a kick? So Black Tom became the scourge of the Moon. He stole, he killed, he raped, and he was damn

189

good at it. For seven years, the Moon was his plaything. But there are always those who are jealous of success, even within criminal society, and so, someone turned stool pigeon on Tom.

In desperation, at age twenty, Tom beat a woman to death and took her ticket on the Space elevator from the Moon to Zenith Center station. He had staked out the ticket offices waiting for a vulnerable victim, someone he could handle easily. Even at age twenty, he was not a very big man. He stood right around 5' 7" and had a slender, compact frame. He worked out and had a fair amount of upper body strength. She was a big-boned woman, probably about five-and-a-half feet tall, somewhere in her late twenties or early thirties he'd guess. She'd do nicely. When she left the ticket office, she had a pleased look on her face.

"She should be pleased," Tom thought, "getting a ticket on the elevator isn't an easy thing. She must have some kind of connections."

Tom followed her back to her home, careful to stay far enough back not to be noticed. But he needn't have worried; she was way too preoccupied with her trip to ever see him. At times, even as far back as he was, he could hear her whistling a merry little tune. It made Tom smile. Tom gave her about ten minutes after she arrived at her domicile then moved to her door and listened. He could hear music playing, but that was it. Tom carefully jimmied the lock and nudged the door open a crack. Seeing nothing, he opened the door wider and slipped inside. Moving quietly, he could hear water running.

"Good girl, taking a nice shower! Well, they say 'cleanliness is next to godliness,' and you'll soon be next to whatever god you worship."

She came out of the shower, her flesh glowing golden-pink in the soft light of the bedroom lamp. She smelled of strawberry body wash. She stepped through the bathroom door into her bedroom. She was whistling that same little tune. She never got to finish the song; she never even had time for her flesh to cool from the hot shower. Tom sprang from behind her door, wrapping one arm around her throat and clamping his other hand over her mouth and nose. She struggled more than Tom would have guessed. She wriggled back and forth, trying uselessly to pry his hand off her face. Honestly, Tom rather enjoyed the struggle. She smelled good and felt great. If he had more time he might have let her live a little longer, but business was business and finally her struggles ceased and her eyes rolled up in her head. Tom held her a couple minutes longer and then released her. She dropped, lifeless, to the floor.

At the ticket office, she had been carrying one of those thin, black-leather briefcase things so many "career" women fancied, and she still had it when she entered her home. Tom gazed down one last time at her.

"Thanks for your generosity, sweetheart."

Then he stepped over her body and started searching for that bag and anything else that might be of use. He found the bag sitting on a chest she must have used as a coffee table inside her small living room. He opened the bag and dumped the contents onto the table. Her ID showed her name was Sarah Jeris.

Tom chuckled softly to himself. "Alas, poor Sarah, I knew her well! Not!" Sometimes Tom just cracked himself up.

Moving things around on the table, he found her ticket, her credit chit, and some pictures, including one of a dapper young man with dark hair. Tom wondered if it was this young man that made her whistle so merrily.

"Well, I got some bad news for you, sport! You'd better start looking for a new girl with a little more life in her. I don't think you'll be seeing Sarah any time soon."

He looked through her closets, finding some clothing that was a size or two larger than what she was wearing.

"Lost a little weight for your boyfriend, huh?"

He dressed in her clothing and shaved close. The clothes were a little snug but not impossible and he found a nice looking blazer with plenty of room. He took her anti-radiation injection, clipped her ID to her stylish blazer, wrapped one of Sarah's scarves tightly around his head to hide his lack of curls, and slipped onto the elevator without a hitch.

What was really hysterical was that while taking the ride up to Zenith, some jerk developed quite an odd

191

problem and couldn't keep his hands to himself. His name was Mervyn McTeague and he put the moves on the lady in the stylish blazer. Tom (now known as Sarah Jeris) played along. When they arrived, instead of going to the quarters reserved for Sarah, Tom accompanied Merv to his temporary quarters.

Tom figured that once they found Sarah's body back on the Moon, the Computer Research Police would follow the trail to Zenith and Sarah's reserved quarters. So, when they got to Merv's quarters, Sarah asked Merv to lower the lights and went to the restroom to "get a little more comfortable."

When Tom was ready, Sarah called out to Merv to close his eyes, because she had something special for him. Sarah turned off the bathroom light and opened the door, entering the darkened bedroom. Tom took a moment to adjust his eyes and could see Mervyn already in bed. He/she had promised Merv something special and that would be no lie.

Tom walked calmly over to the bed, silent on bare feet. He picked up a pillow to use as a silencer and neatly subdivided Mervyn's cranium with his .38 special revolver

Now he had a new identity and a new wardrobe. It was a good thing that Mervyn was only slightly bigger than Tom. As Tom looked through Merv's papers, he got a bit of a surprise. He had assumed that Merv would be taking the elevator down to Earth; instead, the ticket revealed Mervyn was taking the third tether down to Mars.

Tom had never paid much attention, when he attended the Moon Academy, but he knew enough about Zenith Central Station to know that it stood like a camera atop a giant tripod. One shaft led to Earth, one to Mars and one to the Moon. He had no idea what life was like on Mars, or even Earth, other than old stories he had heard. Earth was always depicted as a Paradise. Some of the more religious types had claimed man had sinned (whatever that meant) and been expelled from Earth by angels carrying fiery swords. Those same crazies claimed that the Moon was Purgatory and Mars was Hell, and, as for Zenith Central Station, it was a kind of Limbo in which the souls awaited final disposition. How ridiculous!

"Well, any port in a storm." Mars would be farther away from the military/police authorities of the Moon than Earth.

If there was an elevator shaft leading down to Mars, there must be people on Mars, and that meant fresh victims for Black Tom.

For just a moment, Merv turned philosophical, "I guess there is no Little Tommy Tucker, no Black Tom, not even a Sarah Jeris. From now on, there is only Crime Lord Merv of Mars!"

The newly christened, Merv of Mars slept well that night. When he awoke, he dressed himself in the old Merv's nicest outfit. "I want to make the right impression when I land on my new home." Merv left the quarters early to arrive at the Elevator transit tube. He stopped on the way and got rid of the last remnant of Sarah Jeris in one of the convenient "Dispose-alls." Since he had time, he stopped at a little shop to enjoy a coffee and cinnamon roll, just as he suspected the real Merv might have done. He perused the shop's vid-screen while he sipped his coffee and heard news of a brutal slaying on the Moon. The counterman was also watching the newscast.

"Boy! It's just terrible, some of the awful things that still happen. You'd think with all the modern wonders we have, the bad old days of murder and mayhem would be far behind us."

Merv looked through his new eyeglasses at the counterman for just a moment and then responded, "Well, I guess human nature just doesn't change. But we can all hope for a better tomorrow." With that, he picked up his things and exited the shop, heading for the pod and a new life on Mars.

As he stepped outside the shop, Merv reached into his inside breast pocket intending to double-check his ticket, but before he could pull it out, he was startled by a loud report. At first he feared that perhaps some overzealous minion of the law had found him out and attempted to kill him, but looking all around he noticed nothing at all unusual and continued on his way.

When Merv arrived at the elevator, he was mildly surprised to find that he was the only one waiting to board the pod to head down planetside. He mentioned it to the lovely young woman who was working at the boarding counter. She had a familiar look that Merv couldn't quite place.

He looked at the nametag she wore on her uniform. Pasting a huge smile on his face, he said, "Angel, am I late or early for the passage down to Mars? I seem to be alone, except for you."

She efficiently ran his ticket and ID through her computer scanner, punched a couple of keys, and smiled as she handed them back to him.

"Well, sir, society is becoming pretty civilized. There seems to be less need and desire for folks to head down to a wild place like Mars."

"I didn't realize Mars was that much of a backwater. Guess I should have paid more attention in school, huh?" and he forced himself to chuckle.

Angel's smile broadened, "Oh, don't worry sir. I've checked your credentials thoroughly and I'm sure you'll fit right in with the other denizens. And look, you are right on time to board!"

Sure enough, at that very moment, the doors leading to the pod opened.

Merv picked up his things and headed through the automatic doors. As he stepped inside, he turned for one last look at Angel. She was giving him her biggest smile yet. Her teeth had a dazzling glow. The glow practically blinded him and it was then he realized why she looked so familiar.

"That's odd; she looks a lot like that Sarah girl."

She raised her hand, waving goodbye and said, "Have a nice trip, Tom!"

The doors shut in Merv's face. It took him almost ten seconds to react, "Wait, did she call me Tom?"

All the while, the pod was making its rapid descent through the shaft, headed down to Mars.

"I must have assumed one identity too many. She couldn't have called me Tom. She must have said Merv and I just thought I heard Tom." Still he took out his ID and checked and sure enough, it identified him as Mervyn McTeague. "Crazy! I must be hearing things." Since he also had his ticket in hand, he glanced at it. "Wow, that's bizarre! A one-way ticket to Mars, I was sure it said round trip when I first saw it, after I killed that guy. I may need to get my hearing and eyes checked.

The trip finally ended and the automatic doors whispered open. Now, Merv was really surprised. He had assumed he would exit into a transmission center building like the one on the Moon or the one on Zenith Central Station. Instead, a vast red plain stretched out before him. Miles of nothingness. He stepped out of the pod, meaning to circumnavigate the tube to see if the people and buildings might be on the backside. As he started moving away, he heard the whisper of the doors and felt the slight vibration of the pod starting its return course.

"Damn! I left all my stuff on the pod and now it's headed back to Zenith. Now I have to find that office and arrange to have Merv's stuff brought back down on the next pod."

Merv continued to move around the enormous tube looking for signs of civilization. A gust of hot wind blew red soil into Merv's eyes, temporarily blinding him. Something large, but soft, bounced into his legs and when his eyes had cleared, Merv saw he had become tangled in a large tumbleweed. He tried to extricate himself from the dead vegetable matter, which stubbornly refused to let go of his legs.

Merv began to feel a little frustrated. He turned all around scanning the Martian horizon. Dead plants, dead trees, and blowing red dirt, as far as the eye could see in all directions.

"Wait! That's not possible!" Merv spun around once and then once again. Each time, the annoying rolling plant made the rotation with him. Panic began to rise in Merv's throat like bile. The elevator tube was gone. No sign of it. Not even an impression in the Martian soil of where it had once been.

Merv shook his head to clear it. He had already doubted his own senses of sight and hearing, now he began to doubt everything else.

It must just be the heat, the thin atmosphere . . ., or something. It was so incredibly hot and red. Red everywhere he looked. Were those red mountains in the distance or flames much closer?" He heard a crackling in his head, as if of flames and then he started to hear something else—screams. They must be in his head as well. Were they the screams of his former victims? He heard Merv scream as the bullet entered his brain, he heard Sarah's muffled screams against his hand, he even heard little Tommy scream as the belt fell and rose on his back. Now, he realized the screams were coming from all around him. They were the screams of the Damned. Tom had hoped to reach new heights of his criminal career; instead, he'd reached new depths, depths only the Damned get to see. Black Tom had arrived at his final destination and he howled as the hellish flames seared his flesh, burning him down and down until he was the size of a tumbleweed. The wind caught him and he began his eternal journey around his new home.

Enforcement and Security Officer Rollins stood up from searching the body in the hallway outside the Zenith Central Station snack shop. He turned to the other officer standing further down the hall with his gun still in his hand. Young Officer Marcus Haines had a look of shock on his face

"Well, Marcus, he was carrying a gun, but that's not what he was reaching into his jacket to get. Apparently, he was reaching for his ticket. But, if I were you, I wouldn't worry about it. This was a dangerous man guilty of a number of crimes and two murders in the last couple of days and he was armed. I believe you had reasonable cause to shoot him when you thought he was reaching for his weapon. Anyway, it's not likely that anyone will miss scum like him. You probably did everyone a favor by blowing him straight to Hell."

Randall Lemon took a sabbatical from writing and that period of rest lasted almost three decades. At one time Randall was a regular fixture of the roleplaying community. He was one of the top ranked players from the inception to the end of the RPGA ranking system. He also served as a high-ranking tournament judge, marshal, and coordinator of various events at Gen Con and other gaming conventions. During that time, he was a frequent contributor to Polyhedron magazine, perhaps best remembered for the creation of one of the most beloved establishments in the Living City, "Embrol Sludge's Eatery, and Seashell Shoppe." Along with a co-author, he created the adventure known as "Eye of the Leviathan." Randall also wrote articles for **Video Review Magazine** and the **Quarterly Journal of Speech.**

Hailing from northwest Indiana just across the line from Chicago, Randall graduated from Purdue University with a Bachelor's degree. While at Purdue, he was a winner of the prestigious Purdue Literary Awards contest. He received his Master's degree from the University of Southern California and did some work toward the PhD at the University of Illinois. He taught high school for thirty-four years, has two children and a wife, all of whom he loves dearly.

Now Randall has returned to writing. This time he is concentrating on flash fiction and short stories. Recent publications by Randall include the round-robin novel, **"Gryffon Master: Curse of the Lich King"** and the story, **"A Mouser, a Keg of Rum and a Gunnery Mate"** in the anthology, **"World of Pirates."** Randall will have some of his short fiction showcased in anthologies scheduled to come out in 2014 and 2015 and is currently working on a solo attempt at a fantasy novel.

19. Ascent

Andy McKell

Jim allowed his naked body to soar easily, gliding on insubstantial wings ever higher into the darkening sky. He rose above a vast, rusty desert crisscrossed by dirt roads that microscoped down to slender threads, then melted away as they vanished into the dusty distances of a dream abandoned. Great, dark birds, with wings vast enough to wrap around a house like a black snowfall, circled in the near distance, matching his ascent, chasing him, riding the thermals as effortlessly as Jim rode the starlight. Whether their darkling eyes watched him out of curiosity or hunger, he neither knew nor cared. They would abandon the game, the pursuit, the chase, when their wings ran out of air to curve around, while his star-driven ascent continued.

To the north and east, the ragged mountain barriers became pitiful rockeries. But it was to the far ocean his mind turned, smoothly changing his direction to the west, to the sunset, to the great Star Tower.

Skimming high-hung slivers of clouds for the joy of it, bodysurfing on the ice crystals, slipping between basking sunlight and chilling mist, he released a yell of ecstasy.

He had ignored the strip of greenery and the dismal, gray patches of the urban sprawl below, racing instead for the blue ahead.

He crossed the meandering line of sand and cliff separating the land from the sea; the pale blue of the shallows gave way to the profounder blue of the deeps. Endless Ocean opened up before him. He swooped lower to play ship-spotting; fishing boats and pleasure yachts gave way to liners and tankers; he pushed himself to greater speed—he still had far to go.

He roared through the sky until he arrived suddenly at his destination—the Star Tower!

Like a single piano wire stretched taut between ocean and sky, planet and stars, the cable was barely visible from a few feet away.

It twinkled with aircraft warning lights for the first hundred miles of its length—as though any scramjet pilot, human or automatic, could not know what this was or where it was.

The huddle of ships and air shuttles around the base station carried no interest for him. He knew all about the great laser generators beaming energy skywards to power the elevators—the climbers—that clung to the cable and slid silently between the below and the above.

It was the Tower, the Star Tower, the almost-invisible tower that reached beyond the skies and drew him, moth-like, to its radiance.

He circled the tenuous thread, rising higher, gaining speed, chasing the climber. Through the viewing panels, he saw people moving in the vehicle. He drew level and matched their achingly slow ascent. Someone spotted him, called to the others, pointed. The crowd gathered to watch through the most expensive windows in the world, engineered to handle the extremes of this unique voyage. He saw people smiling, waving to him. He barrel-rolled, spun, cartwheeled and somersaulted, dove and soared, to entertain them, glorying in the applause he saw, and the joy he had brought to their faces.

"*Jimmy!*"

His vision faltered and shattered. His body lost its weightlessness; it sagged, it dragged him down, pressed him prone onto a slightly yielding surface.

"Jimmy Suraci!"

He opened his eyes. Visions of stars and spaceflight and the Tower floated before him. The fuzziness of sleep slowly cleared; he recognized the array of cheap, garish posters on his bedroom walls. His mother's voice rang out again from the kitchen.

He was at home. He was awake. This was reality. It was over.

He had read that astral projection was dangerous. He preferred to think of it as lucid dreaming, taking a dream where the dreamer wants it to go, which was much safer.

A large woman bustled into his bedroom, her voice an unending stream of sound. "Time to get up, my boy, and just you wait and see what the mailman brought you, although I guess it should've been a surprise, I just know you'll get a kick outta it, 'cos you did that contest thing and there's an envelope for you from them and I opened it for you in case it wasn't good news and I didn't want you to be disappointed—"

"Mom! Stop. Take a breath."

"Surely, I will, honey. I'm sorry. But here it is. Do you want to look-see in bed or shall I get you up?"

"Mom, I can open an envelope without getting up." He hated the morning ritual. He was a teenager; he didn't want his mother clucking and fussing around him all the time, as if he was some kind of . . .

"Well, you open it. I want to watch you." She plumped herself down onto his bed, avoiding his outstretched legs.

Jim turned the envelope over in his hands. Recorded delivery? Maybe he had won a runner-up prize? Surely, there would be more fuss for a first prize? Cautiously, as though it might contain a spring-trap, he parted the ragged edges of the hastily opened envelope and peered inside. A letter? But the envelope was too stiff for just a sheet of paper, even quality paper such as this. He drew out the letter spilling a fancy, gold-edged, embossed piece of cardboard onto the covers.

"Oh, Jimmy Suraci!" His mother squealed.

"Is it, Mom? I don't want to look."

She seized the card and beaming brighter than the sun, holding it carefully with both hands at the upper corners to not damage or fingermark it, turned its face to his. The Star

Tower logo glistened and sparkled. The image of the Tower itself, special effects causing it to glow and twinkle like the real thing—or at least the way it appeared in his dreams and on TV.

First prize.

First prize for a ride to the very top of the Tower.

First prize . . . he ran the words around his head, rolled them over his tongue, heard the sound of the words, tasted the sweetness . . . First Prize!

He was going to the top, five days up and five days down. He was going where the stars spangled the sky, undimmed even by the windblown desert dust and the few streetlights. He was going where he could reach out and touch Orion's belt, shake hands with the twins of Gemini, gaze upon the red, white and blue stars of the flag draped across the universe.

He felt a lesser glow of satisfaction that his science project was the best in the land.

Mother and son grabbed each other in a huge celebratory hug, basking in the glow of elation and wonder.

"Oh, Jimmy!" She freed herself and ruffled his hair—a gesture he hated; but he forgave her, just this once. "I'll go make a special breakfast while you get into your chair. We'll wash you later."

The moment shattered like his dream, as his eyes turned to the wheelchair next to his bed.

"Oh, don't you worry about the chair, up there, I'm sure they have facilities, you know, ramps and floor clamps to hold the wheels steady and suchlike. Will there be, you know, turbulence, like in planes? You know, now that I come to think about it, . . ." Her voice continued as the sound faded away into the distance, becoming a meaningless mumble.

Sure, they would have ramps and clamps. Sure, they would have to have them. It was the law. But which laws applied up there, in the heavens? Star laws? Hey, that sounded good.

Having diverted his thoughts onto a more cheerful track, he began the slow process of transferring his body from bed to wheelchair by grasping his knees, one at a time, pulling them in an arc over the side of the bed.

As he wheeled out through his bedroom door, he affectionately patted the poster image of his greatest hero, the one who inspired him most. Not Gagarin, not Glenn, not Armstrong, but Stephen Hawking.

***

The ride to the dock wasn't part of the prize; there was no limo. People from the local news-site tried to take a few words and some footage as they set off, but they wanted to make a big feature of his chair. Jim didn't sparkle and his mother babbled incessantly.

She kept up her constant stream-of-consciousness chatter as she drove their battered truck towards the coast. Jim ignored the background noise, his nervous attention focused on his chair as it bounced and rattled on the flatbed at the back, despite the clamps and straps. There might be facilities for him on the climber, but he needed that chair, his only mobility—and he hated that chair, confining him to ramps and "facilities".

The road took them through occasional clusters of buildings; a few homes, a gas station, and a speed sign. People had landed up here or had been born here and were trapped here, stuck in place, unable to fly free.

They hit the smooth tarmac of the main highway, where he could relax a little. His attention wandered to the endless sands around him. He considered the isolated rocks, also stuck in place, but crumbling down through the ages to mingle anonymously with the sands they rested on. Someday, the winds might carry the grains away to distant places . . .

Scrubby plants struggled to lift their heads closer to the sun, to the stars, to eternity . . .

And there were the freedom bushes. As a child, he had called them freedom bushes. From his porch, he had watched them drift freely from one horizon to the other; tumbleweeds, free to wander as the winds took them, forever in transit, forever moving on to somewhere better.

"What did you say, Jimmy?"

"Nothing, Mom."

"Sounded like 'freedom'. Are you okay, we'll take a break soon, find a restroom, I'll watch out for one . . . "

202

Jim knew she loved him. But she couldn't really cope with it all, even after all these years, since the doctors had told her. She had nursed him for his entire life. And she was lost. He threw her a smile and some encouraging words. He'd give her an extra big hug before the ascent.

**

At the dock, the sky was overcast; the ocean did not sparkle; it looked heavy, and gray, and cold.

After processing, they had joined the other passengers in a reception lounge decorated in a calming, pastel décor, its walls hung with striking images of the Tower, its climbers and the GEO station at the summit. The AstroMining Corps logo clung to every surface. Corporate brochures were the only reading material; the wall-screens ran continual promotional animations.

There were twenty passengers gathered in groups. The GEO station workers sat in huddles, pooling their consoles, or sat alone, tapping away at their wrists. The rest were paying passengers. Jim was the only one who had someone to see him off. It was embarrassing.

Three hosts in blue blazers offered refreshments and bland smiles. Their leader, "Call me Mike", stepped forward to make a brief welcoming speech and run through the legally required safety announcements. He paused, referring to his wrist-panel notes

"And, a special guest today. We'd like you all to welcome aboard this year's prize-winning geek, winner of a free ride into space and back, courtesy of our sponsors, AstroMining Corp, here's little Jimmy Suraci!" He strode forward and ruffled Jim's hair. "Quite a little brainiac we have with us today."

Jim seethed. He burned with embarrassment. He gritted his teeth, lowering his head to hide his face, as his mother blathered out how grateful she was and how proud she was of her little Jimmy.

A few of the tourists "oohed" and "cooed", but most felt the heat of his hostility and kept their distance.

Then the doors opened, revealing the walkway to the shuttle plane for the ride to the base station.

"Thank God," he thought, "a ramp."

There was just time for that big hug for Mom, perhaps less warm than he had intended, then a pretty blonde hostess stepped forward and gripped the back of his chair.

"Now don't you worry, Mrs. Serachi, we'll look after your little Jimmy."

Jim winced; he would have to live with that mispronunciation for ten whole days.

He waved the hostess away. Her corporate composure broke for a moment, as she stepped back in surprise. He ignored her and steered himself through the doorway, leaving her to cope.

He forgot to wave to his mother. Somehow, it had seemed important that he should say goodbye properly, but things never work out as planned—and then it is too late.

***

They were fifteen hours into the ascent and the ocean view had already palled. The shuttle had sped to the offshore installation, located just inside international waters, but, he had traveled faster in his dreams and with better views than endless ocean on every side.

Mike had started his patter, reeling off a stream of impressive, forgettable statistics and simplistic information about the station and the Tower, most of which was almost correct.

"Of course, it's only called a Tower because it's tall. It's not really a tower. It's a sixty-thousand mile band of carbon nanotubes less than an inch thick."

Almost correct.

Jim had been escorted onto the climber first. They had insisted. He was shown his cabin, "the one with facilities", Mike called it. They were shown how to use microgravity washrooms and how to suck refreshments through a straw. They were shown the windows, as Mike called them; armored view-panels, as Jim knew them to be.

The workers—experienced travelers—had retired to their cabins, to work, to rest, or simply to escape the entertainment.

Mike and the hostesses ran through a routine they had all, clearly, become weary of . . . long ago.

"Now, there's no worries about the windows—people are often concerned about the safety of the windows . . . perfectly safe, I can assure you." Mike rapped his knuckles on the glass, as if to simulate the high-velocity impact of a heavy spanner, or other discarded space junk. "I ride this climber a dozen times a year and I'm still coming back for more!" He laughed at his own wit.

A few, weary passengers smiled politely at his hearty, rehearsed patter.

Jim, however, scowled his displeasure. Why draw attention to it, if people are worried about it? Passengers should have done their research; the windows were aluminum silicate glass panels strengthened with transparent nanotube mesh. Pressure changes and micrometeorites wouldn't affect them a jot, but a bigger piece of space debris could rip the whole vehicle apart.

He stared upwards. Night was rolling across the earth; the stars above were becoming visible. Mike, again, spoiled it for him.

"We advise everyone to take a good look outside right now, as we shall be shuttering the windows shortly, and we can all head off for a good night's rest."

"Actually, it's because we're passing through the inner Van Allen Belt," Jim murmured. "and the radiation belts are why they won't let you make more than one trip a month."

Mike ignored him. "And, out there is Icarus!" He pointed. Faces turned, eager for any distraction. Mike turned to face them and slipped into another anecdote. He had a vast stock. The journey was mind-numbingly tedious, once the novelty had worn off. He launched into the legend of Icarus, the boy who flew too close to the sun, wearing wings of wax and feathers, until the wax melted and he plunged to earth.

Jim closed his eyes and called up the images he had seen so many times in his dream-state. He felt the thin wind rushing past, ruffling his hair in the manner he did enjoy. He felt starlight caressing his flesh, felt the distances below and above. Wrapped up in his fantasy, he heard Mike's distant voice trail off. Passengers were asking questions—curious, urgent, frightened.

"What is that, out there?"

"It looks like a person, a boy . . . flying."

"A trick."

"That Icarus thing."

"Is this a stunt?"

Jim opened his eyes.

He saw Mike, agitated, struggling to keep control; there is nowhere to run to on a climber.

He saw what the problem was. Beyond the view-panel was the ghostly image of a naked, human male spinning cartwheels and somersaults.

"No . . . it's, er . . ." Mike's face contorted, as his mind scrambled to find something reassuring to say. "It's a trick of the light, a reflection on the curved surface of the glass . . . maybe a cloud formation . . . strange visuals in space. John Glenn saw fireflies . . ." He was gabbling, gesturing wildly to a hostess to bring the radiation shutters down. But she, too, was entranced by the microgravity gymnastics.

"Mister, that ain't no firefly!"

"My God! It's the science prize boy."

They turned to look from one to the other and, apart from the clothes, they were identical. Mike was defeated, mumbling incoherently, lost for patter.

The gymnast smiled at Jim, beckoned, nodded reassuringly.

Jim's vision blurred. His eyes saw the boy outside, saw himself in the chair, felt a great pull inside; for a moment, there was only blackness in his mind.

Then, he gazed out into the field of stars that surrounded him.

He was outside the climber. He was alone. He was the boy outside.

Something was still pulling at him. Something inside, pulling him upwards.

He realized that he had never tried to launch a dream from such a high place. That had been his problem all along. He had started too low down. He needed to start nearer the sun, to fly even higher.

He gazed into the climber cabin; saw his empty wheelchair and the stunned faces.

Grinning like some manic Peter Pan, he turned his face upwards to choose a star—any star, second on the left will do—and the image of the boy blurred, converting into something beyond pure energy.

Jim Suraci fell up from the earth, and vanished.

Andy McKell is a Yorkshireman living in Luxembourg who was introduced to Sci-Fi as a teenager and whose love for the genre has never dimmed. After raising three artistically gifted daughters and steering a career path through airlines, franchising and computing, he sold his internet company in 2011 to retire early and pursue his interests in writing, acting, and travel.

His short stories have appeared in several anthologies: **No Revolution Is Too Big, Dangerous Days #4, The Future Is Short, Consortium** - *others have been accepted for publication in the coming months. Between writing short stories and occasional acting appearances, Andy is working on a series of far-future novels.*

"Ascent" is a metaphor for the yearnings of humanity for the freedom of the stars - something which grows daily more important to achieve.

20. ELEVATION

Alan D Hickerson

Hix stood with his client at the entrance to the space elevator. He checked the tickets again. Round trip to the upper ring, nearly 300 kilometers. The leprechaun beside him spoke.

"Well, Hix, you had better check with security."

Right! Liam was carrying nearly 4 million hours credits in his golden bag. The casino wouldn't grant the comp if Liam didn't deposit the currency. Hix signaled the security drone. The drone approached and interlocked security protocols with Hix's implant. The passenger list began to scroll on his retina.

Space Elevator Quattro, San Antonio de Pichincha, Quito Province, Ecuador, 5:00 am departure:

Passengers

Liam O'Leary: Leprechaun; Morgan Finance;
Pleasure; to Level 3, MGM Grand Casino;
Nonthreatening (no arms)

Dwalin Wolfe: Dwarf; Virgin Space; Work; to
Level 3, Virgin Space Booster Maintenance;
Caution (assorted tools)

Ralph Chewy: Sasquatch; Redwood Farms;
Business; to Level 2, ADM Agronomy space
division; Caution (personal taser)

Heidi Berg: Human, Norwegian; Pleasure Share Industries; Work; to Level 1, Pleasure Share Industries; Alert (licensed Carrier, several small arms)

Woodrow Hix: Human, British; Hix Investigations; Work; to Level 3, MGM Grand Casino; Alert (plasma sword)

Brock Bradshaw: DNA indeterminate; International Football League; Pleasure; to Level 1, Pleasure Share Industries; Nonthreatening (no arms)

The hair stood on the back of Hix's neck. Something was wrong. He couldn't pinpoint it, but something was off.

Their luggage was whisked away on a freight elevator, while the six passengers filed into the suit room, where they were coated with the underlayment spray. The polymer based shock absorbent material was their lifeline in the event of a systemic failure. A person could step off the elevator at 100 kilometers and fall to earth without harm. During the first few years of use, there was a substantial bounce when a body struck the ground, but those problems had been corrected. Since then, dozens of people had self-aborted, just for the thrill. Next, their implants were fitted robotically with the nanoskin generators. These half-day-lived nano-bytes protected them from the large range of radiation waves they would encounter on their five-hour trip. Their skins glowed silver as the nanoskins grew, feeding off the polymer. The nanos manufactured oxygen to breath, and each person's implants monitored every aspect of their ascent, and then displayed the information on their retinas.

Next, a hard line was attached from their waists to the elevator door, in case they wished to view the ascent. The Elevator was shaped like a giant mushroom surrounding the pillar. There were two people waiting for them in the lounge. The astronaut—all flights to orbit were under the direction of the Astronaut's Union—seemed older but still fit. The steward was a beautiful, very fit, brunette. Hix marveled at her choice of pink carnation for her delta decoration. His had been a simple armored leaf codpiece, whereas the blond had chosen black sequins and tassels. The footballer, of course, had been decoration-less, but the Sasquatch had merely smiled.

They would ascend 100 kilometers in an hour and arrive at the Level 1, Equatorial Ring, a massive geosynchronous orbiting ring of cities, where Earth was "Up". Then, they would wait an hour, for the preparations that were needed before the one hour lift to Level 2—the Polar Ring—with Earth still "Up". The largest space factories were there, sun-side solar factories creating enormous power. Two hours would pass again before they reached the Level 3, Lunar Cycle Ring. Level 3 was the outbound space ring, with its biggest spaceport facing the Moon. At this time of year, San Antonio de Pichincha was the only site on Earth where the trip was this short.

"I want to watch," stated Liam.

"Yes, sir," Hix answered. He took the leprechaun's tether and clipped it to the top of the balcony door's mantle, then opened the door for his wealthy customer. They stepped through the forced air cushion and felt the rush of decompression; Liam slid forward about a meter, and then took a knee to get his balance, before they stepped to the chain link railing. Overhead, the clear dome shunted aside the direct winds from the ascent. They could see New Spain above them, and out over the Pacific the approaching Polar Ring glowing in the morning sun. They were about 20 miles high and could look to the right and see the Atlantic coastline curving away to the east. Hix marveled at the sight. He'd only seen the Elevator in films. The physical effect was quite different. You could feel the acceleration. The Maglev lifters pulled the elevator upward silently, except for the decompression wind. They were still below the radiation levels.

Liam said, "It never fails to amaze me; but I suffer from a fear of heights. Let's go back in."

They went back through the doorway and uncoupled their tethers.

"So, why MGM then?" asked Hix. "There are plenty of casinos earthbound."

Liam smirked at him and answered, "Ach! Have you not heard of rainbows, laddie?" His attention was drawn away by the nearness of a Pink Carnation. He took the proffered drink pouch and plugged it into his implant. "Thank you, colleen. I appreciate you enormously." He fished a ten-hour credit out of his suit. Not easily, but intentionally, then flipped it up to her serving tray. She looked at the small silver coin and a grin formed under her nanoskin.

"Thank you, sir," she giggled. "Let me know if there is anything you need." She walked towards the blond.

"If you ever learn anything from me, Hix, learn this. Do not step on the little people to get where you're going." Liam explained.

"I see. Double meaning understood." Hix turned at the sound of a disruptive argument. Across the room, the footballer was talking to the blond. They seemed to be haggling over prices.

He had learned that she was not to be his share-mate and was haggling for a temporary co-mingling. She was refusing his payment bids. Just as a point was reached that Hix thought was extraordinary, his senses jumped into overdrive. The nanoskins had detected gamma radiation and had reinforced everyone's suits. Hix checked on Liam, who was stroking the steward's flower petals. She didn't seem to be threatening, so he checked the other passengers. Except for the couple arguing, everyone else was watching the Polar Ring get closer; it would soon be hidden by New Spain. Where was the Astronaut? Hix looked around the Elevator and finally found him, waist deep in a maintenance hatch. Hix approached cautiously. He put his hand on his sword, the butt reassuring in his hand. But it was inside his suit. That might be a problem.

The Astronaut sensed him and looked up. He frowned, "We've picked up some kind of vibration in the pillar. Don't know why. I've got diagnostics going all over." The security drone floated over and communicated with Hix. The data download showed a vibration in the 40-hertz range and it had been growing and fluctuating for the entire ascent. The pillar went from about two kilometers deep into the Andes Mountains to 98 kilometers near the ring. At 90 kilometers, the elevator would rotate 180 degrees and descend the last 8 kilometers toward the city ring, where winch cables would be fired and captured by the Elevator, and the last two kilometers would be by cable.

Noting the nametag, Hix asked the Astronaut, "Cruz, is it going to affect the ETA?"

The Astronaut shook his head, "We're going to be about 8 seconds early, and we replaced two generators last month, its cut nearly 15 seconds in transit time. But on that scale, we're about 7 seconds late. Still an hour before the Polar Ring gets here, so no problem. You're going to have to move your feet more purposefully now, because the gravity is gone. We are above 60 kilos." He closed the hatch and headed back into the lounge.

The steward was explaining the gravity transition. The Dwarf decided to kick off; he hung suspended in the air, just floating there. He took about three minutes to be bored, and then had to grab hold of the footballer to get his feet back down. His inertia would have brought him back down, as it slowed, but his stomach wasn't ready for that. He walked over to the wall and covered his ears; he'd forgotten to tell his implant to cancel the alarms.

Liam chuckled, "Does nobody read the manual, Hix? Who's that fellow?"

Hix answered, "Rocket booster techie. He's one of Branson's boys."

"Felix Branson is a disgrace to his ancestors; nobody wants to sight-see the moon. It's for mining and the military. Nothing there but dust and holes in the ground. How many people are going to pay three million hours to circle the moon and then come back? I know exactly eight werewolves with that much money. He can't be serious, can he?" asked Liam.

"Well, I heard rumors that he intends to start a satanic cult resort on the dark side. I don't see the attraction there though, since it's only dark for two weeks at a time," answered Hix.

"There are 8.2 billion of them, so it makes sense. You've got to know your market. In that case, Felix may be on to something," commented Liam. "That's actually very smart. Build a low gravity hotel, ship them up, a cruise-shipload at a time, stop off for the dark side bacchanal, and then send them home. Twelve to thirteen trips a year, that's printing money. And the Satanists practice ritual murder too, so you could figure a way to make that happen. Get a death row inmate - some colleen – and a jurist who would adjudicate it, and you're in business. Whoa, is that the turn?"

"Yes." Hix stated.

Outside the window, the rim of the earth had begun to climb upwards, and the city ring disappeared as the elevator spun slowly on a magnetic axis. After six minutes, the earth was overhead and they could see the ring below them. They began their descent. Hix heard a specific clang and the Astronaut spoke.

"We have cables. We are near the end of the spire. Stand by. Doors secure. Height to station, 1.8 kilometers. 1.2 kilos . . . 6 kilos . . . 500 meters . . . 380 meters." Hix took a breath. He'd been holding it until then. They were no longer connected to earth. They could see the pillar above them glittering in the sunlight.

"100   meters . . . 60   meters . . . 20 meters . . . Touchdown. Thank you all for riding the Pichincha Space Elevator, enjoy your stay." The astronaut and steward spoke over the radio. They filed out across the metal tube and into the New Spain elevator station. Customs had already cleared them, all except the Dwarf, and they were only inspecting his toolbox. They moved as a group to the second waiting room. They said their goodbyes to Bradshaw, the footballer; then Heidi, the blond. Just before she walked out, the Sasquatch gave a woof-bark that echoed through the room as a sad dirge and it lingered in the air as she left with a small wave.

Liam commented, "You just never know about people, do you Hix?"

Hix shrugged, the rest of the trip was uneventful. The Sasquatch left at the ADM station, the dwarf went left toward the Virgin Space Tram, and Hix went with Liam to the MGM's bank. They deposited the credits, and then went to the hotel. When Hix dropped Liam at his door, he wasn't surprised to see the steward from the Pichincha Elevator waiting outside Liam's door. With her nanoskin dissolved, she looked even better.

He asked, "Do you need me for anything else, Liam?"

Liam rolled his eyes over at the beautiful steward and said somewhat smugly, "No Hix, I'm here safe and sound, the credits are in the bank, I'll be staying here till the money is gone, and no one's going to rob me going back to earth. I think I can handle her! So you heading back tomorrow?" he said with a small nod of his head.

Hix got the nod and answered, "Yep, I'll check with security here, then head back in the morning, about eight hours to get home, though. Please call me if you need me in the future."

"I will. My lawyer's got your implant number. So my dear, you haven't had to wait too long I hope." She gave a deep-throated chuckle and preceded Liam into his suite.

Hix slept badly and awoke feeling as if something was still wrong. He salved and rubbed and then dressed in his fairly new traveling jumper, a thermal layer that would protect against exposure to the cold of space. Wouldn't help protect from the radiation, but it would keep him warm in high altitude environments. The polymer spray would be applied at the elevators, as would the nanoskin. Because of the long wait time in the rings today, he would have two coatings and two nanoskins.

A two-hour tram ride got him in position to go up the space elevator to the Polar ring, and then, when he got to the second ring, he waited two hours in the waiting room before leaving for the level one ring. He took the tram ride back to New Spain exactly six hours after he'd left the MGM. The next hour was spent prepping with one other passenger. The Elevator had already been prepped. Hix walked in to find Cruz at the console again.

"Did you get your vibration fixed?" asked Hix.

Cruz shook his head, "Haven't heard back from maintenance yet. Sent them all the diagnostics. It's weird, almost like wind noise on a metal cable on earth. Now this is the tricky part." He drove the Remote Operated Vehicle toward the approaching spire. The ROV held a grappling claw to intercept the pillar. "Contact. We have cable. Lift off from New Spain. 50 meters . . . 100 meters . . . 200 meters . . . 400 meters . . . 800 meters . . . 1200 meters . . . Contact. We are on the pillar. Applying lift." They began accelerating toward earth and then, nearing the

90 kilo mark, they slowed to perform the turn. The lights went out. The security klaxon blared. Hix asked his implant to tone it down and nanos filled in his eardrums. The emergency lighting came on. In the semi-darkness, they could see a bright flash directly above them.

"My god, that's Pichincha!" yelled Cruz.

"Did somebody nuke the town?" asked Hix.

"No, he means the volcano," said the new steward. Just then, the magnetic brakes failed and they started falling down the pillar.

"That can't be good," said the other passenger. He was middle-aged, but fit looking. Hix asked the security drone about him, but it was dead as a dodo. They suddenly noticed that the earth was no longer above them, but starting to arch away.

"The pillar has broken loose! It will fall in the Andes. We're going to have to evac at some point. We have three problems. Going down with the pillar isn't survivable. Winds are out of the west, so if we evac too late we'll fall into the eruption. Not survivable. North or south are our only options, but if we go out, we are pretty much going straight down," Cruz intoned gravely.

"I've seen this before," said the stranger. "Look at this." He sent them each a printed file. "It's a nanoskin enhancement subprogram."

"Who are you?" asked Hix.

"Felix Branson's father, Ricardo." The man answered.

"The daredevil?" asked Hix.

"Unfortunately, got a poly leg because of that. Shall we?" He opened the door to the balcony. Far below them, they could see New Spain and sensed they were falling northwest. "South it is!" yelled Branson as he pushed off from the Elevator. They still didn't have a lot of earth gravity, so it was slow going. He was falling toward earth about two meters per second. The other men launched off.

Hix ran the subprogram. They would have to wait until they got below 60 kilometers, and then stretch their enhanced nanoskin into sails between their arms and legs to get some aerodynamic lift. Hitting the freezing cold jet stream should take them a few hundred miles south before their polymer layers fed too much energy to the nanoskins.

The program would starve the nanoskins when 60% of the polylayer remained. They would need that for the landing.

The drop was breathtaking. They nearly lost Cruz in the Jet stream—he tumbled for two minutes, but managed to stay with them. The Steward broke his ankle when they landed in Puerto Isla Verde. But he didn't mind, it was a nude beach. Because of the Nanoskins, they had only been falling at 1 meter per second when they hit the sand. Across the countryside, they could see the dark cloud of the eruption. Hix struggled to stand.

"Well, I for one am never going to do that again! Let's get a drink, and then go see if we can help anyone." The four survivors of the first Pillar fall walked to the little umbrella covered bar, just as a local cop showed up.

Alan D Hickerson is a Fan Fi and Sci Fi amateur author. Raised in the farmland of Ohio. A father, homesteader, and systems analyst in the real world. Six biological and adopted children now grown to adulthood, with five grandchildren. Married to my bride Jackie for 29 of 57 years.

INTO THE FUTURE

21. My Name is Millec

W.A. Fix

It was late Fall on the Washington Mall, and the chilling wind whipped across the brown grass between the Washington Monument and the Capitol Building. The last leaves had separated from the trees and now tumbled across the grass and seemed to dance with the gusts of wind. Directly between the National Gallery of Art and the Air and Space Museums, the wind mysteriously stopped and the temperature instantly rose ten degrees. Then, without a whisper or the slightest movement of air, the sphere simply appeared. The one hundred foot orb was stationary, yet seemed to hover a foot from the ground. It all happened so quickly and silently that some people actually failed to see it and went about their business, until they noticed others standing silently in open-mouthed shock. Police were dispatched and were quickly relegated to crowd control as the small group of bystanders rapidly grew to several thousand. Within thirty minutes, the police presence doubled, and so did the agitated crowd.

Inside the White House, an emergency meeting was called and a decision made. No one was to do anything that could be remotely considered hostile.

Within two hours, several buses arrived carrying soldiers in Army dress uniforms. They were unarmed and quickly relieved the police. The soldiers encircled the sphere and began moving the crowd back to the surface streets. The orders were to control the crowd and continue to do nothing to provoke the sphere or anything inside it. They closed the entire Mall and evacuated the Capitol Building within three hours. The Secret Service moved the President and Vice President to secure, but undisclosed locations. Most of Congress had left the city within thirty minutes of the appearance, so evacuating them was not an issue. The military guard changed every two hours, in a formal ritual that nearly every television viewer on earth watched.

Two scientists were sent to examine the sphere and, after twenty minutes, they returned with little more information than they already had. They could touch it—it felt metallic—and it was slightly warm. However, the instruments they used in their investigation didn't register the existence of the sphere. Even a surface thermometer failed to detect the warmth they could feel when touching the surface. Baffled, the scientists returned, and waited, with the rest of the world. The sphere neither moved nor made a sound.

After two days, the novelty faded. People around the world began to return to work and continue their lives. On the third day, First Lieutenant Richard Matthews, of Post Falls, Idaho, was the first human to speak "officially" to a being from another world. During the changing of the guard, Lt. Matthews was the officer in charge and facing away from the sphere. Suddenly, the guard being relieved gasped and took a step backward, his eyes fixed on a point above the lieutenant's head. Lt. Matthews had received instructions for what to do in case contact was made. Despite the weakness he felt in his arms and legs, he summoned every ounce of courage, did an about face and found himself looking directly into the chest of an olive green, 7 foot, 400 pound humanoid. He looked up at the face and found it oddly human, but without a nose. Matthews' knees shook and he staggered slightly, and later, he remembered thinking, "So much for *little* green men." The alien was massive. It wore what appeared to be a helmet and light armor over the torso, legs and upper arms. Matthews slowly raised his arms away from his sides, turned his palms to the alien, spread his fingers, and said, "Welcome."

The being extended its right hand, holding a 5" by 7" flat piece of plastic or metal; Matthews could not tell which, but he reached out and accepted the gift. The giant then held its arms as Matthews had, bowed slightly at the waist and in a deep, base voice said, "Thankful." It then straightened up and, with a sound like blowing out a candle, vanished. Matthews read the writing on the paper-thin piece of what-ever-it-was. It said, "Please. This country highest authority. Government. Military. Science. Religion. Must talk. When ready, all come ship."

Two days later six people walked through the guarded perimeter and continued toward the alien ship. They would have been there the previous day, but nobody could agree which religion to send. In the end, three were chosen: Christian, Jewish, and Muslim. The other representatives were the Vice President of the United States, The Chairman of the Joint Chiefs of Staff and The President's Science Advisor. As they walked toward the object, the group vanished in mid stride. Two guards hurried to the spot and found on the grass a variety of pens and pencils, one small pocket knife, one flat ceramic knife about seven inches long, and a small 7mm automatic hand gun.

The group completed the step they started on the grass, and took another step, before they realized they were now in the ship. They shuffled to a stop and looked around in amazement. They were in a crescent shaped room, maybe thirty feet long, with one continuous window along the curved wall. They were looking at the Capitol Building through the transparent hull of the ship. In the center of the room, a grouping of seven comfortable looking chairs waited. One chair was larger and faced the others. On the wall behind the chairs were photographs of every member of the group, with odd-looking symbols below each. The alien appeared next to the large chair and displayed a horribly strained grin. With a wide sweep of his arm, he directed the group toward the other chairs.

The group moved to the chairs and, after some jockeying for position, they all sat. The alien waited for them to settle down then seated himself. When he spoke, it was in a deep base and had the sound of a brass instrument.

"My name is Millec. I do not speak the Earther language of English good, but I try make my thoughts into words you can think. I arrive here five planet spins back, to give words of help. Where I from, I is copper." He paused a moment and looked at each of them for any sign of understanding, "Not good word . . . police, I is police. You planet in future big trouble. Must ready for trouble. Need all on planet must help. I find plan for they steal planet. They kill all. They live here."

The Vice President interrupted immediately, "They steal planet? Do you mean Earth . . . this planet?"

Millec smiled and said. "Yes, Earth." He pointed at the floor. "This planet. They live here. Kill all."

"Okay, let me make sure we understand. Someone is coming to invade Earth. They will kill everyone and everything and then they will live on Earth. Is that correct?" said the Vice President.

Millec thought a moment then said, "They kill you. All peoples. No plants. No other animal. Just peoples."

"Okay," said the Vice President, "Who are 'they' and, why would they do this?"

"They, who, not important. They, why, for they like planet and want."

"Do they need a place to live? Is their own planet dying?" asked the Science Advisor.

Millec smiled wide and said, "No need. They see. They want. They take."

The Vice President said, "Well, we'll talk with them and make them understand that they cannot have our planet. Will you help us talk to them?"

"They no care. They kill all," said Millec.

"Well, you say that you are the police. You stop them," said the General.

"I do nothing can. You planet out circle Millec for." He thought a moment then said, "Out boundary, ahh, out border. No authority." He saw understanding in the General's face then continued. "Millec help some. All planet must work. Build weapon for fight." The alien stood and walked to the opaque wall to his left and reached into a rectangular hole in the wall that had appeared when he extended his arm. He extracted a black cube that was about three inches on each side, and then walked back to the group.

"You, science man, come." The Science Advisor rose and stood before the giant. Millec then placed the cube in his own left palm and touched the top four corners, one at a time, with the first of the three fingers on his right hand. The cube turned white and a hologram of a machine appeared above it. Millec lifted the cube with his right hand and indicated the science advisor should hold out his hand. The advisor slowly extended his hand and Millec sat the cube on the proffered palm. The alien touched the cube in the center of the top, the hologram disappeared, and the cube turned back to black.

"This now for you only. No other can use. Take time will, but you learn" Millec reached out and touched the four corners again, one after the other. Nothing happened. He then pointed at the science advisor and then to the cube. Without hesitation, the advisor also touched the four corners and the hologram sprang back to life. Millec touched the center and nothing happened, then the advisor tried and the cube shut down.

"North America piece here," he said, pointing at the cube. He walked back to the wall and extracted another cube. "South America piece here." He returned the cube to the wall and said, "And Africa, and Europe, and Asia, and Australia all have piece. All build piece. All join piece, make weapon. Fight they before here. Save Earth, you live here."

The Vice President spoke in a low voice, "How long do we have to prepare?"

Millec made almost a growl, "Twenty planet cycles around star. And, maybe five more, but, ready must be twenty."

"Twenty years," said the Vice president, as he almost laughed. "I was afraid we only had a few months."

"Years, yes, twenty years. This," he pointed at the cube, "very big work. Earth need all years. Maybe not enough."

Millec turned back to the others. "You, religion peoples. Like Earth, space peoples has many religion worships. It okay and help many. You MUST say okay each other and help together work. If no help from religions together, all die. ALL DIE!" he said loudly. "All must say, 'okay we help' for all Earth peoples."

There was a pause while everyone thought about what Millec had said.

Finally, he turned to the Chairman of the Joint Chiefs of Staff and said, "Space fight not same. You not before do. Must learn and make all Earth military ready. You, science man come." He indicated for the science advisor to hold out the cube. Millec turned the cube on another side then touched three of the corners in sequence then indicated the advisor do the same. Instantly, four holographic objects floated above the cube: one looked like a spacecraft; another was a 3D picture of Earth's solar system; another a machine with a human sitting in the middle; and the last resembling a football play drawn on a chalkboard.

"Touch." He indicated the corner below the craft. "This how build ships. Must build many." When the advisor touched where indicated, page after page of drawings and schematics were displayed. "Touch page." The advisor reached into the hologram and touched a page. Instantly the page expanded and showed details of a single piece of the craft. "Touch corner twice." The advisor touched and the image went back to the original size. He touched it twice again and the four original objects were displayed. Millec pointed to the cube again, "Much here. Take all twenty . . . years to learn and build. Start now. Time you go."

The giant turned and walked away from the group, indicating the meeting was concluded.

The Vice President called out, "Wait. Tell us more about this enemy. Tell us about your people and your culture. Will you help us build these things?"

Millec turned and pointed at the cube again, "I can no tell more. All need is there and you Earth must do alone."

The group stood and all began speaking at the same time, until they realized they stood on the grass, outside the ship, exactly at the point from which they had vanished. The Science Advisor looked at the cube in his hand and the hologram displayed above it. He touched twice in the center of the up-facing side and the hologram disappeared. While everyone on the planet watched as the small group turned and walked back the way they had come, the sphere vanished. Ten seconds later, the ship reappeared in China on Tiananmen Square and in front of the Great Hall of the People.

The China meeting happened the same as the Washington, DC, meeting. In fact, all the meetings on every continent went the same. When the final meeting in Australia concluded, Millec said, "Remind all, and work together. I return twenty year." This time when the sphere vanished, it did not reappear.

It took five years for the world to accept and organize the required effort. At first, the public resistance in each country was massive, until they all realized that other nations were secretly working as fast as they could. It did not take long to recognize that much of the information they each needed was spread throughout the other cubes. Once they truly began to work together, things moved quickly. Within the first five years, the national borders within the continents began to blur. Financial systems failed, but the work continued. Everyone worked with the common goal and everyone worked. Earth's people soon realized that their most valuable assets were the workers, and so, they fed, housed, and protected them.

The holders of the cubes began the open and free exchange of information. The governments lost control of the project and realized their jobs had transitioned from making war with each other to actually taking care of their people and facilitating the Earth Defense System. With the support of the world's religions, the people swiftly weeded out leaders who were only interested in grabbing what they could.

After ten years, the first ships began to leave earth. They left earth in waves—exploring the solar system at speeds that at first boggled the mind. The time required to reach Jupiter reduced from years to just over six days, in the alien designed ships.

Other designs found in the cubes allowed them to neutralize an object's mass to almost zero and simply tow it behind a craft. When the object was where they wanted it, it was stabilized, and then they returned its mass. Moving objects and supplies to and from space became as commonplace as stopping at the corner market. Artificial gravity systems and radiation neutralizing medications allowed virtually anyone to work in space. And, they did. Floods of people moved to space, built habitats on moons, in asteroids, other planets and either worked on the Earth Defense System or supported those who did.

The Earth Defense System construction was completed on year nineteen, day one hundred and six. The first full system test was conducted on Y19 D234. The entire network was fired at once, without incident, and twenty asteroids scattered throughout the solar system were vaporized. The test was especially impressive because the minimum size of each asteroid, mostly made of titanium or iron ore, was twenty kilometers in diameter.

On Y20 D34, exactly twenty years from his last meeting in Australia, Millec returned. Without a word of warning, his craft suddenly stood on a grassy open space in front of the Earth Defense Command Center in Buenos Aires, Argentina. Two days later, all six of the cube holders walked from the Command Center and were transported to the ship's meeting room, where they had first met Millec. He stood next to his large chair and graciously indicated the six waiting chairs.

"You have done well," he said, "and I have good news. The Trezzak fleet has been delayed. They will not arrive in your space for at least another twenty of your years." The group was jubilant and Millec continued, "This is good and allows more time to prepare." He walked to the wall that revealed a tray with six new cubes. He walked back to the group and gave one cube to each person.

"This is more to help in fight. Learn and work together that will save planet." He activated each of the cubes and demonstrated that they worked the same as the originals. "I return in twenty years. Know you are lucky for extra time. Need all." Suddenly, the six men found themselves standing on the building's steps and Millec's ship was gone.

By Y25 D34, the number of Earth spacecraft rose from hundreds to thousands. The construction of the ships was moved to space. The new cubes had provided two additional spacecraft designs. Both were much larger and the size of them required they be built in space. The materials also needed to be refined and parts manufactured in space. It took almost ten years to create the infrastructure that would support the building of those ships.

By Y32 D200, almost everything used in space was manufactured in space. Earth's primary export was its agriculture, and it fed humanity, wherever it was. Nearly a quarter of the human race now lived and worked in space. Everything focused on the construction of the two new spacecraft and they worked frantically to complete the task within Millec's schedule.

As the time ran out, the people of Earth and the humans in space knew they were not going to complete the ships in time. But they kept building, hoping for more time. When Y40 D34 came and went without any sign of Millec, they kept building. They built for another five years and finally the ships were complete. The ships were tested, crews were trained and they prepared to leave their docks.

Millec returned on Y46 D34. His craft appeared in front of the same building as it had twenty-six years earlier. The name on the building now read, "United Federation of the People of Earth." Within four days of the arrival, representatives from all over the Solar System and from all over Earth met in the building's assembly chamber. The television cameras came on and regular programming was interrupted. Over half of the human race would see this meeting. People everywhere watched as the assembly was called to order, and then Millec appeared. He wore no armor nor anything remotely military in nature. His clothing was loose fitting—a simple light gray in color. When he appeared, the assembly roared in surprise. He waited for them to calm and then began.

"My name is Millec. I first arrived here forty-six of your years ago. I warned you of impending doom and tried to help you prepare to battle for your very existence. You responded beyond any hopes we could have had. I am here to tell you that the battle is over and you have won."

The room rumbled with confused conversation among the delegates.

"There will be no attack. My people have protected your world for many hundreds of years. There has been no real threat from outside your planet for all of that time."

The rumble became louder and some people shouted questions.

"Please understand, the threat to your planet and race was real, but it was from within. You were choking this planet with pollution and you had not challenged your race for a very long time. If we had done nothing, today your Earth would be beyond recovery and your race would be trapped on its surface to die with it."

The assembly began to quiet, as the reality of Millec's words sank in.

"You have completed two ships. The fuel cells are designed for travel within your solar system. One ship is designed for war. The weapons on that ship could defeat many of the races beyond this system and would serve you well to defend against any threat. The other ship is designed for exploration and could be used for many generations to research, explore, and colonize this system." The room was silent. They all knew what those ships were designed for and how they intended to use them.

"My race has one more challenge for you. I have brought with me a single fuel cell. This fuel is of a nature you have not seen. I will give you the technology to convert the engines on one of the ships to use that fuel. With these new engines and this fuel cell, you can reach the stars and the thousands of races that wait there." The crowd reaction began as whispers and grew to a deafening roar as they realized the impact of Millec's words. The same reaction spread across the planet and into space, as the broadcast reached the farthest outpost on Jupiter's moons.

Slowly, Millec held his arms out from his sides with the palms out and fingers spread. The crowd became silent as they waited for his next words.

"Which ship will you take to meet them?"

W.A. Fix is a retired information technology professional, who lives with his wife and three cats in the suburbs of San Diego, California. He has "toyed" with writing all his life and recently became more serious about the craft.

Several of his works appear in online magazines throughout the Web. He has two stories in an anthology of flash fiction, **The Future Is Short: Science Fiction in a Flash,** *which is also published by Lillicat Publishers. Read flash fiction by W.A. Fix at* **The Story Shack Magazine,** *www.thestoryshack.com, where his works, "Born to Play," "Nin's Glory," "Mitzi," and "Testament" are featured.*

22. Heaven's Mountain

J.J. Alleson

When Earth's premier space agency makes you an offer that's out of this world, you don't refuse, and you don't ask questions. You simply sit, on a Tuesday afternoon, at a big desk in a Washington office, nodding dazedly at the ten WSA big guns around you.

The World Space Agency was, admittedly, an ambitious title. Membership was limited and exclusive, with some unexpected inclusions, and some very obvious omissions. But the Agency had initiated several new space-mapping programs, and the meeting seemed to have brought together most of the great, the good, and the hostile.

I watched the undercurrent of nervous tension as ties were pulled, chins rubbed, new haircuts patted, and reassuring smiles forced. Looking across, I espied Ojibwa Senator Elsec Su Li James. James was an advocate of a one-language Earth — therefore not a fan of my work. She must have been persuaded to come along and play nice.

Beside James was her lover and ally, Colonel Jakob Tsien Petersen, Head of One World's Sovereignty Removal Programme. Petersen watched me closely, but those Catalan eyes, framed by the silver-white hair of Norseland, gave little away.

From my own position, I could just about see the Capitol's grey-blue skyline. The view was rendered somewhat hazy by the holographic schematics of an engineering design floating around my eye-level. Clearly, this was a meeting hastily set up.

But then, they had all flown to *me*.

Someone, it seemed, really wanted me to be on this trip.

While my brain struggled to unlayer the two images, I wondered what had happened to create such VIP urgency.

A voice to my left — it sounded like Mike Dugani's — announced very formally, "Thank you for seeing us, Citizen Irena Liu Dem. This is the completed model of the *Bean IV*. As you know, it's our newest innovation in space travel."

I knew. Everyone did.

Mike — it *was* him — leaned in earnestly. "We need you on board. This situation is . . . critical."

Dr. Mikhail Dugani was WSA's Lead Advisor on Strategic Planning. If anyone knew what the deal was, it was him. But as far as I recalled, I'd not been drafted into military service and I couldn't remember signing anything that obligated me to the Agency. I returned his formality.

"Can you tell me a little more, Dr. Dugani?"

"Unfortunately, that's classified."

Mike's tone implied regret and frustration. I steepled my fingers under my chin, a technique I used when trying to squeeze a more substantial response from my students. Then I waited for nature to fill that vacuum she so abhorred.

No one spoke.

I looked around the table, trying to find the weakest link, and came right back to me.

"Uh . . . ok," I said.

***

Three weeks later, tested and innoculated, I was 49,000 km above the equator, on the newest *Bean*. Our on-screen vista showed black space all around, and Mother Earth dangled below like a blue bead of sanctity on the end of a rosary.

I tried not to think about time or distance; normally I needed flight pills for a three-hour hop from San Diego to Mumbai. But a kind of terrorised excitement — and, of course, professional curiosity — had reeled me in. At this point, we'd already passed both Van Allen belts. I stopped

231

worrying about the effects of radiation, and focused instead on a miracle called Méca Popo.

***

I wasn't the only one who'd been invited. Also 'on board' were Yoshi Chén Onisawa, Head of Tokyo's Aoki Institute for Particle Research, and Fan-ye Xua Akinyele, Chief International Liaison from the Dogon Space Institute. Mike Dugani sat with us, hands splayed edgily on the table as he often did during a holo-link report.

Both Fan and I had seen him like this many times. We'd worked with him over the past eight years deciphering linguistic codes, creating new symbols, and developing new syntactic patterns for WSA.

Sharing the minimalised dining space, we played him out. I smoothed down my thermo-suit, and scanned my data-screen of Greek poetry. Fan listened, black ponytail swaying gently, to what we had jokingly termed his 'space elevator' music. Yoshi was silent, although his nostrils flared in a way that spoke volumes. Finally he spoke.

"An odd invitation, Dr. Dugani. Rushed; clandestine; unexpected. When before there'd been no funding, no resources. Now *this*?"

Mike sounded almost apologetic. "There were financial restraints, Yoshi. Money was an issue."

Yoshi's hands slapped down sharply. "*Bullshit*, Mike! Money's a prescriptive commodity! A herd of cows. A string of cowrie shells. Even a promissory note written on paper. Which, contrary to popular belief, *does* grow on trees."

"*Look, Yoshi*, I wanted you in from the get-go, but my hands were tied."

Everyone understood Yoshi's anger. The *Bean IV* was a multi-national project, and Japan's technological expertise well known. But fears of their potential supremacy meant WSA had created a 'gentleman's agreement' that had effectively kept Japan out of the loop.

China was in; but then we were everywhere, having acquired control of most of the world's markets. And Fan was there because just over a century ago, Africa had bullied its way into the space race, their argument being, "We've been treated like another species for so long, who better to be reaching out to Earth's non-human friends?"

232

Under the Dogon Protocol, the continent had wrestled back ownership of 56.9% of its natural resources from international multi-conglomerates. Now every pre-teen from Ouargla to Guguletu aspired to be a 'Moonie' or star-traveller. These days, no one said no to the United States of Africa.

But recently, events had taken a very different turn, and all agreements — gentlemanly or otherwise — had dissolved in the rush to be Japan's new best friend.

"Come on, Mike. Tell us what's *really* going on."

"I'll tell you when we reach the platform. All I can say is that it's *big*."

Yoshi blew out the last of his resentment. "Well, I guess we'd already figured that out, Mike."

***

Our ascent was tortuously slow. Despite other advances, technology still hadn't found a way around the Coriolis force. As the *Bean* ascended, its speed increased, creating an outwards and upwards wobble on the cable. The effect was similar to a gymnast's ribbon of old that twirled more at the top-end than the bottom.

In order to reduce the effect, we were on a go-slow climb, measuring and adjusting as we went. It would be at least another week before we reached geostationary orbit.

With Mike still tight-lipped, the urgency behind our invitations remained a focal topic. In the dining room, while we tried to unravel the mystery, I sucked at a tube of what had been, a few minutes earlier, a dark grey powder. The label showed a celebrated vintage beverage; but since space has a tendency to suck away most food flavours, I let my memory and imagination do the work. "Mmm . . . Coffee, Jamaican blue. They're really spoiling us."

Yoshi grimaced. "We have to ask why. Mike's wound as tight as a drum."

Fan's thick brows met in concurrence. "Do you think some data might have leaked into the wrong hands? Sabotage?"

It was general knowledge that several groups were unhappy with this trip. We spent the next few minutes running down the likeliest culprits.

"God's Hand have accused WSA of actually playing God."

"Green Day. They've subpoenaed nine countries on charges of environmental terrorism." Yoshi had had several run-ins with the pro-Earth group.

"One World want socialist macroeconomics - with payment for services made in kind." We all slid a glance towards where Khasad, James, and Petersen huddled in terse conference. "Works well until there's a lawsuit. *Will the plaintiff accept payment in 30 million yuan worth of macrobiotic viruses?*"

Fan stroked an insulated chin. "Final suspect: World's End. They claim the *Bean* has only been built so that the elite can escape their own environmental messes."

They probably had the most feasible theory. Much of Earth's elite — a group Fan, Yoshi, and I fell into through embarrassing amounts of wealth and influence — lived predominantly in gated ecological paradises.

The three of us went where our work — and curiosity — took us.

"Have you seen the guest list for this trip?" Fan asked. "Several were at the meeting I attended in Cairo."

I'd seen it. "Also interesting that they came to us instead of the other way round. Costly."

Yoshi sucked his grape juice and gave a dismissive shrug. "A mere pimple on their budget. Shows how willing they were to work around our schedules."

Recalling my own cornered stance, I added, "Or make it difficult for us to say no."

"Well, that explains *their* common factor," Fan mused. "But what's ours?"

I had an idea. "A fear of heights?"

The two men waited for me to elaborate. I shrugged, aiming for nonchalance. "Or not."

"Worried about a breach in the hull, Irena?" Fan asked.

"Not really." I'd face that when it happened — although probably not for very long. A human body floating in space would be like a softened pat of butter awaiting contact with hurtling debris.

I tried not to think of the catastrophic end of the Starleap Endeavour, one of Earth's first commercial space elevators.

In 2107, 1,000 km from geo-stationary orbit, the nanofibre cable of the Starleap's first climber had begun unzipping like the kitsch corset of a cheap burlesque dancer.

Twenty-four hapless humans and countless tons of metal had crashed down on other climbers, whipping them earthwards towards Old Australia's Burswood, Kings Park, Booragoon, and heaven knows — literally — where else. Investors had stopped counting costs at 850 billion yuan.

Twenty-three years later, a pharmaceutical company in Shanghia called Tai Inc., developed a drug, which they titled ADva-5. Nootropic based, it was proven in tests to increase neurochemicals in the human brain by more than 300%.

World Health agencies immediately began marketing it as an anti-deficiency vitamin, administering it to every five-year old they could lay hands on. Even before the controversy had died down, the manufacturers were claiming the credit for a global spike in IQ levels. In short, another shot at moving the elevator much closer to science fact.

Fan shook me from my worries. "Be well, Irena. After all, you're the main reason we've made it this far."

"That's high, inaccurate and, quite frankly, comrade, not very reassuring praise."

"You're too modest, Irena. If not for your meticulous studies with the Teqanaquim, how would we have learned the truth about Heaven's Mountain?"

For *meticulous*, read *happy coincidence*.

Ten years ago, as Professor of Linguistics at Peking's Anthropology Archives Agency, I'd been working with the Teqanaquim people, a remote tribe in the forests of Acre, Northern Brazil. A village elder, called Maki, had been describing the Teqa's diet to me.

"Méca Popo leaves make good food. But the tree must be cut often."

The entire village, he explained, worked regularly to keep the rare tree at a height of no more than three metres.

"After that it becomes indestructible." He'd rapped his head strongly. "Impossible to cut."

Curious, I'd questioned him further. And had discovered such a stupendous error in early methodology, it was now the most cited case study in research training. Previous anthropologists, assuming a Western-world centrism, had interpreted the literal translation of the tree's name, *Heaven's Mountain*, as an endearing reference to its short stature.

They had recorded the Méca Popo as a pygmy tree.

The truth was that no one alive had seen the Méca Popo at its fullest height for over seven hundred years.

***

Two days later, we were watching some vintage science entertainment reels, Fan turned to us, his expression illuminated with clarity. "*Not* a world groups' plot, children. *Linguistic diversity.*"

As childhood recipients of ADva-5, we caught on immediately.

I was an expert in obscure and ancient languages. Most of my time was divided between anthropological research, antiquities consultancy, and universities around the world.

Fan came from nomadic aristocracy. His linguistic skills were stupendous. Thanks in part to ADva-5 and exposure to Africa's many complex languages — not counting derivative dialects — Fan could lay claim to fluency in approximately 350 Earth languages.

Yoshi, however, looked uncertain. "But if Earth has been receiving communications from space, why bring us all the way up here to decipher them?"

"And you're not a linguist," I said.

Fan laughed. "No; he just gatecrashed the party."

Yoshi grinned in agreement. He hadn't been involved in initial plans for developing the *Bean 1V*. But once Méca Popo's potential had been discovered, all eyes had fixed on that prize. And then, things had *really* changed.

***

Heaven's Mountain broke almost every rule of botanical physics. It didn't sway or bend under nature's forces. It simply grew straight up. Under carefully controlled conditions, the first full-length tree reached a height of

236

almost 1,000m, automatically re-knitting itself every 15 kilometres into an outer core that even modern tools struggled to penetrate. Its cells, when merged with carbon nanotubes, enhanced their tensile-density ratio by more than 13,000%. Its leaves and bark provided natural anti-radiation properties that left the space energy sector gasping orgasmically.

Unfortunately, because the Teqa refused to relinquish the plant in any discernible quantity, WSA could only gain a miniscule cross section for analysis. It had cost them the GDP of several small countries.

Soon after WSA had bought their sample, Japan announced that they'd finalised (by what some claimed could only have been a pact with the Devil) an agreement with the Teqanaquim. Consequently, Japan now held 15% stakeholder control in all harvesting of Heaven's Mountain.

After that, there was no question of Yoshi not joining us. Africa might have barged through the door; but Japan had kicked the damn thing down.

***

A few days later, Mike came to us, looking even more tense, if possible.

"I'd like you to meet someone," was all he would say.

Silenced by our own curiosity, we followed his taut, officious frame through a previously unseen part of the elevator and down a narrow galley. Minutes later, he stopped outside a sturdy metal door, which he opened using his biometric data.

I suppose I'd expected a team of VIP diplomats, ready to give a gracious salutation and present a long sequence of mysterious glyphic codes received from outer space.

What I didn't expect was the gut punching shock and time-flashes of emotion, from stark terror to elation, at what really waited inside.

Five military staff stood guard around a large object.

It was metallic.

It seemed to be made of rippling fur.

It was turquoise.

Its appearance said clearly and distinctly, *I am a UFO.*

All the unsolved legends of Roswell, Chernobyl and Djibouti rose to the fore. They were followed swiftly by the

knee-trembling concept of being among those who'd been
First to See.

Our racing adrenalin, however, clearly thought
belligerent query was the way to go.

"What the hell *is* it?"

"What *shape* is it?"

"What the hell's *in* it?"

Mike treated all our questions as one. "A spacecraft
with a silicon based hull, interspersed with hydroponic
capacity. It's a polygon. First Contact."

He plunged on. "Twelve equidistant engines allow it to
change course smoothly in any direction. A capacitor force
field absorbs impact like a goddamn sponge and bounces it
back out again. Fully operational, this thing could blow
through space corridors like a puff of air, speeding up travel
and commerce."

"Whoa, Mike, *slow down!*" Yoshi laughed giddily and
tapped his head. "We just got here."

"Sorry." Mike huffed out a long breath. Inhaled again
slowly. "We're not sure if the title is nominative or species,
but he calls himself Thax."

Fan said, "*He?*"

"Sorry, masculine laziness. We couldn't establish
whether Thax's ship has a name. We simply call it The
Polygon."

A small screen allowed us to view Thax. His ship's
interior appeared to be a large sleep pod with slender rod-
extended dials in the ceiling.

"It converts into eight different structures, including a
food and waste processing lab." Mike flipped to a recorded
scene, which did indeed show a lab-like pod. Thax was
preparing something from what looked like barley seeds.

He was reassuringly close to an Earthoid species,
looking like a cross between one of my vintage childhood
teddy bears and a live polar bear. Each digit — he had eight
per limb — ended in three-inch claws. A yellow fur-like
substance rippled down his upper torso and ended at the
groin, giving the impression of a fuzzy pale gold tunic over
dark pebbled leggings. A heavy helmet, however, hid his
facial features, as he moved freely around in the Polygon.

"We believe he's from the Goldilocks zone somewhere around Ursa Major 11. His shuttle crashed on Earth twenty-five years ago."

We all looked at each other. Raised eyebrows and shrugs said no one recalled seeing anything exceptional in the news.

"He breathes a mixture of oxygen, and carbon dioxide. His biology is surprisingly similar to ours."

"So he eats and poops the same way?" asked Yoshi.

Mike forced out a reluctant smile. "Virtually. We've had to experiment with piping stuff in and out. We know he's carnivorous." He added quickly. "But human flesh would be toxic."

Perhaps, but starvation often created suicidal motivation.

"How toxic?" I asked him.

"Imagine yourself eating the root of the belladonna plant and all its berries."

"Okay . . . that's . . . dead toxic."

It was almost funny. It had taken us so long to build a space elevator, that we'd made First Contact first.

Yoshi looked over at Mike in part sympathy, part envy. "It must have been very difficult keeping this a secret."

Mike grinned for the first time since this trip had begun. "It wasn't fun."

Fan simply grunted. "So all those assignments you've been sending recently with urgent deadlines."

"We couldn't establish his longevity," Mike said. "We had others working around the globe, but you two gave us the most promising results."

He was looking tense again. "This meeting was supposed to wait until we reached the platform. Unfortunately, we've run into a problem. Thax's ship has started to deteriorate."

***

Since they wanted us here, there'd been no cost for our tickets. But as my mind chided, *Nothing in life is free, Irena,* I thought of the Starleap Endeavour again.

Yoshi broke the silence. "How long before we reach the top?"

"Approximately three days. At the speed of the Polygon's deterioration, we still have options."

Of course, we did, I thought vaguely. Run like hell. Descend at top speed, unravelling all the way. Blow the whole thing to pieces and martyr ourselves for the cause. Or . . . stay put and see what developed.

Fan was grabbing Yoshi's arm. He had that dawning light in his eyes again. "*Wait a minute. Your samples of Heaven's Mountain. The ones you brought to rub their faces in.*"

No one refuted Fan's indiscreet comment by trying to claim anything else. Our minds conferenced at top speed while I begged forgiveness of my grandmother who had led anti-ADva-5 demonstrations.

"It's worth a try."

"There's enough time. Hopefully . . . ."

"Then let's move!"

Twenty minutes later, we were huddled around a small makeshift lab. There was no time for checking. *Have you carried out clinical tests? Did you examine the patient?*

Yoshi's hands were pale blurs over strips, vials, and containers as we assisted under his direction. Just over five hours later, there was nothing more but to wait for the Méca Popo to knit with the Polygon.

While we waited, Mike brought Fan and I several neatly collated files, which contained all the work we'd done for him. Understanding the real purpose now, and the greater urgency, we experimented, added variations, created shorthand sign languages. As Fan scrolled through a variety of verbal and non-verbal greetings, Thax suddenly became excited, emitting several booming roars.

"I'd say he's very happy to meet you."

Fan was a Moonie through and through. His thin angular face lit up as he said, "I'm feeling just a little tingly myself."

Using my methodology of working with previously unknown tribes, Fan and I began a rudimentary conversation with Thax, as Mike looked on, beaming.

You be well?

Lonely.

240

We established there was a mothership still locked to his shuttle. Whether he'd been alone, or his ship still had life, but had been abandoned, was unknown. But there was hope.

Your main ship where?

Jup. Past.

I looked at Fan. "Jup? Past Jupiter?"

"Or, '*Just up*'. 'Past' meaning '*destroyed*'."

***

Thankfully, the patient survived.

Within two days, Thax's ship had repaired itself sufficiently to disengage from the *Bean*. We surmised the Méca Popo had enhanced other things too, because Thax's yellow fur had changed to a deep golden, and his lower torso now matched the ship's turquoise hue.

His breathing seemed to have adjusted to the oxygen we breathed. Just before departing, he removed his helmet, revealing features more wolverine than bovine. To our stunned pleasure, he attempted verbal speech.

Fan looked highly intrigued as Thax added clicking sounds with the claws on his left hand. "He has a heavier alveolar ridge, but the syntax reminds me of some Xhosa dialects."

I agreed. After adding a few more words to our intergalactic thesaurus, we went back to on-screen communication.

You be well?

I be well. I know — way — from here. Ship safe.

Thax then gave a low soft growl. Eager to show his own linguistic capabilities, Yoshi growled back and was rewarded with a roar. Years later, he would continue to swear Thax's roar had had some Japanese enunciation.

During the flight down, Fan meditated alone to share the news with his spiritual ancestors.

Yoshi and I pored over the screens again.

"He's left us pages of information, Yoshi. Imagine. This could contain his world's history, science, culture, politics, everything. *A map.*"

"The galactic Robinson Crusoe Syndrome: the desire to leave some evidence of self, even if it lies forever undiscovered beside his body on an unknown planet."

241

"Do you think WSA will share this?"

Yoshi considered. "No choice now. They simply need to handle it the right way."

It would be done. Because I couldn't forget the look in Mike's eyes when he'd been able to lay down his burden of secrets. When he'd seen the excitement in our own as we picked up that same burden for him.

Three days after Thax departed, Mike came hurrying up to us, now light and carefree. "We've heard from Thax. He's sent you something."

Yoshi was already up and following. "Something? New technology? A kimono? *Diamond poop?*"

It was none of those. In the communication room, several lines were scrolling on-screen. Each one said the same thing: in Mandarin, English, Spanish, Swahili, Xhosa, Japanese.

In Teqa.

Thank you. Be well. Friend. Thax.

***

There were times when I had wondered just how far the Méca Popo could go. Apparently, as far as an alien spaceship could take it, and perhaps then, a lot further.

Some scientists believed Méca Popo had the capacity to merge easily with both organic and inorganic structures, which made me think of a fiction visio-reel we'd watched a few days earlier. *Invasion of the Body Snatchers.*

I thought of it again. In my version, the cast was a roaring wolverine species with the power of global human communication. And an immunity to toxic but succulent human flesh.

Instead of allowing Thax to die, we'd helped him.

It was a risk.

But everything in life carried some danger. And if Thax's people visited us as flesh-eating plants, or grew their own space elevator down to Earth, well, we'd grown tired of having just our own company. We needed new Thaxes. New Polygons.

We'd take the risk.

As a somewhat maverick UK writer of Barbadian origin, J.J. Alleson ignored her teachers' encouragement to take up writing in favour of the greater nobility of working for the United Nations (never happened.) Somehow, in between working as a legal consultant, ghostwriter and proof-reader, she's had short stories and poems published in several local literary journals. JJ believes that what we imagine can be as fantastic as a caveman's experience of modern day life, or as real as the difficulties involved in space elevator technology. In "Heaven's Gate", she weaves futuristic imaginings and current scientific theory into a fun story that hopefully readers will enjoy. Most of her multi-genre work is available online. Most recently published titles include: Hot Flashes of Science Fiction, Poems to Upset More than Just a Few People; Death Wishes *(a collection of paranormal tales);* Her Cheekbones Were So Pointy: A Guide to Not Writing Romance. *http://www.jjalleson.com*

23. SPACELIFT

Jot Russell

I never trusted it! That meter wide ribbon that extended up to the infinite reaches of space. They say it's a hundred times safer than flying there, but I'd put my money on a scramjet any day; that is if I had that kind of money. A piss-on, female operative like me was not given such luxuries. Instead, my hard work was rewarded with two days of solitary confinement in a capsule that might suddenly drop from the sky. Maybe if my boss had a chance to do some fieldwork, he might unzip his wallet a little. Of course, the agency's excuse was not to draw attention.

I tried not to think about it, enjoying instead the considerably more spacious confines of the train ride to Ecuador. As the tube extended out from the Pacific, the Sun's light exploded in. I squinted and caught a glimpse of the mountainous coastline before we zoomed past. The deceleration process was smooth, but violent just the same. It took only a few minutes to drop from hypersonic within the vacuum tube to standing idle in the station. That's where I spotted my tail. He followed from the platform and over towards the women's room, hiding behind a refreshment stand. I continued in to see only a couple other women. I was hoping for more to help me sneak out after altering my appearance. Without a few of them to leave with, it wouldn't be enough to risk a simple wig and change of clothes. All I'd be telling him was that his cover was blown.

I took a breath and decided to wash up after the tube ride from San Diego. The ride ahead was far longer, and a shower in space is an expense that even my boss would avoid. Ten minutes later, I graciously reacquired my tail and set out to the streets.

The city of Eclipse bloomed out of the former wilderness. *SpaceLift's* port to the heavens created a community of workers that slowly grew into a metropolis. The towers of glass and steel were some of the tallest in the world, yet completely dwarfed compared with the rotating belt to space that carried small containers of goods and the unfortunate souls, such as, yours truly.

I hailed a cab, hoping to lead my tail away from my true destination. The streets still made use of ground vehicles, with the tube being the primary way in and out of the city. Given the delicate nature of the airspace surrounding *SpaceLift's* conveyor belt to space, no aircraft were allowed within a hundred kilometers.

Eclipse's Empire Tower stretched a full kilometer into the sky. The car told me to have a nice day as I left the cab and casually entered the building. I caught a glimpse of my tail from the mirrored doors of a passing elevator car on the lobby level carousel. I stepped to the front of the queue, with the elevator droid asking, "What floor please?"

I looked at him and said, "Cafe; top level."

He projected a circle, highlighting which car to take. I ignored his arm gesture, walking the long way around the carousel. Finding the car, I jumped in and ducked into the front corner. I gave a sigh, voicing, "That was easy enough." A simple change of floors in the sky level would bring me down another elevator path and allow me to exit from a different side of the building. I took a few deep breaths to flush out my nerves and control my heartbeat. I moved to the back of the car and turned to watch the doors close. Just before they did, he stepped in!

The man who had been following me stood a full two meters, and practically doubled my body mass. We gave each other an innocent smile, but he followed with the typical male response of allowing his eyes to drift down

245

across my figure, before looking away. The shudder of the small car was almost non-existent as it slid back and up towards one of the six primary elevator shafts. Just the same, I let out a little chirp and pretended to lose my footing. He gave a surprised look and instinctively put out his arms to keep me from falling into him. His mistake.

My knee hit its mark, causing him to double over from the pain. Without hesitating, I shot both of my forearms up, catching him in the jaw. His head snapped up and hit the wall. I quickly retracted my arms and joined my hands to swing them together at his head. Miss!

My motion carried me around, leaving my side wide open. He jumped left from his duck and grabbed me from behind. I tried to lean down, but could gain no leverage against him. As I struggled to break his bond, he leaned forward and whispered in my ear, "Can I buy you a frozen coconut colada?"

I relaxed my struggle and he slowly let go of his grasp. He stepped back, groaned, and gave a grimace.

I shrugged my shoulders and said, "Sorry about that. I was told my contact would meet me at the station."

"Yes, the tube station. But you didn't give me a chance to tell you the code phrase. Luckily, I guess, I caught you before you ascended up the beanstalk."

I smiled. "Why, are you claustrophobic?"

"Sitting a couple days in a two meter tall, one meter wide box is enough to make anyone claustrophobic. Heck, I can't even stand upright in that thing." As he attempted to straighten his legs again, the grimace reappeared on his face.

The elevator doors opened on floor 198. I smiled and said, "Again, I'm sorry. How about you let me buy you a drink? It's a little early for a colada. Care for a coffee, instead?"

He forced out a smile and motioned me out of the elevator.

The box he so accurately described would be better defined as a coffin. I rechecked my gear, including the urine recycling system, before stepping inside and strapping myself to the collapsible launch seat. The gatekeeper checked my harness and cycled through the typical launch prep speech. I provided the required thumbs-up and he bid me a nice flight. With the door closed, the countdown began: "Ten; nine; eight." Even though I had done this three times before, my heart raced, and panic induced chemicals attacked my nerves. "Six; five; four." I found myself hyperventilating with the count. "Three; two; one; lift-off!"

If I could, I would have screamed. The force of the launch arrested my breathing. I forced my eyes open and looked out the capsule screen to see the building windows screaming by. Within thirty seconds, I went from zero to close to that of sound itself. Finally, the g-force subsided and I felt the latching mechanism take hold. For a moment, I felt a gut wrenching weightlessness, until my senses adjusted to the familiar pull of Earth's gravity. I worked to control my breathing while taking in the view outside. The towers disappeared below, replaced with the coastline in the distance. As I continued up, the curve of the Earth was slowly taking shape.

It only took a little over five minutes to reach the vacuum of space. I surveyed the chamber, listening for the sound of leaks. There was none. No sound but that of my faint breaths. I also started to notice the slight evaporation of gravity. It would take some time before that completely faded, only to flip and strive to push me away. I thought about how the station would fly away into oblivion, if and when the cord ever snapped. I tried not to think about it.

I let out a deep sigh and said, "Only forty-eight hours to go."

The stasis pill provided a sleep like no other. However, the drawback to getting a full thirty-six hours is that you wake with enough energy to climb a mountain. I would have settled for a three meter pace, but I didn't even have enough room to stretch my arms. With gravity slowly reversing past nil, I decided it was as good a time as any to invert myself within the capsule. I tucked my legs and threw my arms down into a spin. Without effort, I spun like a tumbleweed until my feet brushed the wall. I stretched back out, flipped the launch chair, and settled in. With Earth but a large ball in the distance, I switched off the external view to the display for the latest news. My jaw dropped as I read. The machines were at war!

The factories in China, that had been running day and night to create them, suddenly turned into the front lines of a new type of warfare. But, instead of waging this war against humanity, as many had feared they would, their pride and bigotry against each other's programming had created an evolution of unnatural selection. The competing companies that had strived to wake up their own form of artificial life didn't understand how this competition was bred into their being.

I knew this, because I had helped to steal the two opposing internal designs. Although both used the same quantum optical lattice processors, the logic housed within was as different as day and night. Compulet reduced all human languages into simple computer structures for the purpose of understanding the thought behind every word ever written. Mentalque used a statistical approach to represent every potential decision and determine the least weighted path towards the best solution or outcome. Taken to the extreme, within these new unlimited quantum processors, two alternate forms of artificial life were created.

On the planet, the built-in telepathy of each processor marked its programming like the color of skin. The growing resentment and breakdown of cooperation between the Compulets and Mentalques paved a path towards destruction that only my boss seemed to foresee. We had attempted to share the logic of both, but the infiltration from neighboring self-aware computers saw to its demise. However, fifty-thousand kilometers away housed a quantum computer that ran but simple programs and was isolated from the interference of artificial intelligence.

As I neared my destination, the wars had extended to cities and towns throughout the world. With reports of collateral human casualties, I feared the escalation of our involvement might lead the machines to override their prime directive of protecting us. I suddenly felt even more closed-in and vulnerable. If either breed of AI realized the nature of my mission, they would sever the cord and send me, and the station, off into the cold depths of space. The tension in my nerves built. It felt as if the tiny box in which I found myself, was closing further in upon me. The sudden announcement in the quiet chamber made me nearly jump out of my skin.

"Pod 308, you are approaching SpaceLift Station. Please strap in for deceleration."

I took a deep breath and felt my nerves settling back down. "Acknowledged, *SpaceLift*; ready for docking procedure."

The soft detachment turned into another violent change in velocity. This was half as strong as the launch from the planet, but my acclimation to zero-g made the change seem just as bad. After a minute of hell, the force subsided and my coffin door was opened. I stepped out into the weak gravity and rejoiced in the feeling of stretching my arms and unlocking my soul from that box.

"Welcome to SpaceLift Station. Let me show you to your room and comfort station," said the attendant.

"Later, please. I need to talk with your captain right away."

He looked at the badge that I handed to him and nodded. "As you wish," he said, directing my way.

The ride home would be much the same torture as that coming up, but I happily accepted the trip, knowing there was a world to return to. The conjoined program that combined the seed of Compulet and Mentalque bloomed into new life. Once it was aware and made witness to the destructive war waging below, it provided an answer for its parents' salvation, as well as our own. By mimicking the host program within each quantum computer, it was able to transmit itself there and upgrade the programming until each understood the logic of the other. Using the human examples of man and woman, black and white, straight and gay, the programs learned to accept and embrace their differences.

As I was preparing to board the pod, the captain came up and offered, "For your service, *SpaceLift* would like to upgrade you to a first-class seat on our scramjet, *Liberty-1*."

I smiled and said, "Lead the way."

Jot Russell is a writer of Science Fiction and Political Science, and is the creator of the Science Fiction Microstories Contest. His works include Terra

Forma, Open Source Government, The Future is Short, *and the anthology,* Consortium. *Although a world traveler, Jot lives in Long Island, where he was born and raised. A software engineer by profession, he also enjoys a love for mechanics. He is currently working on obtaining patents for his new internal combustion engine and elevator designs.*

24. ENOUGH

Thaddeus Howze

She was as sharp and crisp as a newly printed dollar bill; edges still firm, resisting folding, spindling, or mutilating. Dark brown skin, high firm cheekbones highlighted in the lobby's early morning light. Her power suit, purse, and pumps indicated she was ready to work.

Right out of Dartmouth she came highly recommended from her several externships with local media companies. In another life, Francis would have considered her pretty, in that cold professional way women have begun to be seen. A man wasn't supposed to notice what they looked like. Only what they thought about.

In this way, women had finally achieved parity with men. They now had the freedom to be completely ignored. So Francis did. He was only interested in her academic qualities, her scholastic abilities, and her sociopathic tendencies. She rated seven on the scale; selfish enough to put her own survival above anyone else's but charismatic enough to make you believe she cared.

She was perfect. He hurried down from the mezzanine to meet her.

"Good morning, Ms. Ross. Are you ready to begin work?"

She assessed him. Quickly, visual scan from shoes to hat. She lingered on his wedding ring, an imperceptible

251

second, and then made her way to his eyes. Cold. Centered. Focused. She held his gaze before smiling and extending her hand with the perfect amount of pressure. He responded and reflected her back. No more pressure than necessary.

She smelled of honeysuckle. Surprising.

"Yes I am, sir."

"Follow me. We'll be using the executive lift."

She was being watched and she probably knew it. Thirty psychometric teams were scanning her, watching her every movement, every micro-expression. They had to know if she could be the one. The last three candidates had failed to pass muster and were . . . retired. They had high hopes.

He decided to take her to her workspace. They had tried to ease the previous workers into the idea of their job but that had failed. Today, he decided they would do something different.

"How was your flight to the ship?"

"It was fine. I didn't expect to travel quite so far but the crew was really nice and the accommodations were wonderful."

"Good, I think we will skip the normal office tour and introductions and take you straight to your workspace, if that's okay? You can meet the team later."

"That's fine, I am eager to see what a Resource Management Specialist does for Colcorp."

"Besides manage resources? You will be determining the fate of a world."

Her micro-expressions revealed blushing and her small but well-managed afro vibrated with her amusement. Her activated hair implants were capable of emotive response. Only the best for this lady.

When they arrived at her door, the security guards scanned them and then gave them access to the control panel.

With a brief handprint and retinal scan, he was identified. "Colson, Edward Francis, President."

She took her turn. "Ross, Marilaine, Director, Resource Management, pending."

The door opened. It was a huge vault door, similar to the ones used by banks. It opened outward, with the solid

252

steel rods retracted and barely visible at the edges. The air smelled crisp, cold, highly refrigerated. Servers could be seen in the distance lining the outer edge of the room. An entire wall was filled with monitors, flipping between multitudes of constantly changing images. People of all colors and economic backgrounds could be seen. Different countries, famous landmarks, social catastrophe zones, were all equally represented.

There were two people working in the office already but they did not turn away from whatever they were doing and did not acknowledge the CEO or the director at all.

The most important wall was on the left of the main door entrance. On this wall were counters. Hundreds of them. Almost all were counting down. A rare few were counting up. Many were dark; a couple went dark as the two of them drew close. They were immediately replaced with new counters.

"How do you like it?"

"I'm not sure what I am looking at."

"The resources of the entire world. Everything we will ever need, ever use, ever want. Every widget, every technology, everything. If Colcorps can find it, manipulate it, or destroy it, we track it here."

"Excuse me?" Her face revealed her incredulity. Her sharp mind was already wrapping itself around the impossibility of the statement.

Start with the truth—lie later. "It's the year 2104. You have seen what is left of the world, as we once knew it. Your native Haiti has all but vanished under the rising sea level. Colcorp has consolidated the best technologies, the best surveillance systems, and our specialized resource algorithm, which allows us to predict which resources are going to vanish or become unsustainable next."

Pause for effect. "Look at that gauge. It is tracking desertification worldwide in feet per year. ISSAC, if you would, explode 'desertification' please."

"Desertification, exploded, broken down by region, deserts, sustainable or unsustainable, temperature ranges, exploited or still pending." ISSAC's response was especially modulated to invoke calmness, no matter what he might be displaying.

The graphic flew from the wall and was suspended in three dimensions. She could see graphs of the world's oldest deserts and newest. How fast they grew, where they were growing, who lived near them, what effect these deserts were having and whether solar facilities had been established within them to take advantage of their only resource, vast amounts of solar energy.

Matching screens on the walls flashed to different feeds of the deserts, some showing sustainable areas where, if sufficient water were available, some level of life for humans could be maintained. Unsustainable deserts, like most of the Sahara, only showed the rippling of the sand, like a crystalline ocean, its waves frozen on its surface.

"Haven't you noticed it? Your food should be your first clue. How many things from your youth taste as good as they did then?"

Marilaine had never given it much thought until this moment. She had spent a little time in her native Haiti before it was lost in a superstorm and remembered her grandmother cooking the native plants and animals. When she moved to the Allied America, the first thing she had to get used to was the machine-prepared food. But now that she was thinking about it, the quality of food had changed recently. Bread was flatter, less flavorful, as if the ingredients were being stretched across neutral filler, bereft of flavor.

She looked around the room, reading the displays, until she found what she was looking for.

"ISSAC, please expand aqueous plant fillers."

This was one of the few numbers rising instead of falling. Once broken out, she could see most of this was seaweeds and plankton, much of it grown in artificial inland seas, or in the few remaining unpoisoned ocean areas. Carrageenans were expanded and utilized in almost every processed food as a binding agent—a bland, tasteless filler.

She was beginning to understand. Marilaine moved around the room looking at each of the displays, her face unchanging as a stone. ISSAC complied with her requests and she found her way to a section of the room where displays were winking out. One of them was marked

Humanity. One of the counters was down to single digits. She waved her hand and brought up the display. It showed two aged giraffes in a zoo. Both looked sickly and the zookeepers stood by with rifles in hand. With the two mercy rounds, the last two giraffes vanished from her display board and the counter fell to zero.

Her composure began to crack.

"What do you want me to do with this? Am I supposed to sit here and watch as these things become extinct? Or as the population of Indochina is wiped out by the next super-typhoon?"

And here's the lie.

"No. We want you to manage this. We want you to find ways of slowing this erosion of the Earth. Figure out ways to divert resources, move people, harness skills. You have five different academic degrees and a level of synergistic thinking we have never seen. You have the ego to believe you can do something like this and the willpower to carry it out. Every resource at our disposal is yours to command. You answer only to me."

This was the first time she appeared to be the young twenty-eight year old woman she actually was. Her face softened, her eyes lost their steely glint, and she leaned on a console casually, her composure momentarily gone. "Why are you lying to me?"

"I don't understand."

"I have been here for little over an hour and I can already see this is impossible. And that most of what you are claiming has already failed. Computer technology is already on a downward spiral. Your space program can't get the rare earths you need for your engine prototype designs. Food quality and nutritional value is diminishing. People are starving faster than you can create empty calories for them to eat. From where I stand this project is stinking of failure."

"ISSAC, please reveal Genesis. Ms. Ross, this is what we need from you. To save Genesis."

***

Forty years later, the human race died; right on schedule.

Marilaine Ross helped wind down the world. She saved lives when she could. She gathered the remaining scientists, thinkers, engineers, and leaders. The best the world had to offer. In the end, governments failed. Corporate power waned and humankind fell to barbarism.

Billions died. She worked tirelessly, knowing her time was running out. The three starships of Project Genesis would be her last work. As the gauges went out and the displays died, the control room grew darker and darker until only a few remained. The last timer counting down was Genesis.

In ten days, the last of the three ships would be gone. On day eight, the senior Colson, her husband of twenty years, died.

He died protecting the last computer components from the roving bands breaking down the walled enclave where ISSAC and Resource Command were located.

Their son, Francis, carried him back. There were no words exchanged. He dropped his father's body inside the vaulted room and went to install the final components for launch.

Project Genesis, Resource Command, no longer bustled. It was cold and dark, protected only by automated systems. The younger Colson would be her final passenger. The great ship hung in the sky, next to Space Elevator Omega, barely visible with the naked eye, filled with tens of thousands of humans in a perfect stasis. Bound outside of time they waited. And they would wait. For as long as it took to reclaim the world.

Francis shuttled to the ship high above the Earth, plugged the last module in, and stepped into his stasis chamber. "Goodbye, Mother," were his final words to her.

When Genesis reached Jupiter, with a final dive into the planet's mighty gravity well, the great ship, like its two brethren, would slingshot around the giant, taking advantage of the gravitational boost, and head for its new home.

The last artificial intelligence, ISSAC, would do its best to ensure a quiet journey. As the most powerful Mind ever created, it was certain its arrival in a new star system would be anything but uneventful. It would dim the lights onboard for its long journey before dreaming of electric sheep on virtual plains.

As Genesis turned outbound from the solar system, it would begin its spin-up to seventy percent the speed of light. It would still take nearly a hundred years for them to arrive at their destination, an Earthlike planet, larger, with more water, capable of supporting human life.

Fifty thousand humans, one hundred thousand embryos, fifty thousand Mechasmic Minds, the labor force of Project Genesis, the sum total of the best knowledge, and all the tools for rebuilding civilization. It would not be Earth. Its gravity was stronger, its climate wilder, it would be a struggle for survival. But she knew her son. He would never give up.

He was his father's son.

Only when the last timer reached zero and the last monitor shut down, did Marilaine Ross detach herself from ISSAC, complete the AI's upload, and climb from the nutritive bath that had sustained her semblance of youth.

Then a new timer started up. It had a one hundred year clock. Marilaine took the holographic timer down from the wall of her office and transferred the countdown for Genesis and its estimated arrival time to her inner chronometer. It would be decades before she would need to check on it again.

She finished drying off and dressed in the last advanced technology on Earth.

She walked outside for the first time in fifty years and looked toward the heavens as Genesis pulled away from the boundaries of Earth's gravity. Howling bands of humans screamed and tore at the fences, sensing this final change in their fates. They would be alone with a Stone Age future ahead of them.

Marilaine Ross strode down the street, breathing in the air, filled with the sharp tang of degrading toxins. With major industrialization gone, the sky was still cleaner than it had been in decades. As she approached the city walls, the people outside the gates were unsure of how to deal with her.

She was utterly fearless, her long, braided hair whipping around her head like serpents. Her brown skin shown with an inner light—she was no longer Human and anyone seeing her would know this. They would feel it, deep in their bones, the same awareness they would have used when confronting a deadly predator, when there were such predators. The last big cat died forty years ago. She was now the most dangerous creature on Earth.

Her body had changed during those years in the nutritive bath. She was stronger, carbon laced her body, she was smarter, her neural net augmented by nano-technology. Barring catastrophic injury, she would live long enough to see Genesis reach its destination and beyond.

But that was not her goal. Her goal was to restore the Earth. To bring humanity back from the brink. There were approximately ten million humans left all over the world, living in burned out cities, scavenging from the remnants of the world that was.

Hers was the harder task. The once-ravaging hordes outside the gate followed this tiny and strange woman, from a discrete distance, of course, weapons falling from their hands. For the first time in generations, someone had a plan. They could sense it.

Her plan was simple: to give her son and the people of Genesis a home to return to—if they wanted it. Even with her modifications, she was certain she would not live to see their return, if they even could.

She had to live in the present for the first time in a long time. No time delay, no decades long planning, no schemes to secure rare materials, no remote viewing. The vicissitudes and struggles would be hers.

A group of younger teens had already come closer to her than any of the others and signed if they could touch her. She hadn't touched anyone in decades. She welcomed it. The scent of wild honeysuckle lingered on the breeze. She smiled. They came.

At the end of the world, with no future in sight, with humankind sitting back at the Second Stone Age, Marilaine Ross-Carlson came to life.

Thaddeus Howse is a California-based author whose non-fiction work has appeared in magazines, including Black Enterprise, the Good Men Project, The Examiner.com *and online at* Astronaut.com.

His fiction writing has appeared in blogs, such as, the Magill Review, ScifiIdeas.com *and he maintains a prodigious amount of non-fiction work at his own blog,* A Matter of Scale. *He answers questions on the* Scifi.Stackexchange.com *and Quora.com.*

His collection of short stories can be found at Hub City Blues *(http://hubcityblues.com/). He has recently led a monthly challenge called "30 Cubed" (http://30cubedsf.wordpress.com/).*

His speculative fiction has appeared in numerous anthologies including The Future is Short, Visions: Leaving Earth, Mothership: Tales of Afrofuturism and Beyond, Genesis Science Fiction Anthology, Scraps, and Possibilities.

He has authored a collection of short stories called Hayward's Reach (2011) and an e-book novella called Broken Glass (2013).

He has also been a tabletop roleplaying game designer, magazine publisher (Interface Magazine) *and written materials for* Cyberpunk 2020, Dungeons and Dragons, Warhammer 40K, *and* Hero Games.

Favorite Quotation:
"A human being should be able to change a diaper, plan an invasion, butcher a hog, conn a ship, design a building, write a sonnet, balance accounts, build a wall, set a bone, comfort the dying, take orders, give orders, cooperate, act alone, solve equations, analyze a new problem, pitch manure, program a computer, cook a tasty meal, fight efficiently, die gallantly. Specialization is for insects."
--Robert Heinlein

25. I RIDE THE NIGHT

Thaddeus Howze

Those in the know call it "riding the night."

Standing on the surface of asteroids as black as the night that surrounded us, we drank in the feeble light the sun deigned to share so far from home. We mine asteroids for conflict minerals long exhausted on Earth.

It's as dark as the sea at night with a cloud-filled sky. As dark as the heart of a coal salesman during the worst winter in a century. Back when we had coal. Or salesmen.

Stretching, I checked my energy levels. Satisfied with my power reserves, I drew my light-absorptive wings back to my body.

It's been about forty years, give or take, since I came to work at the edge of the asteroid belt. There's no gold watch at the end of this rainbow—no happy retirement. As a matter of fact, one hundred and fifty days from now I expected to be dead.

My daily survey concluded with checking my skin for micrometeorite strikes. As usual, the repair system performed adequately while I slept. Mining the Trojan asteroids, I reset the drones to compensate for Jupiter's interference and they flew off to relay telemetry for transport, while sending a signal back from Resource Control.

The drones take two hours to reach the right distance and arrange themselves for signal relay. By then, my last shipment of rare earths was set up and launched magnetically toward their destination.

It will take one hundred and eighty days of constant magnetic manipulation before they would slam into the moon's surface. Collected, they'll be sent to the Genesis project for future manufacturing.

I heard the first squelches of received radio signals carrying encoded messages. My navigational HUD took a reading and calculated where Earth was in relationship to my position.

As the comm-link was established, I waited to hear her voice. The voice I have heard more often than anything else since I came to work here—the voice of Resource Command and Control.

Yes, there were still a few live broadcasts sent out here to the Belt. Back when they still played sports, we could get them sent out by laser on a three-hour delay. I wasn't even a sports fan until I got out here.

As governments broke down, organized sporting events became rarer and eventually all such low priority transmissions ceased.

"This is RCC, reporting on Belt Ore Reclamation. All units are to finish their operations and report for pickup at your appointed locations. Set your launch systems for shut down upon completion. It's time to come home."

Her voice was the only thing that held me together in these last years, as Earth became increasingly inhospitable and time grew short.

***

I lived in Shanghai until the plagues came. The Chinese government firebombed Shanghai attempting to eradicate a virulent strain of hemorrhagic fever sweeping through China.

Their efforts met with failure. My mother, a researcher, lived in Shanghai. She fell in love with my father, an African businessman during one of her many business conferences. She died soon after the bombings.

I was away on a school trip in Africa visiting my father who was a vice president for an international bank. We didn't spend much time together but when he learned my mother had died, he did his filial duty and I moved to Kenya. I never returned home.

I went to university in Kenya and my father used his influence, coupled with my grades, to get me into the South African Space Program. The program deemed me capable of enduring the genetic alteration necessary to take part in the Exotic Metals Recovery program.

Getting into space wasn't like when my parents were kids. They didn't use rockets anymore. Now, machines carried men into orbit. They were literally elevators into space. Mind-boggling physics was required to tow massive cables into orbit while using lasers and fervent prayer to move the cars.

The cables terminated at geosynchronous space stations. There, humanity's greatest projects were being built: three star-ships preparing to take a select few to the stars.

I was gene-engineered after my training in South Africa. The program was on an accelerated timetable. Food, water, and populations were under assault from humanity's excesses. Too many people and not enough places to live or grow sufficient food. Plagues swept the globe decimating populations. No one was safe.

It was dubbed the Holocene Extinction and considered the end of humankind. We could no longer pretend climate variations were not our fault. We stopped using cars, reduced our energy emissions, and finally embraced renewable energy. But like all closed systems, the Earth would need time to adjust. Time, like all other commodities on Earth, was in short supply.

Once the space elevators were finished, geo-engineering attempts included a solar shade project. While I was being turned into more machine than man, the space program launched thousands of satellites to block the sun to try to cool the Earth. Geo-engineering could not stop global heating; it was merely a stopgap to give us more time to work.

Billions perished. Starvation, flooding, minor wars sprung up everywhere. The Four Horsemen reaped lives like wheat from the field.

The final gene engineering altered my body in ways I barely understood. My tolerance for radiation was increased. My skin became black and energy absorptive. My musculature and bones were made harder and stronger with carbon fullerenes, but my healing would be slower. I would need a repair infrastructure, not just an immune system.

This came in the form of nanites—microscopic machines I could control, send into injuries, augment my physical capacities, even use them to sense the environment and gather information. My body was changed in such a way, my need for a spacesuit was eliminated.

My brain was altered as well; woven into it was a cortical network computer, designed to control all my artificial technologies. My planet-side training, once my augmentation was complete, lasted another three years. I had to learn to live all over again.

I no longer needed food. I was nearly one hundred percent photosynthetic. My unused organic systems were crystallized within my body and could be restored in a few months using the same process that took them offline. The rest of me was reinforced and augmented with a nano-factory stored within what used to be my lower digestive tract.

My body could manufacture everything I would need to live on, using a chemical substrate supplied every three years from a drop pod. During that drop, compressed media was also delivered to help keep me sane. It barely helped.

**

It was over a decade since I was last on Earth. The last time was when my father passed away. I hadn't seen him in years. He left everything to me.

The ships, for which this constant stream of mineral wealth was being drawn from the Belt, were nearly finished being built in orbit. They were more than the skeletons I remembered.

Each ship was designed to hold a little over fifteen thousand souls in stasis and another fifty thousand as nothing but Mechasmic Minds. A quantum computer replicating the mind it copied; pure mind, divorced from a physical body, a thing of silicon, ceramics and just a tiny

263

bit of quantum chaos. MMs copied people who were too old for the trip and willing to make the sacrifice of their body's dissolution. You had to die to inhabit an MM. MMs were how a portion of humankind would take to the stars.

These MM frames would become the workforce of a new world. With new robotic bodies, they could survive the elements. They would be the shock troops of the human race, capable of dealing with whatever conditions the world had to offer. They would build the habitats of these future humans.

Being an MM meant, you would defend a way of life in which you would no longer be a participant. I understood that all too well.

As my shuttle pulled into Space Elevator Omega's station, it was only with the help of my internal computer that I could make sense of what I saw, the space elevators reaching the geosynchronous points, sixty-two thousand miles into space. The trip planet-side will take fifteen hours.

My father's attorney said it would be necessary to manage his vast estate. I think he insisted I be there to prevent his many wives from getting anything. He thought I would be like him.

A good provider, he had taken multiple wives and his favorites thought he would leave his vast holdings to them.

They met me at Space Elevator Omega, each jockeying for favor. They pretended not to be disturbed by my appearance. I could hear their gasps of horror as they approached. Their hugs could barely hide their revulsion.

Granted, I was difficult to see, fresh after my three-month trip from the Belt. My skin was still a photon-absorbing matte black. On the trip, I had returned my skin's texture to something resembling human flesh.

Lacking proper calibration, I could only approximate the texture of human flesh. I had the physical appeal of a freshly cooling corpse.

Adding to the insult, I no longer sported my father's powerful build. I was only four feet tall. I'd altered myself to conserve energy and to navigate the mining tunnels on asteroids. I was thin as a rail; appearing more skeleton than man. They brought me some traditional African clothing, which hung loose and looked strange with no flesh to fill it out.

I ignored their conversation on the way home. Their chatter was little more than birdsong to me. I was completely enraptured with being home. Genetic engineering made it possible for humans to live in other environments. But it didn't take away our psychological hunger for familiar surroundings.

I missed the simple things, like the pull of gravity on my entire body. Working in micro-g for so long, it felt as if I had rediscovered a partner I didn't know had left me.

I loved the flow of air across my face. In space, you can feel the solar wind but it's ephemeral compared to the wind tossed South Pacific of Space Elevator Omega. The storm drove the rain with the force of small bullets and I cherished the feel of every drop as I climbed into my father's wives' chartered plane.

As far as my/his wealth? None of it mattered to me. I divided the estate and gave each wife an equal share. He would have hated that I did it, but I walked out of the room with knowledge none of them possessed.

No amount of money would get them on a starship.

In a decade or less, they would be among the hundreds of millions left behind on a planet without infrastructure or the skills to maintain any of it. They might as well be comfortable in their dotage before the planet returned to the Stone Age.

***

I rode the night for another ten years after his passing. I counted down the days, listening to all the reports from RCC. I noted fewer general broadcasts as environmental pressures took their toll on people across the planet. In my last year in space, it was only RCC that came across the channel.

People asked, why use rock jocks at all? Why not let computers and AI do all this work? It's hard, solitary, difficult work requiring extensive alterations to a human's body and mind. But a machine couldn't do what I did.

In those last years, I spent less and less time on the surface of the asteroids. I conserved energy for work. I used my third and fourth arms as sensors, scanning for more of the rare earths to meet my quotas.

Feeling the veins of ore, sensing their richness and their density—all this happened in my inner eye. The sense of yttrium is bitter blue-black, indium, a yellow green sticky sensation, dysprosium, a hot red, europium, violet in scent and in color.

These are wired to my neo-cortical implants to recognize them and decide if the supplies are worthy. Drones scour the Belt seeking samples. My job starts with determining if they are worthy enough to drop drilling probes.

I determine the quantities by releasing nanites into the soil. I trace rich veins of pure ore. Using my sensors, I listen to the asteroid's metallic heartbeat and call probe ships down to help with the elemental extraction.

Once the asteroid is clear of rare earths, they are launched into space along travel lanes. The routes are cleared with powerful lasers and low quality AI watchdogs who are smart enough to recognize a problem, and capable of handling them.

Contingencies are why I was needed. No machine could be trusted with the fate of the human race. RCC's all too human voice reminded me why I was here—why she needed me to do this impossible job.

***

The final trip home took ninety days, half of what was normal. I was barely able to complete the re-acclimation program needed to live on Earth.

Then I remembered why. They didn't expect me to go to Earth, but to transfer to a Mechasmic Mind. I was expected to die in space.

My shuttle approached the last of the three starships in orbit. The other two had already left, staggered apart by weeks, as a fail-safe against disaster or human intervention.

I looked down on the brown and dying Earth. The oceans were an unhealthy blue-green color, the land parched desert dry in some places I expected to see green. I could see the wreckage over the coast of Africa where one of the space elevators failed due to terrorist attacks.

"Chen Enkufu." It was the voice of RCC, the sound of all that I knew to be Earth. "You are the last to arrive. You are to report to MMC for retasking and download to your MM frame. The last of the Genesis starships will be leaving in 48 hours. Please respond."

An opportunity to speak to RCC. In all the time I had worked the Belt, I had never needed to, until today. "Resource Command and Control, this is Enkufu. It's good to be home."

"Welcome home, but we don't have time for chitchat. Final evac is taking place and you will need to report for processing."

I had thought about this for months. My father hadn't put me into the space program out of the goodness of his heart. Just the opposite. He wanted to be sure that his lineage would be one of those that escaped the Earth.

He didn't do it for me. He did it for his name. It was our last conversation, which helped me decide.

"I don't want to hear about how much it hurts. I paid a lot of money for you to become part of this program. You have no idea what prestige this brings to our name."

I was in a chamber undergoing the last modifications I would need to become an asteroid cyborg. My neural network was augmented with an artificial analog. There was no way to prevent the pain and I needed to be awake to assist the doctors in checking their work.

They brought him, thinking he would comfort me during this crisis. They didn't know him. He thought more of himself and his family line than he did of any person in that family line. He had dozens of children, and none could qualify for this program, but me.

I was in a recuperation chamber awaiting my next treatment. I floated in zero-g, since nothing could be allowed to touch me during this time. I could see him floating outside and I knew he was getting nauseous.

"Baba, I didn't mean to complain. It has been a while since you have come to see me. I'm glad to know you're well."

He pinched between his eyes and I noticed a bit of yellow there. "I had planned to stay on the medical satellite until the end of the week. But I have to leave tonight for an important meeting in Sweden." Somehow, I wasn't surprised he was telling me this.

"Baba, the most critical surgery will be completed within another five days. It's the most important part of the re-integration process and why they called you here at all. You mustn't leave."

"It isn't something I can put off. This is how I am paying for your MM transfer when this is all over."

The emphasis on "your" and the venom with which he spat this out wasn't lost on me. He was too old for any of the technical upgrades needed for a Mechasmic Mind transfer. No amount of money could buy him a frozen slot on any of the three starships either. Frontier planets don't have much need for accountants or business executives.

"As usual, Baba, you've made time to visit, cast a bit of blame, questioned my choices, then disappeared in a puff of greasy smoke after depositing a bit of guilt. Nothing's changed with you at all."

His answer was curt and tense, "I've made a survey and a cortical transfer will answer most questions you need answered. It should be more than enough. Good luck, son." He pressed on the glass and then pushed off toward the suite door. "I'm proud of you." He said while floating out the door, not looking back. That was the last time I saw him alive.

"RCC, this is Chen Enkufu. Is it possible to return planet-side?" There was a long and uncharacteristic pause. There was no static, no alternative commands issued on complementary channels. Just silence.

"All spaceports are closed. All the Elevators are offline and Omega will be making its final trip up before going offline. Please stand by."

My robot transport was not planet-worthy so landing in it was impossible. I felt the change in the direction of the shuttle before anything was said. I was being redirected from the MMC and I could see the lights go off in the central processing dome.

"Chen Enkufu. This is RCC. There is one small shuttle arriving at SE-Omega. It has my son on board. It will have enough fuel to get you anywhere you want to go on the planet. But you might want to hear what I have to say before you make the Drop."

There was a moment while she delivered final counts of resources arriving from the belt and directed the rare earths on board Genesis. They would be used in computers created when they arrived at their destination. The last of my work had arrived home.

"It's been ten years since you've been back. In that time, billions have died. The only power left on the planet is solar. More than two thirds of the planet is blacked out. There are no real governments left. There are still plagues, internecine fighting, starvation and people wandering the planet in shock. There are still people down here fighting the good fight, but for the most part, it has returned to the Stone Age. This isn't your home anymore. Take the MM conversion. Go to the stars. You of all people have proven you could make it—being more machine than man. You deserve it."

I could see her son's ship arriving at the platform for SE-Omega from the planet's surface. I extend my vision and I saw him helping to coordinate the last minute arrivals.

I won't give my father the satisfaction. He wasn't saving me. I'm done. "Clear them for launch. I want to come home, RCC."

On my final approach, I watched the Genesis pull away from the SE-Omega as the autopilot directed me into the station. I flew across the station, boarded the shuttle, and detached, before the Genesis had completed its final outbound maneuvers.

I was the last human being to see Humanity's peak development—our exit from our home solar system. Would we survive? Just by being able to leave, we had altered Fermi's paradox and our chances of meeting our alien neighbors should increase just a bit.

I set my course for the planet and strapped in, making myself as durable as possible. I had no idea what to expect when I arrived. The heat of re-entry soon removed any concern for the future.

***

I ride the night.

But now there is a dawn. It moved slowly, gloriously across the ruins of the city.

There are people out there. Most that see me with my wings extended, absorbing the morning sun, flee. I might look like a gargoyle immobile in the morning light.

On the second morning, I noticed a couple of abrasions and my internal computer indicates they are likely bullet wounds. I hadn't noticed. I was frozen in the ecstasy of being home; I had become involuntarily aphasic while my mind adjusted.

Then I saw her. I knew who she was when she crested the hill at the end of the park where I stood. Her hair standing high above her head, likely a nanotech construct, waved in the morning breeze. She walked with several people, a few armed with guns, others with nothing more than fierce determination to survive.

I suspect I was a bit of a sight as well. The weather had cleared after my crash landing. The return shuttle didn't have quite enough fuel to go anywhere I wanted. I had guided it in for a pretty nasty landing here at Resource Command.

While I was returning to Earth I realized the voice of RCC was planet bound. I remembered learning this once I became part of the program. Much of the technology used to make us had been already tested on her.

She was woven into the infrastructure of Earth's computer networks so she could do her job monitoring Earth's stockpiles. Everything humanity would need for the trip, she could lay her figurative hands upon.

I knew there was only one thing left for me.

I had to meet the voice of Resource Command and Control. I warmed myself up and retracted my solar wings as she approached. Her hair was endlessly fascinating as it danced above her head, absorbing solar radiation the same way my wings did.

"I don't know if you're lucky, stupid, or both." She smiled when she said it and her teeth were brilliant in the morning sun. A beautiful Black woman with a mild accent I knew every corner of. A voice that had permeated my days and nights and shaped my world for the last forty years.

Nothing she could say could ruin the moment. "What do you mean?"

"You could have chosen to land anywhere on the planet, but crashed here instead. Did it even occur to you to consider landing near a medical facility to replace your nanite stores? You have been without a recharge for nearly three years. I know . . . I looked it up."

I checked my internal displays and she was right. I would last about six months if I was judicious in their use. I hadn't even thought to consider stockpiling them while they were plentiful. Without them, I would have to start eating food and quickly.

"I'm going to go with 'stupid.'"

She smiled that smile at me again and handed me a small bag. "Fortunately for you, I watched your return flight and realized you had changed your trajectory at the last moment. I wondered if you would survive the landing so I thought I would bring you a gift, just in case you weren't just taking the classy suicide route of burning up on re-entry."

I looked inside and she had brought me the only gift a girl could get a guy who was already a self-contained ecosystem. "I meant to get you something but there wasn't anything at concessions."

"That's okay. Remember, I am the woman who had everything."

I had to laugh. Here was a woman who had just saved humanity and she could joke about it in the ruins of that same humanity.

"What do I call you? I guess RCC won't cut it anymore."

She took my hand, her strength was impressive and yet comforting. "Call me Marilaine."

The early morning light dimmed in the cloud cover of an impending storm. I noticed the people starting to get antsy as the day darkened. They would need to take cover once the rain started.

"Marilaine, where are you going?"

"That way."

"Doesn't seem terribly specific."

"Specific has been my catchphrase for fifty years. For today and the next couple of weeks, 'good enough', is enough. I'm on vacation."

Can't argue with that. I clutched the hand of the voice of my dreams and sought cover with the rest of our new family.

Thaddeus Howse is a California-based author whose non-fiction work has appeared in magazines, including **Black Enterprise, the Good Men Project, The Examiner.com** *and online at* **Astronaut.com.**

His fiction writing has appeared in blogs, such as, the **Magill Review, ScifiIdeas.com** *and he maintains a prodigious amount of non-fiction work at his own blog,* **A Matter of Scale.** *He answers questions on the* **Scifi.Stackexchange.com** *and* **Quora.com.**

His collection of short stories can be found at **Hub City Blues** *(http://hubcityblues.com/). He has recently led a monthly challenge called "30 Cubed" (http://30cubedsf.wordpress.com/).*

His speculative fiction has appeared in numerous anthologies including The Future is Short, Visions: Leaving Earth, Mothership: Tales of Afrofuturism and Beyond, Genesis Science Fiction Anthology, Scraps, and Possibilities.

He has authored a collection of short stories called Hayward's Reach (2011) and an e-book novella called Broken Glass (2013).

He has also been a tabletop roleplaying game designer, magazine publisher (Interface Magazine) *and written materials for* **Cyberpunk 2020, Dungeons and Dragons, Warhammer 40K,** *and* **Hero Games.**

Favorite Quotation:

"A human being should be able to change a diaper, plan an invasion, butcher a hog, conn a ship, design a building, write a sonnet, balance accounts, build a wall, set a bone, comfort the dying, take orders, give orders, cooperate, act alone, solve equations, analyze a new problem, pitch manure, program a computer, cook a tasty meal, fight efficiently, die gallantly. Specialization is for insects."
--Robert Heinlein

www.ingramcontent.com/pod-product-compliance
Lightning Source LLC
Chambersburg PA
CBHW062136170626
46813CB00002B/723